Caroline Stickland was born in 1955. With a degree in English and American Literature from the University of East Anglia she became involved in adult literacy tutoring. Her first novel, *The Standing Hills*, was runner-up for the 1986 Betty Trask Award and the Georgette Heyer Historical Novel Prize. Her second novel was *A House of Clay* and her third *The Darkness of Corn*. Her previous novel, *An Ancient Hope*, is also published by Black Swan. Caroline Stickland is married and lives in Dorset.

Also by Caroline Stickland

AN ANCIENT HOPE

and published by Black Swan

The Darkening Leaf

Caroline Stickland

BLACK SWAN

THE DARKENING LEAF
A BLACK SWAN BOOK : 0 552 99607 6

First publication in Great Britain

PRINTING HISTORY
Black Swan edition published 1995

Set in 11pt Linotype Melior by
County Typesetters, Margate, Kent.

Black Swan Books are published by Transworld Publishers Ltd,
61–63 Uxbridge Road, Ealing, London W5 5SA,
in Australia by Transworld Publishers (Australia) Pty Ltd,
15–25 Helles Avenue, Moorebank, NSW 2170
and in New Zealand by Transworld Publishers (NZ) Ltd,
3 William Pickering Drive, Albany, Auckland.

Reproduced, printed and bound in Great Britain by
Cox & Wyman Ltd, Reading, Berks.

For Alitia

'   : fierce extremes employ
Thy spirits in the darkening leaf,
And in the midmost heart of grief
Thy passion clasps a secret joy'

'In Memoriam' Tennyson

Chapter One

February 1847

It was no night for travelling. The carriage that was labouring to make headway against the gale had long since had its lanterns blown out by the violence of the south-westerly wind. The driver, hunched into the collar of his coat, urged the horses forward with words that were swept into oblivion as he spoke. Thorn-trees, deformed by previous winters, wrenched at their roots as the salt-laden gusts bent them inland, narrowing the road. There was no shelter here, beyond what little was offered by the rise of the Chesil Bank before it dropped to the sea, but it was not the hardship of navigating by the fitful light of an obscured moon that troubled the coachman, nor the misery of holding harness made slippery by the sluicing rain. In the roar of storm and ocean he could not tell whether he truly heard a more ominous sound.

The sea was close, beyond the bank of shingle, and the crashing of breakers that dragged and sucked the stones into the undertow was thunderous in the turbulent air. The relentless boom of the waves filled the darkness so that the crack of breaking branches, the grating of iron wheels, even the scream of the cold Atlantic winds were overpowered and submerged by the frantic waters but still other sounds suggested themselves to the driver. A cry, a shattering of wood, a rending fall – all vanished before he was certain they were there and twice, flitting to one side, the shadows took a human form. Isolated above the straining horses, he sat alert and listening.

Inside the carriage, a man and woman were stoically enduring the discomfort of the journey. The jolting of their passage over the rutted road and the buffeting of the gale that beat in sudden squalls against the right door, made the body of the old-fashioned vehicle more like a ship's cabin than a private coach. The windows were too begrimed by the weather for the travellers to watch their progress and, except when the clouds revealed the moon, they sat in sombre dusk.

The woman touched the man's arm and leant towards him. Wrapped as she was in a cloak and beaver-skin rug, her figure was indistinguishable, but her dark eyes gleamed in an instant of moonlight. The man bent to hear her.

'Do you think we'll reach Abbotsbury?' Her voice was deep-toned and even, carrying no hint of fear or the blame that her companion believed was justified.

'We must. There's nowhere for refuge until then.' He spoke grimly. Concern for the woman's good name had made him risk pressing on towards his cousin's house instead of finding an accommodating farmer to take them in, and it seemed that it might cost them their safety. 'I'm sorry, Philobeth. I should have turned back when it took so long to find a smith.'

The wind beat against the carriage and, slipping icily round the door, blew a strand of hair over her face. She pushed it away with a gloved hand. 'How could you tell the storm would be so intense? I can't remember a night as harsh as this.'

The fur had fallen away from her as she raised her hand and she drew it back to her waist, pushing its thick folds into position about her. She was not afraid of the gale, but her courage did not come from being unable to imagine its consequences. Philobeth Alleyn was naturally daring and, though she regretted the storm because of the danger it presented to the driver and horses, it did not occur to her to be timid on her own account.

This was not the first occasion on which she had been threatened by the elements. Her father, the portrait-painter George Alleyn, was periodically gripped by a desire to interpret landscape, and the twenty years of Philobeth's life had been divided between her home in Dorset and the rigours of artistic travel. Mr Alleyn enjoyed his creature comforts and his intention was never to suffer for the sake of his Muse, but his haphazard organization and his insistence, once seated before his easel, upon staying until the light faded, had involved his daughter in perils not normally experienced by a young girl. Six months spent touring Scandinavia had provided Philobeth with materials to furnish a most alarming journal. A night lost on foot above the English lakes had grown tame when compared with a Norwegian blizzard unexpectedly encountered in August, or rafting the swollen rivers of Sweden.

She did not complain about these hazards. Her coolness in times of jeopardy was matched only by the warmth of her usual emotions: her zest for living made her ready to prevail over whatever adversity fell into her path.

It was a fall that had caused their present predicament. Loose stones had slipped from beneath the horses on the steep slope out of Burton Bradstock, and one had lost its footing, casting a shoe while lunging to get up. Hauling a carriage over rough tracks, with knees already bruised by the accident, would have ruined the animal's leg if it had not been re-shod, and the search for the absent farrier had meant that night was upon them before they resumed their journey.

Being used to late returns from her excursions, Philobeth had accepted her companion's decision to continue, but he was cursing himself for having made it. Frederick North was accustomed to having charge of other people's lives. At twenty-nine he had already enjoyed full control of his West Country estates for eight years, and he carried the occupation of land-owner with such ease that he did not find it absorbed all his energy. He wanted his days to be more challenging, but did not stir himself to seek out duties that would demand more of him. It was this unsatisfied part of his character that drew him to Philobeth and made him sensitive to any censure that she might suffer because of his actions.

His home was Holcombe House, the elegant and extensive residence that his great-grandfather had caused to be built when he had acquired more land to the north of Dorchester than his neighbours believed to be good for him. A spur of his grounds touched the road that led to the hamlet where Mr Alleyn had brought his family. His mother had grown attached to Mrs Alleyn, despite a constant suspicion that the charming woman might break out into an undefined but agitating originality, and the stone stile in the park wall was often used by the female Alleyns during the first years of their stay. The loss of both ladies while Philobeth was still young enough to hold her nurse's hand had ended familiar intercourse between the households. Frederick was away for much of each year during Philobeth's childhood – at school, Oxford and touring Europe – and it happened that, when he came into his property, there were few families of his class in the area prepared to admit an artist's daughter to their circle. He greeted her civilly if they chanced to meet out of doors, but it was not until she was eighteen and he encountered her curled upon a silk divan in the drawing-room of their neighbour, Mahala Graham, that they could be said to have spoken to each other.

Her unembarrassed and supple uncoiling from the cushions attracted him in a way that shyness and formality had never done. He liked her dark and heavy hair, her unusual, slightly medieval, gown, the way her eyes showed, in an otherwise still face, her enjoyment of what she heard. She was found to be a particular friend of the caustic and shrewd Miss Graham, and to have that distinction meant much in her favour. His possessions and birth had made him coveted as a husband but the unmarried women of his acquaintance left him with the same feeling of vague discontent that he got from the routine of his life.

Philobeth stirred him. Her company was at once soothing and stimulating. He stayed that day until the forthright Miss Graham had told him to leave and as he walked out of the room, where the lamps now shone on the Indian hangings, he felt that he had drunk of a potion that was heady with unknown spirits.

He began to call more often on his old friend and she did not scruple to tell him that she knew why. Philobeth was glad that he came. She was neither coy nor forward but frank in a manner that he had not met before. Her love for him was plain but unstated, and his for her was first unrecognized by him for what it was and then kept as a secret marvel for his private pleasure.

If Philobeth had come from a conventional family, their courtship would have taken a different path, but the unorthodox nature of her upbringing that had made her what he desired also prevented him coming to the point. He did not need to use marriage to unburden himself of chaperones, for the freedom and trust she was granted by her father allowed them to be more intimate companions than many a legal couple. They used each other's Christian names and were aware of the sensations they excited in each other; they walked together on soft, summer evenings and sat together on fire-lit winter afternoons, and always the inertia that kept him from breaking out of the habits laid down by his ancestors held his tongue from the question he most wished to ask.

He blamed himself for this, as he was blaming himself for their present situation. It had been necessary for him to go to Devon on business. As Philobeth had wanted to visit friends in Uplyme and collect a package from Weymouth that Mr Alleyn would not risk by carrier, he had arranged to take her to her destinations in the course of a round-about route to and from Exeter. She travelled without relative or maid and he was painfully conscious of what would be said of her if they were benighted. He believed himself to have been cavalier with her reputation and, as the carriage strained and rocked in the gale, was more occupied with the thought of what verbal injury could be done her than with any physical harm they might come to.

Philobeth was not concerning herself with such fears and would not have thanked Frederick for his. It was not his concessions to society that appealed to her but the potential to rebel that she recognized in him. The wildness of the night aroused her, and suspicions of evil-minded rumour did not intrude on the intensity of her interest in their experience.

The carriage lurched, swung to the left and stopped. As the passengers righted themselves, the door on Frederick's side was opened and the driver, holding the handle tightly as the wind dragged at the hinges, looked in.

'Sir,' he said. 'There's a wreck on shore.'

Frederick sat forward, ready to get out. 'Has it beached?' he asked.

''Tis being dragged on and off.'

Opening the door had made the noise of the storm crueller and more immediate. The pounding of the sea upon the shingle and the wailing of the wind were overlaid by the crash of a vessel breaking against the stones and the splintering of wood.

Frederick turned to Philobeth, who was poised and expectant. 'Stay here,' he said, 'while I see if there are survivors who need the carriage. Burnett will be on guard.'

She was tying the hood of her cloak beneath her chin. 'I'll come with you,' she said. 'It may take two to carry a seaman, and I couldn't calm the horses as Burnett can.'

He wanted to object, but her argument was reasonable and a welcome reaction to the violence of the night. As he stepped out into the darkness and handed her down, he had time to be grateful that she was not as other women he had known.

They went round the coach and into the face of the gale. Their heads were down as they climbed the ridge of pebbles that separated them from the sea but once, as they paused to regain their balance on the treacherous ground, they looked up and glimpsed a mast swaying in irregular arcs against the sky.

At the top of the bank they stopped to take in the scene. Philobeth held Frederick's arm, her skirts flattened against her and her cloak straining behind, and they rocked in the turbulence of the storm as their feet sank in the stones. It was the worst of winds on this shore. A storm beating in from the south-west gives no quarter to ships caught against the eighteen miles of Chesil Bank. From the cliffs of Bridport Harbour to Dead Man's Bay, there is no haven for a stricken vessel to run to, and the deep waters that reach to the land are made deadly by the strength of the undertow that snatches ship and crew back beneath the waves and down into oblivion. A captain who knew this coast would run hard ashore, hoping to ground high enough upon the ridge for his men to leap to safety, but common graves in the shingle mark the failure of man against the sea: wherever a traveller stands upon the Chesil, the dead may be close by.

The clouds driving across the moon had grown more sparse and the cold light that glinted on the churning ocean showed no sign of lives that could be saved. The brig, that was floundering as it was drawn back from the beach, was broken-backed. One of its masts had fallen and was acting as a vast rudder, slewing the vessel as the rollers deluged its decks. The other was upright, but its rigging had been torn from its ties and was whipping savagely through the air, smashing spars with the force of its lash. No-one could have stood upon that tilted planking as it reared and fell with the breakers that cascaded over and around it;

no-one could have survived below deck as the sea flooded into the gashed hull, dragging the cargo out into the waves.

Philobeth put up her hand to protect herself from the spume that was being caught by the wind and flung against them. The spray hit her face, brine stinging skin already made raw by the gale. The sea was alive with loose barrels and crates that rolled and crashed together, colliding with beams ripped from the dying ship. She searched amongst the debris for a human form, dreading to find what she sought, only to witness the helpless extinction of life, but the brig might always have been crewless for all that she could see.

Perhaps a score of men were engaged upon the beach, hauling what boxes and timber had been cast to the land onto higher ground. More were appearing steadily from the east, some leading pack-horses, and, hearing the squeak of wheels intruding on the storm, Frederick turned to see a cart labouring along the road from Bexington to stop near his carriage. It was a situation that could turn in a moment from good to evil and he wanted to take Philobeth away, but he could not leave without being certain that no survivor was lying unattended amongst the wreckage.

He pointed down the slope and Philobeth, understanding his thoughts, nodded. They started down the bank, supporting each other as they slid, ankle-deep, in wet shingle. On the other side of the ridge they had been shielded slightly from the rain but here it sluiced them, indistinguishable from the spindrift that careered in the wind. The noise of the storm and wreck; the incessant motion of air and water, of men and ship; the undeniable presence of death inspired a sensation

17

of terror and awe undiminished by the mundane occupation of those loading the restless horses with sodden bales of tobacco and cloth.

They walked unmolested amongst the looters. The mood of the first men who had come to the beach was not malicious; they worked diligently collecting the bounty of others' misfortunes, but they would have thrown a rope had they seen a sailor in need. Further along the shore there was a sourer greed amongst the latecomers, a conviction that they had missed the best of the cargo. Voices were raised as claims were staked upon crates newly hurled upon the beach. Arguments broke out as bundles were filched from unguarded piles.

Frederick was about to turn back when Philobeth pointed at a group of men to their left. Some stood and two were kneeling, but all looked intently at what was spread in the midst of them and, between their legs, Philobeth saw an uncertain gleam of flesh. They approached the men and stood slightly behind one of those who knelt.

A woman lay before them on the stones. Naked and lifeless, her death was more poignant for her exposure and the bruising on a body that was both young and mature. Her hair had been drawn away from her face. Long strands covered her right breast and clung to her waist; another was taken by the wind and writhed above her head. Even stained and bloodied, her features were of such delicate loveliness that she seemed to Frederick more a creature of myth than one who had breathed common air. Her hands were held by tinkers, who were trying to force off her rings. Lasciviousness pervaded the atmosphere, lust and avarice filled the eyes of the watchers. Shadows moved across her skin, giving phantom expression to the horror of her plight.

Philobeth pulled at the fastenings of her cape. Pity for a woman displayed in death as she would never have been in life, made her ignore the cold and drag the billowing cloak from her shoulders to cover the corpse. She was gathering it into her arms, when there was movement amongst the men. The younger tinker, unable to twist the heavy ring from the hand he held, took a knife from his belt; he laid the blade against the base of the middle finger. As he began to sever it, there was a stirring amongst the onlookers and Frederick, who had been standing entranced, reached forward and jerked the knife away. The woman's hand, incongruously encrusted with jewels, fell onto the shingle and redness seeped over her palm as if her rubies were liquifying into the night.

Both tinkers started up but, awakened by Frederick's reaction and recognizing him as a Justice of the Peace, the local men held them back.

'Bind the pair of them,' he said, the authority in his voice undiminished by the ferocity of the storm that snatched it. 'A guinea for anyone who will keep them for the excise men and another for those who'll carry the body to my coach.'

Philobeth was covering the woman as he spoke, but a ploughman, eager for a reward that had no risk of arrest attached to it, removed the blanket that was tied around him and, giving her back her cloak, wrapped the corpse. A length of tarpaulin was brought from higher up the bank and the woman placed on it. Four of the men, ashamed of the nature of the covetousness that had overtaken them, lifted the corners and began to walk along the beach.

19

As she turned away from the gale so that her cloak was blown around her, Philobeth watched the men struggle with their burden while she waited for Frederick to see that the tinkers were secured. The rain had soaked into her clothes and its iciness chilled her spirit as well as her body. She shuddered with cold and repugnance for what she had seen. The breakers surging against the shore and pounding the carcass of the ship no longer seemed inanimate forces of nature but the personification of an evil intent. In this roaring darkness a woman had been robbed of her life and cast down for humiliation by strangers infected by the corruption of the storm. Tomorrow the woman would lie at rest and the men return to their toil, but always, outside in the night, the wind would be ready to rise.

Frederick touched her arm and together they followed the makeshift bier. When they reached the carriage, they found the men standing exhaustedly in the small shelter it afforded, while one of them shouted explanations to Burnett. The woman lay on the road and was the one still point in the landscape.

Finding his master beside him, Burnett indicated the body. 'Sir, is the poor lady to be inside or out?'

Frederick turned to Philobeth. 'Inside,' she said, 'I can't bear to think of her more cold than she is.'

'We'll have to ride with her. Aren't you afraid?'

She shook her head. 'There's nothing to fear from her now.'

The body was lifted into the coach and arranged on the seat facing the one where Philobeth and Frederick had sat. The carriage was too narrow for it to lie outstretched and it slumped awkwardly against the window, one of the ringed hands that had so tempted the looters protruding from the blanket. God knows, thought Philobeth, as she took her place beside Frederick and the door was closed upon them, I feel compassion for her, but I wish the night were over.

The horses moved forward and the carriage once more began to labour over the sodden track. Their swaying, buffeted progress resumed, but inside the coach a new solemnity settled on the passengers. The piercing cold was harder to endure when sitting passively than it had been on the beach, and carrying death through the darkness made their hearts bleak. When Philobeth put her arm through Frederick's, he pressed it to him as if he were drowning and she had thrown him a line.

They could not keep their eyes from the figure before them. The movement of the carriage and the fleeting moonlight gave the wrapped form an illusory life so that, at every moment, it seemed about to raise its arms and rear up. They had not covered the hand that had fallen outside the blanket and it lay, white and forlorn, against the plush. Philobeth found herself staring at it compulsively, imagining the fingers, with their ornate decoration, clenching and unclenching with the rhythm of her breath. She watched in dreadful fascination as the shadows passed across the hand until, slowly and with a sensation of shuddering hope, she leant forward and placed her own hand over the woman's.

'She is – Frederick, she's alive!'

The woman twisted against the back of the seat. There was a sound of choking. Frederick stood up, bracing himself against the door, and put his arm under the woman's shoulders as Philobeth pulled the blanket from her head. Sea water was running from the woman's mouth as she convulsed with retching coughs, and they held her down over the carriage floor until she was quiet and her breathing dry. They knelt together, cradling her, gazing at her pale, unseeing face as if she were their first-born.

'I wonder who she is,' Frederick said.

Philobeth touched the woman's wounded brow. 'I think she'll hardly know herself. But there's one certainty. We may thank God for this day.'

Chapter Two

Philobeth was standing before the wide, stone fire-place of Mahala Graham's drawing-room, scrubbing vigorously at the hem of her skirt with the hearth brush and kicking the resulting fall of dried mud into the grate. The wet March weather had not been kind to walkers and the path that connected the homes of the two friends was so treacherous that Philobeth had borrowed an old shepherd's crook, that her father used in his more bucolic figures-in-a-landscape, to support herself on her way.

'If I'd seen anything of him in the past fortnight, I could give you a better idea of his actions,' she said. 'Or of how interested he is. But I suppose his absence is an indication in itself. Not a welcome one.'

Mahala was lying on a chaise-longue to one side of the fire with her legs covered by a paisley shawl. A fever had prevented her receiving Philobeth for over a week and it surprised her that Frederick should not have called during that time. 'Is he away?' she asked. 'It's odd that he should have vanished completely.'

Philobeth flourished her skirts at the flames so that the last of the loose dirt was thrown onto the coals and, dropping them back into place, sat in the chair opposite Mahala.

'He hasn't, of course,' she said. 'I've seen him on five days since the wreck, but once was when we met by accident as I was walking to the village – and I believe I'll come and go by the roads from here until the paths dry. I'm not an acquatic animal.'

'I'll have the roan mare saddled for you. The boy can fetch her. And the others?'

'Apart from the afternoon when he came to the studio and brooded – really, I dislike being watched, but being stared through is much worse – his appearances have been brief and full of fidgets. On the other hand, I'm told his visits to his grandmother have increased strikingly since a mysterious and half-drowned stranger was taken there. The truth is that my attraction has lessened because I'm not a beautiful young woman in need of rescue.'

'You're not in need of rescue but I've seen worse in my time.'

Mahala rested her head against a velvet pillow and tried to take a deep breath. There was a wearisome pain in her chest, but the exhaustion that afflicted her body did not affect her mind and she was glad of Philobeth's company. In the dim, tapestry-hung room with its vaulted ceiling, her white face burned like the moon at twilight. The consumption that had killed her mother two decades before had come upon Mahala so gradually that only she and her doctor suspected that this, her twenty-sixth year, would be her last. Her condition gave her a look of fragility that made strangers want to take care of her, but in all matters, except the combating of a disease for which there was no cure, she was well able to fend for herself.

In many ways her life had been wasted. Not only was she a prisoner of illness but, in her days of good

24

health, she had been subject to a father who would have appreciated all her qualities if only they had been contained within a male form. James Graham was a nabob who had returned to his native England, after making his fortune in India, with the intention of marrying to found a dynasty. He had arrived in Dorset with a fondness for lying disreputably on cushions in loose pyjamas and it was soon rumoured that he had kept slave-girls. This was a calumny – he had no need to own a woman to treat her as a slave. His wife was a gentle spirit, who withered under his scorn and died fearing for her daughter. She need not have been afraid. Mahala had exactly the set of mind her father would have admired in a son and, although she was often angrily frustrated by the confines of her allowed behaviour, she was undaunted by her sire and never cast down her eyes in his presence. She expected her father to marry again in the hope of achieving male offspring, but Graham had gained such a distaste for being tied to a wife that he remained a widower, passing much of his time in London and travel, and leaving Mahala alone to calculate her opportunities when she came into her inheritance.

When she was eighteen and, unnoticed, the first heralds of disease were stirring within her, her oppressor died and she discovered that her freedom was not absolute. Her father's low opinion of women had caused him to make a will in which she was left a substantial sum yearly for the upkeep of herself, household and estate but was prevented from having control of the capital until she was thirty or married. The trustees for the astonishing amount that she could not yet touch were her solicitor and Graham's two middle-aged, tediously narrow-minded and respectable nephews.

Her hearty and well-founded dislike of her surviving family did not endear the arrangement to her and, now that she was convinced that she would not live to be thirty, the thought that they would benefit from her death played on her mind. Her father had stipulated that his money should go to his nephews if his daughter died before receiving her wealth and, as she lay on her sick-bed, Mahala amused herself with plans to thwart them.

Her determination to have her own way in this matter, and her relish of her relations' future outrage at her action, were typical of her character. She had days of fury and bitterness when she would shut herself away from the world, but she despised such weakness and usually hid her regret at having so short a life with sharp-tongued courage. Her illness, she said, was a grave business but did not take the flavour from a peach. She had suggested that Philobeth paint her portrait and entitle it *A Disappointing Summer*; it was illustrative of their friendship that Philobeth had laughed.

It was of benefit to both women that they lived so near to each other. When George Alleyn, a quarter of a century before, had chanced upon Combehays Manor and been romantically possessed by the squat and solid edifice that had been declaring its importance for four hundred years, he did not guess that the infant eating daisies on the lawn would come to be the solace of his daughter, not yet in existence. He had been refused entry by Mrs Graham, who had been instructed by her husband that no travellers were to be shown round, and, unruffled, had taken the footpath that Philobeth had used today to be enchanted by an empty cottage at the neighbouring hamlet of Buckland Chantry.

He had bought the house with its rose-blown garden on an artistic impulse, and though over the years he had as often been away from it as in residence, privately preferring to leave the joys of rural life to the females of his family, he had done the county the compliment of naming his child from an ancient register of his chosen parish.

The bearer of the antique name was raising her eyebrows at her friend's remark. She was irritated by Frederick's distraction, and the beginnings of jealousy did not incline her to take oblique compliments gracefully. That five meetings in a fortnight should seem to be desertion, showed her how much she had grown to expect his presence. Despite the lack of a formal understanding between them, she had come to take it for granted that they would marry, and this change in his attentions chilled her.

'I'm spoken of badly in the village,' she said. 'Did you know?'

'I have had it mentioned to me,' Mahala's voice was dry. 'But no-one says it twice.'

'Frederick told me that we drove on through the night to protect my reputation. He doesn't see that I'm already considered scarlet because of our familiarity.'

'You've never been worried by the opinions of others before. Your own judgement of your actions has been enough.'

Philobeth slid the flat of her palm along the chair-arm. 'It's started to occur to me late at night that perhaps Frederick thinks of me as artists are often thought of. The kind of woman it isn't necessary to marry.'

Mahala stirred slightly against her cushions. It was her nature to demonstrate her feelings by touch and it cost her dearly to be continually crushing her impulse to reach out. She wanted to comfort Philobeth by taking her hand, but would not even sit close to her. Her decree that no-one should be infected by breathing her miasma was absolute and broken only by Dr Carmody and her nurse. Her habit of covering her mouth with a handkerchief or fan to prevent tainted air reaching those who were with her was one of her many generosities.

'I often see horrors in the dark,' she said, 'but in the morning they're not so terrible. Frederick may be a laggard in love but I don't believe him to be a dastard. He's never offered you any insult. I imagine he's bedazzled by the romantic circumstances of the rescue and will consider the young woman his private property until it becomes plain that she's as mortal as the rest of us. The sooner her family claims her, the better it will be.'

'Unfortunately she has none, and so is not only the victim of a dramatic calamity but is forlorn and unprotected. What gentleman could resist?'

'I hear that she isn't entirely friendless,' Mahala said, thoughtfully. 'Dr Carmody tells me that Mrs North is acting unlike herself. There are strange rumours that she's making her guest feel welcome. Now, I wonder if she's really feeling amiable or whether she's simply trying to draw Frederick away from you.'

'I believe the latter,' said Philobeth. 'It's beyond me how he puts up with her. If she were my grandmother, I'd insist that I was actually a foundling. And if Dr Carmody spent less time giving you gossip and more in finding a treatment that works, he'd be better occupied.'

'My dear, he comes by the usual method of taking

the road; he doesn't walk across the lake. We mustn't expect too much.'

A sadness more threatening than Philobeth's vague fears began to be intrusive, and Mahala drove it away firmly. She pointed her fan at Philobeth. 'The reason that you choose to disapprove of Carmody,' she said, 'is that he makes sheep's eyes at you.'

'I wouldn't use that description.'

'Nor would I when I consider it. There's nothing of the mooning youth about him, but he does pine after you while I, alas, am merely a collection of profitable ailments.'

'You're a disgrace. You're both more suited to palace intrigue than decent society, and if I imagined for a moment that you truly had a *tendresse* for him, I'd advise him to run for his life.'

'You're a heartless creature,' said Mahala, approvingly, 'and more than a match for Mrs North and her protégée. If I were well enough I'd visit the ladies and make mischief. As it is, I'll rely on you for developments. I'm sure you can carry the fight alone.'

The bleak afternoon was settling into dusk as Frederick drove towards Dorchester. Brown woods, whose first suggestions of leaf were too indecisive to be seen across the sodden fields, stood heavily before hills that were fading into one deepening shade. In the town, lamps were being lit in shops and offices and curtains pulled in private homes. The stable-yard of The King's Arms had the industry of a well-run establishment in the throes of an occasion, and as Frederick gave his reins to an ostler, he was hailed by several other prosperous-looking men who were having their horses unharnessed. One of them walked over to join him.

'Thorne.' Frederick nodded to him and they both stepped aside to allow an elderly bay gelding to be led past. 'That's old Unsworth's,' said Frederick. 'Don't tell me he intends to ride back tonight.'

'I hear it takes his groom and three lads to get him into the saddle these days and only the most pressing need to get him out. His man will see him safe.'

They began to walk towards the rear entrance to the inn. It was noticeable that, as they moved through the throng that was blocking the doorway, more easy greetings were made to Thorne than to Frederick. One man, hawk-faced and gaunt, pointedly turned away when he recognized Thorne's companion. Frederick did not appear to be affected, but the slight gingered him. His walk was firmer as he woke from the reverie he had fallen into during his journey. The veiled antagonism he saw in many eyes put him on his mettle. In this collection of J.P.s and landowners, gathered for a gentlemen's dinner in honour of Sir James Lasdun's thirty years upon the Bench, it was inevitable that his presence would bring this reaction.

It was not yet a year since the Corn Laws had been repealed, and Frederick's outspoken support of a measure inimical to the wealth of his peers had earned him outright hatred from some and angry disapproval from most. He had acted from principle, believing that to discard protectionist laws, that kept the price of bread too high for the poor to live in comfort, was a duty that must be carried out. His promise to the tenants of his farms, that he would review their rents if their incomes suffered severely from free trade in corn, had further estranged him from those who thought him a traitor to his class. Had Philobeth moved in the same society as he, she would have realized what courage and tenacity had been required for him to swim against the stream in this manner, but she saw him only basking in the shallows and, indeed, although he had been surprised to find that confrontation stimulated him, he had not roused himself for any other enterprise.

Inside the hall the crush was too great for insults to be given or received with any satisfaction. Old names and good bank balances – not always united in the same person – were arriving by the moment, and the assembly was at that stage when it has not yet divested itself of its wraps or finished giving orders to the staff. Men were pausing with one arm out of their greatcoats to salute a new influx of their acquaintance whilst maids held out their hands for hats and waiters chivvied the crowd towards the stairs. The smell of roasting beef gusted from the kitchens as doors opened and closed, and trays, laden with full glasses, were appearing above the heads of the guests as their bearers tried to edge through the press.

Frederick and Thorne, who had known each other all their lives and had survived many a banquet and ball unscathed, reached the first-floor dining-room without mishap and took their hot brandy into the bay window that, supported on pillars, jutted out over the street below. They had not met since the night of the wreck, and Thorne was under instruction from his wife, who dearly loved a gothic novel and had shuddered deliciously when she heard of the supposed corpse reviving, to tax Frederick for a full account of the adventure. Thorne himself was romantic enough to be moved by the rescue, and his curiosity had only been whetted by the newspaper report he had read to his shivering lady in the warmth and safety of their drawing-room; but he had warned her that Frederick was unlikely to be forthcoming at such an event as this.

'Amelia would like the three volumes of your experiences in the storm,' Thorne said. 'I'm not to go home without them.'

'I thought as much.' Frederick was not irritated by this interest. Although the frivolous and laughing Mrs Thorne was not to his own taste as a wife, he liked her and would not have wanted to disappoint her sensation-seeking had developments not complicated the straightforward telling of the tale. He would have to decide what he wanted to make known before he opened himself to inevitable questions on what had happened since Philobeth had reached out in the carriage to find life.

'She regards you as a hero,' said Thorne.

'I can't fault her judgement.' Frederick moved further into the bay as the room filled. 'Tell her to invite me to one of her comfortable suppers and I'll thrill her to the marrow.'

A surge of latecomers issued from the landing, and the commanding voice of the head waiter, who had shepherded many celebratory diners to their places before the white soup was cold, was heard urging the guests to take their seats. Frederick and Thorne drew up their chairs, neither wishing to give an evening to a man whose sympathies were not theirs, but both resigned to the necessities of clanship.

'North!' A solid, middle-aged man, whose figured waistcoat was already straining at its buttons before the eating had begun, called from his position on the opposite side of the table.

Seeing who had summoned him, Frederick

anticipated no pleasure from their conversation but nodded with cold civility. 'Corbett.'

'I hear you have a naiad in your protection.' Corbett was tearing a roll with thick fingers. His neighbour murmured a comment, with salacious eyes on Frederick.

'Miss Farebrother is recovering at my grandmother's home.'

Until now Frederick had encountered only pity for the plight in which he and Philobeth had found the unfortunate woman, but the expression on the faces of those watching him made him realize he had been naive.

'And have you recovered?' Corbett had taken a mouthful of bread and was chewing as he spoke, his forehead glistening. 'I hear she was as ripe a piece of flotsam as was ever washed ashore, and all clad in sea-foam.'

Beside him, Frederick felt Thorne tense. His colour heightened with disgust. 'Keep your remarks for the tap-room,' he said. He turned his chair slightly towards Thorne, clearly cutting Corbett who sat up to reply, but was restrained by the man next to him.

'He hasn't forgiven you for the repeal,' Thorne said, glancing at the huffing Corbett. 'He's always one with an ill word for those he dislikes.'

'I'll stand for none about Miss Farebrother. Half of this company holds me personally responsible for the Whig government, but that cannot excuse slurs upon a lady.'

'It was the Irish that caused Peel's downfall,' said Thorne soothingly.

Frederick laughed. 'Come, that horse won't run without corn. What a fellow you are for peace-making.

33

You don't agree with me but you wouldn't have me blamed for the world. Amelia must—'

A rapping on the table silenced them, and the Reverend Mr Durrell rose from his seat beside Sir James to say grace. Frederick stood and bowed his head with the rest, but his mind was no more upon his devotions than it was upon the dinner that followed or the speeches that rang in the increasingly convivial room. He talked happily to Thorne and politely to Stockwood, who sat to his left and whose admiration of Frederick's acres kept him from impudent inquiries, but his thoughts were elsewhere.

It was not only a ship that had been wrecked on that violent night on the Chesil Bank; the simplicity of his expectations had been shattered against the cold shore and he felt himself adrift upon the currents. His dissatisfaction with the women of his acquaintance – that same dissatisfaction that had made him so susceptible to Philobeth's originality – had kept him from affairs of the heart and given him a reputation for a coldness unsuited to his years. It was undeserved. His blood was as hot as that of his fellows, who had wedded their friends' sisters or entangled themselves in ways that women whispered to women and men to men, but his imagination was too vivid to let him settle for the ordinary. He desired romance and mystery. The strangeness of Philobeth's world, her freedom of movement, her ease when alone with him, even her ambition to earn a man's status and payment for her work set her apart from other women, and appeared to grant him what he wished. Since the day she had risen, sensuous and dishevelled from Mahala's divan, he had wanted her presence. She gratified his senses and rewarded his mind. He laid claim to the tone of her low voice as she talked, to her laugh – round and mocking – as she read out portions of her father's gossiping letters, to the suppleness of her walk, to the scent of her dark hair, to her stance as she stood back from her easel: one hand in the small of her back, the end of her brush between her teeth. He believed her to be his, and it was his intention that they would marry, yet the inertia that prevented him from rebelling against his staid life by doing more than hold unpopular views, held him back from the commitment of a proposal.

There had seemed an eternity in which to bind themselves by contract, but they had taken the coast road on a night of storm and uncertainty, and the future was now to be seen through a glass darkly.

It was not that Ellen Farebrother had been at the mercy of the most vile of men and circumstances when they had rescued her that attracted Frederick. It was not the helplessness of a young woman without family, whose entire wealth had gone down into the sea, nor her gratitude for her care in a house where Philobeth was not welcome. It was not her beauty – although he could not deny that part of his disgust with Corbett had been because images of her fragile nakedness intruded upon his private thoughts. It was not the drama of their meeting that was causing his obsession. It was all of these things merging into a vulnerability that cried out to the chivalry in his nature that Philobeth did not need.

He loved and wanted Philobeth; he wanted Ellen. There was guilt and confusion within his breast and as he sat amongst men, applauding and raising his glass, he felt the hands of women and heard the distant raging of the sea.

Chapter Three

The girl walked carefully. A shepherd, describing her later, said that she looked as if she feared the ground was treacherous, although there had been no rain to speak of – nothing but a shower an hour before. He had a notion to shout to her, he said, but she was ever a maid for dreaming and she was out of the meadow and gone without lifting her head. 'Twas no business of his, he thought, if she was wandering, God forgive him.

She took the path up from the valley, past newly ploughed fields where barley had rustled about her last summer, through meadows whose young grass was sharply green in the March sunlight. She knew the way well – better than many who had lived there far longer than the year she had been on the farm. The walk was lonely, hidden for much of its length by hedges that lay between the track and the few buildings on this remote ridge. Barlow had brought her here for the first time in July, when honeysuckle was withering amongst the briars and the scent of meadowsweet had mingled with her shyness, to make her dizzy and short of breath. She had stung her hand on a nettle and he had dipped his neckerchief – red silk that she protested was too good to spoil – into the trickle of water in the ditch and held it to the rising blisters on her skin. It had been hot that day with a waiting stillness and he had laid the wet silk on her neck and throat, pressing gently so that drops of water ran down between her breasts and shoulder-blades.

'There now,' he said. 'That's cool, bain't un? That's cool, this weather.'

Before she entered the wood, she turned and looked back the way she had come. The morning was cold but piercingly bright. Her world was beneath her. From this point she could see beyond her farm to the ranges of hills enclosing other valleys where other lives were lived. She gazed impassively at the richness, noticing, without pain or pleasure, the glitter of sunlight on the lakes at Holcombe House and Combehays and the sudden lift of gulls from a brown field.

'This'n's our place,' he said. 'Don't no-one come up here much – not enough to see.'

There was birdsong in the wood. The ground was damp and twigs bent, pressing into the mould, before they broke under her feet. As she raised her head to the sudden flight of a thrush, shadows of branches and sprouting leaves fell across her face like a net.

Beyond the copse rough pasture ran along the spine of the ridge. The soil was poor, thin and stony, and no sheep would be grazed on it until later in the spring. She hesitated at the edge of the trees. In the clear light the place looked desolate, and for an instant there was expression in her eyes, but the anguish died as soon as it was born and she walked on across the short grass towards a small barn that stood isolated within the meadow.

It was not locked, as she knew it never was. She unlatched the door and swung it open, sliding inside and pushing it to behind her. There was nothing in the barn but a platform built half across the tie-beams to make a loft, and a bed of straw that had rotted in the winter rains seeping up through the earth floor. It did not smell as she remembered. She crossed to the ladder and climbed.

'When was she found?' Dr Carmody looked down at the body on the trestles.

' 'Twas no more than two hours since.' Holden was standing beside him. 'Missus thought 'er gone from the kitchen an uncommon long time and couldn't rest easy. Said there'd been sommut not right all the morning. Fair gave 'er the shudders, she d'say. Then Martin said Shepherd had seen 'er going up Far Leaze, all dazed like she were shrammed with snow and feared of falling. So I sends men out searching and next thing one on 'em comes running back for me a-saying 'er's hanged herself and will I come? I gets there and there she be dangling from the loft with 'er head all to one side and a red silk scarf knotted to a rafter. I tell ee it made me sick to my stomach. I been tenant of this farm twenty-odd years and there ent never been nothing like this. Nothing. And that poor girl's not seventeen. Not seventeen till April nor ever will be.'

Distress made Holden talkative, but a tightening in his throat silenced him. He was not an imaginative man and the blunt fact that lay wrapped in a sheet before them was more shocking to him than if his mind was used to seeing possibilities. Mary Taylor, who had moved about his house so silently, whose smile spread slowly beneath her lowered eyes and had not spread at all in recent weeks, who was never chaffed roughly by the men because they were gentle with timid lambs; Mary Taylor, whom he had carried, heavy and silent, on a hurdle down from the hill.

'Who reached her first?' Dr Carmody asked.

Several farmhands with strained faces were standing bunched together beside the trestle-table. One of them stepped forward stiffly at the question, as if grief had frozen his limbs.

'Was there any sign of life when you arrived?'

'No, sir. She'd gone on – 'twas plain.'

'You're Thorpe, I believe?'

'Yes, sir.'

'It must have shaken you to come upon such a sight.'

Thorpe made an abrupt shrugging motion, raising his hands as if he could not express himself adequately in words or gesture. 'It turned the blood in my veins, sir. I thought my own heart would stop, 'twas so sorrowful to see. I never heard a quiet like there was in that barn.'

Dr Carmody turned back to Holden. 'What could have made her do this?' he asked. 'Was she of a melancholy temperament?'

There was a general stirring amongst the men, and Carmody heard the name Barlow several times.

'She were lovesick, poor maid,' Holden said. 'Barlow was courting she off and on and when 'twas on 'er was glad as a bird, but that's been off these two three months and 'er's faded like a lily-flower.'

'Does Barlow work here?'

'He do. And he can work with the best when he sets himself to it. 'Tis the only reason I d'keep him on.'

'Then he's not of good character?'

'No. You couldn't rightly say he's bad, but he's of a foul-mouthed, sneering cast with a temper on 'n. We all thought 'twas a change for the better when he took up with Mary. She were a bashful girl, not forward, not like the pieces whose skirts he usually followed after. Seemed to calm 'n somehow, but it didn't last and she were a-moping and pining after 'e. Still, I didn't never think 'twould come to this.'

'I'll examine the body now, if you'd oblige me by waiting outside.'

When he was alone, Dr Carmody uncovered the girl's face. He had not recognized her name, but he remembered having seen her walking down into the village and sitting amongst the farm servants in church. Her features were undamaged and it seemed extraordinary, even to one of his profession, that this young creature would not open her eyes again. He thought of Philobeth reaching forward in the dark carriage to touch a woman she believed to be dead and he, who was no stranger to shrouds, shuddered, feeling a momentary reluctance to be about his business. Looking up at the rafters where cobwebs straggled in a shaft of sunlight, he pictured the youth and shyness that had been harboured by the flesh and bone that lay before him fastening a noose about a narrow throat.

He did not think it was in him to feel such desperation. Neither his mind nor his body had yet suffered any pain except the ordinary ills of childhood and, though he pitied the vulnerable and afflicted, his compassion was slightly detached. It did not affect his skill or his determination to bring his recent training to bear upon the sick of his practice, but his sympathy was sometimes stunted by a lack of complete understanding of a weakened spirit.

Deep emotion had not touched him. The ills that sapped his being were the dissatisfactions that, though they could turn a base man to greed and a fool to bitterness, were balanced in his character by the reserved sympathy that had drawn him to medicine. He resented the comparative poverty that had brought him to this remote place. His inheritance from extravagant and pleasure-loving parents, who had never thought of the morrow and were now ten years dead, had been enough for his training and the purchase of a cheap practice but, for a gentleman, he was poor. He was ambitious both to cure the sick and to gain a name for doing so – a name that would bring him the income to let him command the luxuries he remembered from his boyhood. He wanted the wine that he drank to be good and to come from a well-stocked cellar; he wanted the linen that he wore to be fine and always fresh; he wanted the woman at the foot of his hospitable table to be handsome and dressed without regard to cost. There seemed no way to achieve these comforts and so discontent tarnished his benevolence, making him abrupt with men of his own class, who enjoyed easier circumstances, and giving a twist to his speech that did not trouble Mahala, but which made Philobeth wary.

When he had finished his examination, he had found what he suspected. It was the old story. Barlow's betrayal had ended not one life but two. He wondered whether she had told her lover of the coming child before he had cast her aside. It was probable. She had reached that stage of pregnancy when she would be in daily expectation of discovery, and Holden had said that it was only two or three months since Barlow had lost interest in her. He was exasperated by the waste before him. Had no-one thought to protect the girl? He covered the body again and was wiping his hands on a cloth when there was a knock, and Holden half entered the barn.

'Miss Alleyn's here, sir,' he said, 'asking to come in.'

Carmody was always ready to meet Philobeth, but these were not the circumstances he would have chosen. 'Does she know of Mary?' he asked.

'That she does.' Holden lowered his voice. ''Er's got her painting-box, sir.'

It was obvious that Holden considered this improper, and Carmody disliked his tone. He thought art a fitting occupation for gentlewomen, providing as it did both physical and mental exercise and, if only Philobeth could be persuaded to take her talent less seriously, it would be an excellent pastime for her. If she had heard the news while out sketching, it was natural that she would arrive with her equipment, and her appearance did not warrant disapproval from her inferiors.

'Then show her in,' he said.

Realizing that he had said something amiss, Holden retreated without comment and a moment later Philobeth came in. She was carrying the light wooden case that doubled as a drawing-board and a container for pencils and paper. Her face was calm as she looked first at the shape on the trestles and then at Carmody, but her eyes were full of sadness. She had been told of the suicide by the servant, who had been dispatched to Holcombe House with the news, and had immediately gone home to fetch her case. The ability to see beneath the skin that made her portraits so telling had flooded her with horror for the suffering of the girl who had deliberately walked to her death, and for those who would mourn her. It was her way to react to disaster with a practicality that belied the heat of her feelings,

42

and she had come to the barn to perform a kindness that would make many think her cold.

Carmody was intrigued. He did not expect a woman of twenty to have had no experience of the dead, but Philobeth's composure in the face of a hideous destruction of life, that united sin, crime and desolation, startled him. He had been inclined to believe her part in the revivial of the victim of the wreck exaggerated, yet she had chosen to come into the presence of this violence and stood before him, cool and grave.

'You're surprised to see me here, Dr Carmody,' she said in the low voice that acted upon him like the stroke of a hand. 'If I'm hindering you, I'll leave.'

'No, please. I've done all that's necessary.'

Philobeth looked back at the wrapped form on the table. Outside the barn there were sounds of footsteps and hushed voices; inside, silence seemed to rise from the body as if stillness could infect the air and numb the senses.

'Is it true that she hanged herself?' she asked.

'I'm afraid it is.'

She raised her face to the beams beneath the roof. 'Was it here?' she asked. 'I was told it was the barn.'

'It was the one in Far Leaze. She was carried back.'

Philobeth continued to gaze upwards, putting her fingers to her neck. 'She used to sing when she thought no-one was listening,' she said. 'I heard her several times. She had a voice like a linnet, but if she saw you, she lost the note.'

Carmody said nothing. His own knowledge of the girl did not extend to such details and it disturbed him to have them mentioned. That song had come from the throat now fatally marked and stretched made the life that had fled more vivid.

Philobeth was looking at Carmody again. 'Was she with child?' she asked.

'Yes,' he said and his indignation at the waste returned. 'Why wasn't she guarded better? She was a fine-looking girl. It should have been obvious she was a temptation. Why did they let her fall?'

'You've been away from London almost a year, Dr Carmody. You must be aware that many brides of Mary's station are in such a condition. They go on to become faithful wives. Respectability or shame lies in the gift of the men they trust. Mary trusted unwisely.'

There was an edge to her words, but when she next spoke it was gone. 'I met her one day as she was taking a cheese to Combehays. I was painting the great elm by the railings. She looked so fresh and young that I said I'd sketch her, and she told me she'd like one to give to her mother, who had no likeness of her. I've come to do it now so that the poor woman can at least see her daughter's face on the wall.'

She waited for a reply, but being given none was struck by what might be implied by Carmody's hesitation. 'Is she too disfigured?' she asked.

'No, her neck broke at once. There's no sign of strangulation or bruising from a struggle to die. That's one small mercy she was granted.'

The thought of the limpness of the neck beneath the face she was to draw made Philobeth shiver but, finding that Carmody raised no objections, she went forward to the table and, putting down her case, lifted her hands to uncover the girl's head.

Carmody came to her side. 'Let me,' he said. 'I'm more used to this work.' He folded back the wrappings and they both looked solemnly at the calm features with their hint of discolouration. 'Forgive me,' he said, 'but you're an unusual woman, Miss Alleyn. This must be abhorrent to you, but you'd do it for a stranger.'

'It's true – I do recoil, but that's my foolishness. The dead can't harm me, and it would be ungenerous not to do this small thing to give a mother a keepsake.' She opened her case and rested it on an empty barrel while she drew. Her hand was firm and sure, and her eyes did not flinch from the details of the stiffening features. Watching her, Carmody did not know whether to admire or be chilled.

The sketch was finished, and Philobeth was placing it carefully between two clean sheets of paper when Frederick was shown in. His face was pale, and this sign of anger pleased Philobeth. Her composure hid a desire for a revenge upon Barlow that she was powerless to take, but Frederick owned the land that Holden rented and, if he chose to exert himself, Barlow would suffer.

Frederick walked over to the table and looked down. Mary's face was not yet covered, and he stared at it fiercely as if he wanted to issue a challenge to her death. Unlike Carmody, he had known that she could sing. Although he was not the most approachable of men, he was paternalistic through a real interest in the lives of those connected with him, and he had a more intimate knowledge of the workers on his estate than most landlords would have wished. He remembered the girl's slow smile and from whom she had got the red silk kerchief that had broken her neck. It enraged him that despair should have rooted itself amongst the domestic duties that ought to have been her security; Barlow would get no leniency from him.

He had not expected to find Philobeth there, and her action touched him. Since he had become familiar with Ellen, Philobeth's independence had irked him, but it was her lack of need of his protection, not her professionalism, that he found unsatisfactory. He did not wonder that she had been able to sit beside a corpse and produce a portrait that was true to the face before her, yet softened by a vitality its subject would never feel again. He recognized her talent as a fundamental part of her nature and would have disapproved if she had not used it. Just as he had not been surprised by her coolness in the storm, he was not disturbed by discovering her at a task that he would not have suggested to another woman. He wanted to join her in her kindness, and offered to have the drawing framed.

'Take care that you have it done cheaply,' Philobeth said, closing her case. 'Or the mother will sell the frame and the loose paper will be ruined. Dr Carmody, perhaps you would wrap her now.'

The three went out into the yard. Frederick had questioned the men who had brought back the body before he had gone into the barn and they had left to resume their work, but Holden was waiting, surrounded by a murmuring group of labourers and passers-by. Several women were standing in the kitchen doorway, talking with grim expressions and folded arms. Philobeth noticed that one whom she had seen plait Mary's hair, had reddened eyes, and looked towards Frederick with the same hope of anger as herself.

Holden came across to them, followed by his wife making her curtsy to this accumulation of gentry in her yard.

'Is he here?' Frederick asked.

'No,' Holden said, 'but he's sent for. Shouldn't be long now. Will you stop in the parlour, sir, or shall us send him on?'

Mrs Holden was hovering at Philobeth's side, whispering of tea and, hearing her accept, Frederick said that he would stay. He had barely spoken to Philobeth for three weeks and the habit of her company was too strong for his new neglect of her to assert itself on an occasion such as this. Carmody made his excuses and, promising to call at the vicarage with the news on his way to the village, left Philobeth and Frederick to be taken indoors.

The parlour was cold with the damp chill of a room that was more ornament than use. Philobeth sat on a sofa hard with horsehair, while Frederick stood by the fireplace, staring at the can of embers that Mrs Holden had brought in as a gesture towards comfort. The hearth was piled with decorative wood-shavings and, as the farmer's wife went out, the closing door dislodged a paper-thin twist which fell into the embers and fizzled into a sudden curl of red.

The dankness of the room, the dark, heavily patterned wallpaper and the badly executed paintings, suspended from crimson ribbons in a manner horribly reminiscent of Mary, had a depressing effect upon them both. There was a nearer approach to a morgue in this unsuccessful attempt at luxury than there had been in the simple presence of the dead.

Philobeth felt that there had been another death. Neither knew how to begin to speak, and the silence between them was not the easy silence of friends but awkward and intrusive. They had not touched and, close as they were, the small room seemed filled with their care that they should not do so. It was not only the sympathetic grasping of hands that they avoided, nor the small caresses that had crept upon them, but the casual brushing of her skirts against him and the reaching out for the same object. There was to be no accidental contact between them of the kind that would not be noticed by those who did not want to embrace.

A heaviness settled on Philobeth that she had not suffered while in the barn. Then, she had been actively engaged and the usefulness of her talent protected her from the bleakness of the suicide. Now, in this enforced passivity, trapped by her civil acceptance of refreshment, she felt caged and helpless, as if she were one of the submissive women that Frederick had rejected. She thought with bitterness that her passions had deceived her. It had been extraordinary good fortune that she, who was unlikely to be accepted by a lover as an equal even if he were a fellow artist, should have had her love returned as she desired. In this atmosphere of loss and treachery, it seemed that her feelings had blinded her. A man of Frederick's position in the county might entertain himself with such as she, but he would marry one of his own kind.

When the tray was brought and Mrs Holden, bashful of gentry, had again retired from the room, Frederick forced himself into speech. 'This is a sorry business,' he said.

Philobeth, slowly stirring her unwanted tea, sighed. 'Yes,' she said. 'It is.'

'I've sent for Barlow.'

'I imagined you had.' She raised her eyes to his. 'Will you dismiss him?'

'Indeed I shall. I wish I could do more. He deserves to be hanged.'

The decisiveness with which he spoke pleased Philobeth as much as the sight of his anger had done, but her approval was tempered by her remembrance of his behaviour towards her.

48

'It would be just,' she said. 'A false lover should suffer as much as the woman he betrays.' She set down her cup. 'Dr Carmody says she should have been protected. What do you think? Should a girl be fettered for her own good?'

Frederick leant his elbow against the overcrowded mantelpiece. He was aware of her meaning and it provoked him to have his faltering attentions cast in his face as if they were on a level with Barlow's seduction. He wanted to rebuke her, but it did not help his anger to know how frequently he had longed to have her hair across his pillow nor how often now his thoughts changed that hair to a gold that writhed in the night wind.

'She shouldn't be left defenceless,' he said, guardedly.

Philobeth gave a half smile. 'How true,' she said. 'The world's so dangerous. We can never tell what storms we may encounter.'

His face tightened, but before he could answer shouts broke out in the yard and a clangorous drumming resounded in the room. It was so sudden that both went to the window, forgetful of their self-imposed aloofness. Their view was screened by the budding branches of an elder, but through them they could see Barlow, livid with rage and humiliation, being dragged towards the barn. To each side of him, jostling the men who had him by the arms, women were banging saucepans together and beating ladles against irons.

'It seems the general judgement's the same as ours,' Frederick said. 'If I'm to please you, I'd better go and take the lead.'

Chapter Four

An artist's good intentions are often thwarted by the pace of her enthusiasm, the need to finish a work or a knock at the door, and the orderliness of a studio is apt to creep back from the area most used. Philobeth's work-place was no exception to this rule of recurrent chaos, and on a still morning, a week after Mary's death, she set herself to banishing the confusion.

The studio was a long room of wide windows, built onto the cottage for Mr Alleyn, who rarely painted there, and was filled with the dull light of a day that needed vigorous activity to ward off dejection. As she moved from shelf to cabinet to cupboard, Philobeth glanced out through the Gothick panes in the hope of increasing brightness but, as yet, there had been no improvement. The sky was a pallid grey, and distances were obscured by the haze that is not quite mist and threatens that the weather could be dismal if it roused itself to try.

There was a strong smell of turpentine in the air and this, with a row of clean palettes lying on a trunk of costume for historical tableaux, and the streaks on the sleeves of her smock, testified to the most hated task of removing dried paint having been done first. The studio, graced as it was by a pair of elk horns that

Mr Alleyn had carried back from Sweden, to the annoyance of all who shared a carriage with him, could never be elegant, but the regularity that was supposed to be its norm was appearing in patches that would soon make a whole.

Outwardly, Philobeth showed the thoroughness that was habitual to her in this place, but her mind was chasing a number of linked subjects in a wearisome circle. Wherever she was in the room, she was conscious of the low plush armchair where Frederick used to lounge while she worked. She missed him; she wanted to feel him watching her, to see the line of his legs as he rested his crossed feet on the sill, to hear the irritating tune he tapped with his fingernails on his match-case when he was growing bored. The sadness that had settled on her since leaving Mary gave her no confidence in a return of his interest and, although she did not wish that Ellen had been left to die upon the beach, she did regret that it had been they who had found her. Jealousy was like a fist within her, crushing the breath from her body. There seemed no way for her to fight back. She was handicapped by Frederick's wealth. Knowing that success would bring her riches and standing as well as love, she was too proud to pursue him as she would have a poor man. She could not confront Ellen, who had never come to thank her, or even visit her, to let Frederick judge them side by side, for Mrs North would not receive female artists. In the dark watches of the night, she thought that when she had reached out in the carriage to touch the cold hand, death had left it and killed part of her.

Philobeth had the worst of characters to make a woman happy. She was ambitious and loving: a combination that promised almost inevitable heartache.

Spinsterhood had few attractions for her, but she was not sentimental, and the ability to find a baby ugly or sit dry-eyed at a wedding meant that she could not hide from herself that marriage would not be enough to satisfy her.

She was more than her father's daughter in her devotion to art. The skill that Mr Alleyn had been delighted to recognize in his only child and employ in completing backgrounds for his figures was fed by more passion than he had ever known. The confident and alluring society portraits that were the backbone of Mr Alleyn's patronage, were of a quality that justified their high price, but the blood did not beat in his temples during their execution as it did in Philobeth's as she strove to make full expression of her vision in paint. The elusive, indefinable reason for straining for excellence in art did not concern her, her own shortcomings did. She worked in fear of being second-rate, of her pen never capturing the thoughts behind an eye, her brush never giving breath to her colours. She wanted a viewer to fan himself in the heat of her sun, to smart in her salt winds, his mouth to cringe at her green apples. Her style was not yet fixed and she was tormented by the idea that the flowering of her talent was a twist of thought away and might wither from her own blindness to what she must do.

Her impatience to unite inspiration and craft made her twenty years weigh heavily upon her. Had Frederick come now, as she moved slowly to and fro pondering her future, he would have seen her handsome face looking as vulnerable as his chivalrous spirit could wish. If he had known how much she yearned for him and how fiercely she rebuked herself for loving a man who had turned from her, the strength of his shame would have told him the truth of his feelings. He did not come and she forced her thoughts to the plans she was forming for a life without him.

She did not need to consider the direction she would take, for it went without question that she would dedicate herself to her work. Her difficulty lay in deciding how this course could be carried out. It was not necessary for her to struggle to overcome the obstacles that disapproving families put in the paths of young women who wanted to rise above the accepted amateurishness of ladies' art. Mr Alleyn would welcome her in London and encourage her endeavours, but the calls on his time were too great to allow him to give her the tuition she believed she needed, and money slipped through his fingers too easily for him to work less. She had already had several commissions to paint the children of her father's sitters and did not doubt that she could earn a living from this orthodox female field, but she did not want to commit herself to that subject.

Providing for herself was not an immediate problem, for Mr Alleyn assumed that he would be financially responsible for his daughter until she became a wife. However, although warm-hearted, Philobeth's love was not given readily. She wanted Frederick and no other. Now that it seemed he was lost to her, she looked boldly at the time when her father would die, leaving her without an income. She knew his extravagant, impulsive habits and expected that, despite his good intentions, no money would have been set aside for her. It was her purpose to achieve a comfortable independence through her own efforts and, to uncover the bedrock that her work would rest upon, she thought that she must study to improve her technique. Her sex barred her from ever becoming a member of the Royal Academy and the schools of art, where students were groomed for this precious and profitable distinction, would not welcome her because of it. There was more freedom on the Continent, and she was inclined to use her father's introduction to enter a studio in Paris.

Even there she would not have the liberty of a man. She could not be accepted into the fraternity of artists who called upon each other casually in a manner that a lone woman could not do, and the flow of criticism, the news of developments and patrons would reach her as a trickle.

It chafed her that she should be constrained. In moments of depression, when the demands of talent and the distaff clashed too fiercely, she thought herself a freak. Mahala had suggested that they see the world by hawking themselves through the fairs – 'The Beardless Wonder and the Disappearing Woman' – and the remembrance of her friend's dry gaiety prevented her feeling sorry for herself. Despite her disappointment and difficulties, she was strong in mind and body. Her life might not give her all that she desired, but it was likely to be long and full of diversion. She suspected that Mahala's health was worsening more swiftly than she wanted to be known, and that her years of near-captivity would soon draw to their close. The love the women bore one another made it simple for Philobeth to postpone her departure until that grievous and scarcely imaginable time when there would be no acerbic presence at Combehays.

The pain that gripped her at the idea of her world without Frederick and Mahala roused her to renewed industry, and she was sorting through her port-crayons as Slater came through the door, holding a letter.

54

'Your father's written, Miss Phil,' she said. 'And not before time, as you may tell him from me.' She passed the letter to Philobeth and, taking a stocking from her apron-pocket, began to darn rapidly, plainly intending neither to leave the room before she had been told the gossip nor to waste the time she was waiting.

'You can tell him yourself,' Philobeth said, breaking the seal and unfolding the paper. 'If he hasn't been delayed, he should be here on the heels of the post-boy.'

Slater raised her eyebrows without looking up from her darning. 'We've had letters before,' she said.

'Yes,' Philobeth agreed with a sigh, 'indeed we have.'

Hearing the unusual tone of wistfulness, Slater glanced up and her mouth hardened as she returned to her stitching. Forty of her fifty-four years had been spent in service to Mrs Alleyn's family, and she considered herself the guardian of their welfare. On marrying his Georgina, Mr Alleyn had been aghast to find that she came to him complete with a maid of forthright opinions and no scruple in telling them. He had soon found the young Slater to be as capable as she was plain-spoken and the ideal lynch-pin of his erratic household. Nothing could be fiercer than her devotion to the infant Philobeth and the anxiety, if not the anguish, of losing his wife had been removed by his perfect faith in Slater's practical loyalty. It did not occur to any of the three that Slater would ever leave them, and she would not have thought it safe to do so, for she believed simultaneously that her employers were near to genius in their talents and utterly unable to look after themselves. She was disturbed now because she foresaw a trouble that she could not drive

55

away from her beloved girl. It had seemed to her completely fitting that Frederick should fall for Philobeth. Arguments put to her in the village that her mistress had neither the wealth nor station to make her suitable for such a landowner received short shrift. She had liked Frederick and been glad that Philobeth was to be spared the poverty that so often afflicted artists, but her approval had turned to a readiness to hate him with all her heart. He was hurting her child and she knew that, although Philobeth would appear to recover, the wound would weep within her.

Philobeth had seated herself on the edge of a table as she read the large, assured writing. Her face showed nothing but the grave serenity that was its natural and deceptive form, yet Slater was able to tell from the quality of her stillness that she was disappointed.

When she had finished reading, Philobeth refolded the sheets and laid them aside. The hands that had been so occupied all day lay in her lap. 'He's sold the three views I did of Weymouth Sands, and the sketch of Corfe,' she said. 'That's something, but he isn't coming. I suppose we might have expected it.'

Her voice was flat. She was surprised by her reaction to news she had received so often before. Her father gave her love and enjoyable companionship when they were together but her commonsense had outstripped his years before and she had never looked to him for support. She had not told him of the cooling relations between Frederick and herself, and his joshing remarks about her lover were more galling because she could not complain of his tactlessness. Telling him seemed to be an abandonment of hope, but she realized she had had an unrealistic image of sympathy and protection in her mind. A memory of her younger days, when she would curl up in her dressing-gown upon his knee to be petted, was enough to stiffen her. She was no longer of an age to be comforted with stories and cocoa.

'Well,' she said, 'we must manage on our own. There's nothing new in that.'

Some five miles to the south, a scene not unlike the remembrance of Philobeth's childhood was being enacted at Mythe, the home of Mrs North. The romance of the ancient house was lost on Frederick's grandmother, whose fantasies, although as dark and inconvenient as her dwelling, were of an order that would not lend themselves to the visions of courtly love that were fashionably drawn from medieval piles.

Had a stranger looked through the deep-set windows into the room, known somewhat dashingly as 'the Scarlet Boudoir', his sentiments would have been agreeably touched by the tableau within. A frail old lady sat, dressed in purple velvet, in a wing-chair. At her feet, a young woman of a delicate and ethereal beauty reclined on a long stool, her limbs extended and her head resting on the edge of the chair so that she was the delineation of grace from her clear, white brows to the narrow slipper that protruded from her silken skirts. The older woman was stroking the younger's golden hair. It was a portrait from a fairy-tale and, as in many such tales, if the stranger valued his safety he would be advised not to enter in.

The air in the chamber, overheated and dense from the smoke of smouldering pastilles, was not conducive to physical health, but it was the moral climate that was dangerous. In all her seventy-two years, Mrs North had not taken to anyone as she had done to Ellen

Farebrother. Steeped as she was in selfishness, it had not pleased her to have her household roused in the early hours of a February morning to receive a victim of drowning. It had taken her maids some time to convince her that Frederick had not arrived in possession of a corpse, and when she had been persuaded that the lady was living, she agreed to give her shelter only because Philobeth was present. She was violently opposed to Frederick's attentions to Philobeth and had instructed him that 'the creature' would be turned away should she ever try to gain admission to Mythe. On that foul and stormy night, it had not occurred to her that Philobeth remained in the carriage because she was too proud to enter a house where she was unwelcome. The glee she felt that Philobeth was ashamed to show her face to a respectable woman was increased by realizing how pointedly she could favour the invalid over the rescuer by taking her in. Her mind had been made up by learning from Frederick, who had no great faith in her charity, that, despite the additional journey, they intended removing the unknown sufferer to Philobeth's home if Mrs North would not accept her.

A queer jealousy had overtaken Mrs North at the thought that she might lose her unwanted guest to Miss Alleyn. The venom she felt for Philobeth was not only because her station was too low and her conduct too unorthodox to fit her for a North, but because she was causing Frederick to choose for himself. Mrs North did not like her grandson. She held it against him that he took after the mother of whom she had disapproved, and would often gaze at his dark features with her head slightly to one side and remark that the true Norths had always been fair. This attitude did not prevent her exploiting Frederick's sense of duty to her advantage, nor did it make her less conscious of his value as the bearer of the family name. She wished him to have an heir, whose character would prove the consanguinity of generations by resembling herself, and this desire made it seem her right to choose his wife.

It appeared that Fate had played into her hands. When Ellen Farebrother had recovered enough to tell her story and had revealed herself to be not only of good lineage and exceptional beauty, but of a temperament to make Mrs North believe her hospitality was the essence of her real self, it soon seemed to both women that Ellen should be mistress of Frederick's heart. Mrs North congratulated herself upon her find. Small-minded and susceptible to Ellen's flattery and insinuating ways, too lazy to do other than take what pleased her at face value, Mrs North was an easy prey for Miss Farebrother. Mahala, having fewer scruples than Philobeth, could have countered Mrs North's baseness more easily than her upright friend, but neither could have beguiled her as Ellen did – for the woman who called herself Ellen Farebrother was without conscience.

It would not be true to say that Ellen was a wolf in sheep's clothing; she was closer in nature to a cobra, and it was nearer the mark to say that Mrs North was nursing a serpent in her bosom. The serpent was dazzling. She had an almost mesmeric influence upon those around her, as if her self-absorption was a whirlpool that sucked in observers who strayed too near. Her movements were all as though she were luxuriating in the sun, and her eyes, unshadowed by doubt, were deep and full of promises.

She admired her new name. For twenty-one years

she had been first Margaret Miller and then Ann Marsh, but neither had carried with it the life she intended to have. She was born of servants on a rich Virginia estate, where her delicate prettiness and playful ability to learn the manners of her social superiors had made her a pet of the lady of the house. Her childhood had been spent avoiding the work her mother set, curling at the feet of her mistress on pale-pillared verandahs, riding in open carriages beneath creeper-hung trees. There was a son in the family, a single heir to mansion and land, and she early decided that his affections were the easiest route to wealth. As her girlishness was shed and her ripening attraction caused men to pause in smoking their cigars, the son succumbed and, for fear of his parents, a run-away marriage was arranged. Both were convinced that forgiveness would follow when the deed was done, but their plans were discovered and Margaret found that she had misinterpreted her lady's fondness for her. Both master and mistress were horrified that she should have aspired to a legal union with their boy. Saved only by the colour of her skin from being as lowly in their eyes as a slave, she had been an amusement to them, a decoration and addition to the lady's dress as was her lap-dog and string of pearls. They could not sell her, but she was given a day to leave the plantation and the young man, who had sworn to love her, grew anxious for his inheritance, making no argument against his removal to a Maryland aunt and no farewells.

She had not cared for him, but she believed herself cheated of her entitlement and when she left she took with her what jewellery she knew would not be missed until she was too far to be traced. Being too young for a reputable trader to believe she had come by it honestly, and too inexperienced with the disreputable, she did not receive a good price for her spoil and it was not long before she was destitute. Soft-living had not fitted her for hard labour and her good manners did not serve her where gentility was not required. She could have sold her body, but an undaunted determination to rise in the world kept her from accepting the risk such a course involved. For a brief space, when money given her by a man who did not know the tavern had a back-way, enabled her to look respectable, she was a lady's maid in Boston. It seemed another door had opened. Her mistress, young, indolent and weak-spirited, was wax in her hands and the imperceptible slide from servant to confidential companion in possession of remunerative secrets was in wily progress when the husband was indiscreet enough to make his ardent pleas where his wife could hear.

Adrift once more, her contempt for the world enflamed by its thwarting of her, she travelled to New York and there her fortune changed. It occurred to her that her nationality might make her a novelty in London and, her social origins disguised by foreign-ness as well as courtesy, a good match might be easier to come by.

It was while she was seeking a passage that she encountered Ellen Farebrother. Miss Farebrother was in a friendless condition. Her parents had come from Lincolnshire over thirty years before and now that they were dead their only child, forlorn and yearning for 'the old country' of their reminiscences, had sold their Massachusetts property and was sailing to make a new life. At the last moment, her maid had refused to go with her and, distressed by the thought that she would

61

be the only woman upon the ship she had chosen, she pressed 'Ann Marsh' to take her servant's place.

Miss Farebrother was five years older than Ann and lacked her boldness, but their build and colouring were similar. Ann had always been superstitious and she saw her employer's pallid resemblance to herself and solitary situation as a gift that she would do well to accept. Without having a clear idea of how she could profit from Ellen, she took the maid's position and the two women sailed as the only passengers on a cargo ship.

From the moment of departure, Miss Farebrother was laid low with sea-sickness. She kept to her bunk, stricken alike by illness and alarm at the step she had taken, and clung to her sympathetic maid. Ann soothed and nursed her, encouraging her to remind herself of old happiness and future plans by recounting all details of her past and hopes. Their meals were brought to their cabin and, in their perfect privacy, Miss Farebrother grew to trust her servant enough to have her read aloud personal papers that were too much for her own aching eyes. She was grateful to the maid, who was showing such ready devotion, and anxious that they should not be parted on shore.

Ann went on deck only at night and wrapped, at Miss Farebrother's insistence, in her mistress's thick cloak, let herself be mistaken for that lady. She had come to no decision upon how she could turn her victim's attachment to her advantage, but as she stood in the bows, watching the cold starlight glint upon the waves, the rising surge of the ship fed her fierce and unaccountable anticipation.

When opportunity came, she did not hesitate. The winds that hurled the brig upon the Chesil were not more merciless than the woman, who killed when her own life was in peril. As their cabin filled with dark and swirling waters, Ann took her weakened mistress by the throat and held her head beneath the intruding sea until shock had gone from her staring eyes. It seemed that no-one would survive, but still she stripped the rings from the dead fingers and put them on her living hands. She tore the nightgown from the body and was exchanging it for hers when the storm claimed her, and a new Ellen Farebrother was cast out of the deep.

There was no-one in England to claim Ellen. A journey made to her parents' lost youth had had no living relatives waiting at its end. Ellen was sure her deception would not be discovered. The only two others rescued from the wreck died of their injuries as they lay upon the beach, and a finger broken by the looters could excuse any slight difference in her often-practised signature.

To her chagrin, there was little to sign. Her mistress had rashly carried all her wealth aboard the brig and nothing was recovered. One dream of gain, presented so suddenly, was thus as suddenly snatched away; but her situation had changed. Her acceptance as a lady gave her some claim upon the kindness of the gentry, and the good fortune that had borne her into Mythe showed her two paths to security.

It had taken her several days after the storm to emerge from the fever and nightmare that kept Carmody at her bedside, and another to gather enough information from the maid who sat with her, to know that it was safe to reveal herself as Ellen. When she did and found it necessary to be grateful to a rich, unmarried man and his foolish grandmother, she thought her ship had indeed come in. It was plain that Frederick was entranced by the romantic nature of their meeting, and it seemed an easy matter to beckon him to the altar. She did not waste her thanks or fears on Philobeth, who had no benefit to give her, believing that a woman earning her own money and travelling unchaperoned at night would not be considered as a wife.

It was her desire to wear Frederick's ring, but she had learned that ambition could be thwarted unexpectedly and she needed to ensure that his loss would not harm her prospects. Mrs North's opinion of her grandson was soon made plain and Ellen, as she fawned upon the old woman, held in reserve an intention to become her heir if she could not be her granddaughter-in-law. Pretty speeches and tender confidences had already passed between them on the subject of Frederick. With lowered head and rising blushes, Ellen had admitted to a regard for her saviour that was beyond the natural gratitude of the rescued. Sighing, she mourned the impoverished state that made it impertinent to think of him, and it was with difficulty that Mrs North coaxed her into believing that her name allowed her to aspire to his hand. She trod a narrow line on which the display of a proper affection for her future husband was balanced by sharing Mrs North's scorn for men in general. They did not whisper in corners, but many of their conversations had that tone and Mrs North, stroking the golden hair that flowed across her knee, lived in a spirit of gloating conspiracy.

They heard the sound of hoof-beats with stirring expectancy. The visitor came at all hours and was never refused. Ellen writhed in Mrs North's lap, pressing her cheek against the velvet skirts, but did not move to put up her hair. The old woman grasped the young shoulder that raised itself to her and turned to the maid, who had come in.

'Mr Frederick's here, ma'am.'

Mrs North raised her head in exultation. 'Let him be shown in,' she said – and the women looked towards the door.

Chapter Five

'I saw him last week,' said Carmody. 'Henderson was short-handed and took him on to clear that low field of his for turnips. It wasn't past noon, and I'm sure he was in liquor.'

Philobeth closed the lich-gate behind her. 'If it was remorse that was making him drink,' she said, 'I might have some sympathy, but I hear he thinks himself hard done by and talks slightingly of Mary.'

'I'm afraid Barlow's one of those who can never believe themselves at fault. He harbours a grudge against the world.'

They began walking back towards Chantry, Carmody leading his horse. It was a fine May afternoon, warmer than the day that Mary had hanged herself, but so like in appearance that Philobeth had been reminded of her and had walked over to put flowers on her grave. She, who could suffer for love but would never be defeated by it, often thought of the girl she had drawn in the barn, and the warmth of her own pierced heart flowed out in pity for that still face. It pleased her that Frederick had insisted that the grave should be in the churchyard. There had been some talk in the village against a suicide being allowed into consecrated earth, but the living was in Frederick's gift, and the vicar, who wished his son to succeed him, saw fit to agree with the squire. Mary now lay beneath a green mound in the far corner of the enclosure where holly blossomed whitely around her and violets spread beneath the sheltering wall. Philobeth had taken bluebells – the token of remembrance that Greeks had carved upon their tombs in distant years – and her gloveless hands were still damp from their sap when she met Carmody.

He was riding down the lane that passed the church and had reined in to hail her as she made her way through the angels and crosses of the graveyard's more favoured occupants. From the direction he was taking, she thought it likely that he was going to visit Mahala and, having questions she wanted to ask about her friend's health, she greeted him with more eagerness than usual. She was always civil to him, but his interest in her was an annoyance that made her feel a little ashamed of herself. Considering the pain she was suffering from the suspension of her own hopes, she believed that she should feel compassion for a man whose affections she could not return, but his attachment only caused her irritation. It was the more exasperating because she thought that she could like him if only he would look at her as dryly as he looked at Mahala, and talk with the same acerbic tongue.

Carmody was encouraged by her readiness to answer him. Dismounting at her first smile, he had kept pace with her to the gate. He was not a sentimental man and had not said plainly to himself that he was in love, but Philobeth occupied his thoughts to a surprising degree and altered his demeanour and pulse when she was near. In his youth he had been inclined to think a wife an encumbrance, but manhood had brought an ability to learn from observation, and he had seen that women are various and more vital than circumstances seemed to allow. He had not reached the belief that the female sex was equal to the male, but he was prepared to accept that certain women had that distinction and he numbered Philobeth and Mahala amongst them.

It puzzled him to find such animated characters in the wilds of Dorset. He had not been down from London long enough to have shaken off the idea that a city is the proper place for vigour and decision. When he had finished his training, and financial constraints had meant that he must buy a cheap practice, he had felt the frustration of thwarted ambition. He wanted to cure the sick, but his vision encompassed an infirmary following the most modern theories under his direction, and did not rule out personal and increasing wealth. It enraged him that he could do no more for Mahala than make her ebbing life more comfortable than nature intended. Day after day he sat at her side, cool and quick, matching her mockery of the world with his own wry fancy, and all the while his anger that he could not save her beat beneath his sardonic smile.

He was afraid that Philobeth would ask about Mahala. There was small doubt that Miss Graham would not see the end of the year, and he had her permission to tell Philobeth so if she should ask. He knew Philobeth to have the strength for sorrow; he had heard of her hand put out to the corpse; he had seen her stand firm and unflinching in the presence of death, yet he shrank from revealing impending grief to her when he longed to give her hope and returning health. He watched her as they walked. She was thinner than she had been, and there was a suggestion of sternness in her expression; but the changes did her no harm in his eyes. Her movements were supple and she held herself with the confidence of one whose body had always done her bidding. Her closeness made him conscious that they were man and woman, and the need to touch her made him tighten his fingers on the reins.

Despite her appearance, Philobeth was tired. At all hours, her thoughts ran upon Frederick, constantly presenting her with pictures from their past, and to counteract this obsession she was driving herself to work long days in pursuit of her elusive form and subject. Slater would find her at dawn searching for the colours of the flushing sky or standing transfixed, staring at the veining of a leaf. She prowled the house at night, candle aloft, reproducing the shadows that a single flame could cast. Her exertions were bringing her to that point of exhaustion when sleep is no longer possible and the imagination that would be dissipated in dreams springs forward and releases inspiration into the waking mind. There was expectation surging behind the barrier of her self-discipline, but always she longed to turn, in her coming triumph, to a lover who would share her joy.

She could feel Carmody watching her with more than the attention of a casual companion. Though she did not want to attract him, she did not find it necessary to be cold. She could sense a tension that might lead to his being less careful of her sensibilities and treating her as if she were Mahala. Easy conversation, unhampered by the unspoken fears and accusations that now hindered her intercourse with old friends, would be a relaxation for her and welcome, despite its origins. Complications might arise, but it was enough at this moment to be cordial and forget tomorrow.

'I've heard that Mr Alleyn's visit is to be delayed again,' Carmody said.

'I'm afraid so.' Philobeth noted that her father's presence had grown so rare that his promised arrival could not be called a return to his home. She was chilled by this further sign of change, but resolutely told herself that she was, after all, planning to spread her own wings. 'Mrs Gilbert Anderson asked him to paint her daughter on her coming of age and he says the girl has too interesting a face to refuse.'

'Then you take after your father in your choice of subject as well as in talent. You both understand the human countenance.'

'I've no great wish to be a portrait-painter,' Philobeth said. 'Though,' she added, dryly, 'in historical composition it can be rewarding. I often think of Judith slaying Holofernes.'

Carmody was not averse to hearing her speak sourly in this manner. He knew whose face she would choose for Holofernes and felt no compunction in hoping that should she ever draw Boaz covering Ruth with his cloak, another cast of features would suit her purpose.

'However,' Philobeth went on, 'there's an advantage to having such a close connection in the portrait-buying circles. I sent papa the series of heads I had done – my own amongst them – and the dealer sold them all. I'm a woman of substance – but temporarily, for I have nothing left to sell.'

She glanced at him wickedly, aware that he was uncomfortable with the fact of her earnings. He had raised his hand to fondle his horse, occupying himself to hide his distaste, but when he saw that she was teasing him, he was again encouraged. A woman is not mischievous with a man she dislikes. This reflection interrupted his caress and the horse nuzzled him to have it continue. Philobeth reached out and cupped her palm over its soft muzzle, smoothing the short hair with her thumb. She was wearing a tight-fitting velveteen jacket and as she raised her arm the sun gleamed on its blue-black surface like the sheen on a peacock's feather. Carmody had always preferred exotic flowers, and he seemed to see himself pinning orchids to her breast. There was an instant's hidden confusion as Philobeth realized how close to him she was standing and he wondered if she could read his thoughts.

She moved a step away. 'I'd been hoping to meet you,' she said, more seriously. 'I'm concerned about the change in Mahala's condition. Can you tell me what it means?' She was looking at him directly, trusting him to be honest, and it filled him with compassion.

That best part of him, dedicated to the cure of suffering, was fleetingly naked in his eyes as they walked on. 'Yes, my dear Miss Alleyn,' he said. 'I can tell you what it means.'

The work that Barlow had been hired to do in Henderson's fields was not carried out to the farmer's satisfaction, and he was turned off before the job was completed. Carmody had been right to suspect him of being in liquor before noon. It was usual for labourers to drink heavily during the day, but outright drunkenness that slowed progress and caused resentment amongst the other men was not to be tolerated. Henderson had been obliged to have Barlow thrown into the road by two broad-shouldered carters used to dealing with protesting and recalcitrant creatures. The tale of the threats and obscenities Barlow had shouted as he was dragged from the meadows spread amongst the farmers at the next market-dinner and it was generally held to show extraordinary patience on Henderson's part not to have taken any legal action.

The incident made it still more difficult for Barlow to find employment in the area. Since being dismissed at Mary's death, he had had only casual labouring work, with a day here and week there offered by masters who found a sudden need for an extra hand greater than their disapproval of him. There were those who believed that girls in Mary's predicament had only themselves to blame but, whichever side they took, no-one renting Frederick's land would have dared risk giving a permanent situation to one he had personally condemned.

Barlow had brought his misfortunes upon himself, but guilt did not figure in his reasoning. He had always been of light morals, and the doxies he consorted with had laughed at respectability, mocking girls who clung to their maidenhead, and, unless they were maudlin with gin, affecting a brazen self-reliance. When Holden had told Carmody that he had thought it a change for the better when Barlow had abandoned the forward pieces he usually followed for Mary, he had not known his man. The gentle maid had been piquant to Barlow's jaded tastes, but he had not understood that the contrast between her and his fancy women was more than skin-deep. He despised her for having taken her life. Other girls had had bastards before now and been none the worse for it. Love and betrayal were mere words to him, but the reduction in his circumstances from the ordinary poverty of a labourer to a hand-to-mouth grind was real, and festered in his mind. His violent nature made the scorn of those who pitied Mary hard to bear. In his anger he needed a living person to hate and, as he could do no more hurt to Mary, his bitterness focussed upon Frederick. He brooded incessantly upon the injury done him and, through long nights of sodden dreams and longer mornings, his grievance grew.

One evening, before the bluebells had withered on Mary's grave and while Philobeth was being accused by Mahala of having deliberately let her win at cards, Barlow decided to visit The Swan. He was living in a back room over a chandler's shop at the poorer end of Buckland Weston. The shop, with its tallow candles and adulterated tea, catered for those as impoverished as Barlow himself, and its owner was glad to cram his family into three small rooms for the sake of a few shillings a week from a tenant. Barlow's savings were almost gone, and those few shillings were growing to be a hardship, yet he did not choose to solve his problems by leaving the district. He was a strong, healthy man and could have found work easily by going to a hiring-fair, but a misplaced stubbornness kept him to the one valley where his bad character was recognized. The smell of rabbit often drifted from the pot hanging over his grate and this poaching was his only satisfaction, apart from the drinking that ate his erratic income.

Before he had been publicly disgraced, he had taken his rum-and-cider in The Swan when he had not had an inclination for low company. The Swan acted as a club for the artisans, petty tradesmen and farmworkers of Weston. Raucous behaviour was not expected, and the landlady looked askance at any 'falling-down-drunk', unless it were in celebration of a first-born child or despair at a tenth. Farmers and dealers would occasionally look in if they wanted to speak to a regular, but it was rare for a woman to be seen in the bar if she were not employed on the premises. He had not shown his face there since the suicide, preferring more disreputable beer-houses where he could be certain of sympathy.

Tonight, a belligerent mood made him want to challenge his accusers. Four days road-mending had put money in his pocket that ought to have been set aside for necessities, and his inability to see tomorrow made him feel purse-proud. He could not grasp that the disgust felt by the good-natured for his shaming of Mary was genuine, and it seemed to him that if he went amongst them boldly, he would be accepted, especially if he could pay his way.

Defiance of the scorn in which he was held made him dress himself carefully. He steamed the kersey-mere jacket he always wore to go courting and, with a feather in the band of his billycock hat, looked as devil-may-care as if no shadow fell upon him. A moment of spite made him knot round his neck the red silk kerchief that was sister to the one he had used to cool Mary and that later had taken her last breath.

He entered The Swan soon after nine. It was Saturday night and, despite the needs of their beasts making Sunday little different from other days for many of the men, there was a general feeling of liberty and license amongst the drinkers. There was a lull in the talk as he walked to the counter and a leaning together of heads as eyes followed him. He was self-conscious as he put down his coins and the unexpected

sensation made him ask for his cider more aggress-
ively than he had intended. Mrs Lomas, the landlady,
looked towards her husband before she reached for
a glass and he, judging that Barlow was likely to
be troublesome if refused, nodded coldly. Barlow
received no greeting as he was given the cider and he
made no attempt at conversation. Picking up his glass,
he sat defensively facing the length of the pub. At one
end of the table he had chosen, a harness-maker and a
joiner were playing draughts, and their expressions as
he tossed his hat onto the bench and stretched out his
legs, made it plain he was unwelcome.

He rested his back against the wall in a swaggering
attitude and raised his drink to the company, but he
was shaken. His custom had not been refused but the
change in atmosphere as he was noticed, and the slow
return to their talk of the other drinkers, showed him
that he was ostracized. He looked down the dim room
at groups sitting at other tables and in the settles beside
the hearth, where a can of ale was warming in the
coals. Mrs Lomas was passing to and fro lighting
candles and as each flame threw another face into
distinction, he saw insult and contempt. He had not
bargained for such disdain in a place of men. There
were no women here, except the landlord's wife, to
force lip-service to respectability, and no tenants of the
squire's land, yet blame was loud in every glance. In
this masculine society, he had thought to have the ruin
of a maid winked at, but he had chosen the wrong
class of men for that attitude. The wives of many of
the drinkers had been with child at the altar and their
husbands might joke of being 'caught' or cast it in
their women's teeth during quarrels, but each had lain
with one to whom they had been true. There was a

struggling decency in the room that was not to be found in the low beer-houses. These were men whose hard lives had not blunted their ability to understand misery in others and, in Mary, they had seen their own daughters. They were rough in their speech and justice and, when the news of the girl's death had broken, there had been demands amongst them for punishment to be meted out to her seducer. There were ways to deal with a libertine, and only Barlow's absence had saved him from them so far.

Nothing of this was apparent to Barlow. He felt the condemnation but believed it to be insincere. The enjoyment of someone's discomfiture, with its feeling of spurious superiority, was familiar to him and he thought the scorn in which he was held was a form of gloating over his downfall. It filled him with loathing and, as he drank the strong cider, an insolent urge to provoke the assembly and show up its smugness got the better of him.

The pub was becoming more crowded. The air was thickening with tobacco smoke and the warm, greasy smell of cooking. As more men entered and drew back from the empty seats around Barlow, his isolation was emphasized and his resentment was like a second heart within his breast. A sailor, travelling inland to visit his sister in Sherborne and unaware of who Barlow was, sat beside him at last, causing him to make room by sliding along the bench until he was next to the joiner. The sailor had ordered a basin of broth and, feeling convivial as he ate and contemplated his holiday, he asked Barlow to take a glass with him.

They fell into conversation and, as their jug emptied, the good humour of his companion made Barlow more truculent towards the other drinkers. The sailor's easy manner and flow of anecdotes made Barlow feel accepted and seemed to justify his conviction that he was being treated unfairly. He began to talk of himself and the sympathetic response he received to his tale of unemployment encouraged him to expand upon the reason for his dismissal from Holden's farm. His description of Mary was lewd and his contempt for her despair was venomous. His gaze was ranging round the room as he spoke and he did not notice the antagonism growing in his listener's eyes. It startled him when the sailor stood up abruptly.

'What?' Barlow asked. 'Another jug?'

The sailor stared at him. 'If I hear much more—' he said and broke off, shaking his head and gathering his glass and bag. He moved away, his face set, searching for a place to sit. A ploughman from Holden's who had taken in the scene with Barlow, pulled over a stool for him and the sailor pushed his canvas holdall under the round table and sat down. A question from the ploughman, answered in a few sharp words, caused the men who heard them to turn and look at Barlow.

The shock of the sailor's departure was the straw that broke Barlow's back. He slammed his glass onto the table so violently that cider slopped onto the wood and ran onto the draught-board beside him. The noise and the springing up of the players as they found cider dripping into their laps attracted the attention of everyone in the room. Barlow was suddenly the focus for the hostility that had been caused by his presence but, until this moment, not purposefully directed at him.

'What are you staring at?' he demanded. 'Like to throw me out, would ee? But doesn't dare? North not

77

here to do it for ee? Not but what he'd have been afeard if all was equal. I'd have set en down sharp if e didn't have his money to hide behind.'

There was silence in the room. Mrs Lomas, wiping a tankard with a cloth, stood arrested with her hand inside the rim. Nothing was said, but the atmosphere grew heavy and close. Lips parted and skin flushed as if the watchers expected an act of passion. Barlow, pressing his back against the wall, knew that there was nothing now that he could do to protect himself and, even in his dread of what might be done, he was glad that he had aimed a pinprick of insult at Frederick. These were men who needed the cheap bread that Frederick had fought for, lauding him for it, and it pleased Barlow, as his body cringed in anticipation of blows, that he should have mocked their hero.

Davis, Holden's ploughman, took his pipe from his mouth. 'Mary was a proper good maid,' he said quietly.

'She was a whore and be damned to 'er!' Barlow's voice suddenly rose high, leaving the impression of a scream in the stillness.

There was a moment of waiting and then the men got to their feet. They went for Barlow as if their individuality had dropped away and they had merged into one being with one intent. Barlow raised an arm across his face as the first hands reached him, but he did not struggle as he was dragged to where a space had been cleared amongst the tables, beneath the central beam that supported the ceiling. He saw a cowman tying a loop in a rope and sweat broke beneath his arms and on the palms of his hands. There was no strength in his legs and he felt his bowels loosen. A whisper of hanging was passing from one mouth to the next, becoming more insistent as it changed into a chant. He waited for the noose, his throat contracting, but when it came it was looped around his ankles and he was upended and lashed to a hook in the beam. He flailed his arms and they were grasped from behind and bound to his sides. There seemed no sound possible in the world but 'Hang him! Hang him!' and no smells but the pungence of leather and cattle that suffocated him as the men pressed near. He shut his eyes but a thumb was thrust in his mouth and he opened them to see the cauldron of broth on the floor by his head. His jaws were forced wide and a full ladle tipped in. The broth flowed out over his face, running into his hair, and rough fingers held his nostrils shut so that, as the next ladle was poured in, he swallowed as he breathed, choking on broth that blocked his nose and lungs. There was another ladleful and another. The chanting was louder about him and soon there was no sensation but drowning and the darkening of his sight.

Chapter Six

Towards the end of May, Mahala haemorrhaged. The loss of blood was small and had stopped by the time Dr Carmody had been roused from bed to attend her, but both knew what it heralded. It was rare for Mahala to show she was afraid, and Carmody understood what it cost her to be unable to suppress the trembling of the hand he held. He sat with her till morning, as she lay with the taste of blood in her mouth, stifling coughs that might start the bleeding again, and by dawn she had control of herself once more.

What was a shameful show of fear to Mahala was remarkable stoicism to her friends and a lack of a suitable solemnity to her relations. Hearing of her turn for the worse, the two black-clad cousins who were to inherit from her by command of her father, descended on Combehays to enjoin her to cast herself upon the mercy of the Lord and to take a mental inventory of what would soon be theirs. The visit cheered her greatly. Agreeing that her illness was lamentable, she outraged them by announcing the price of everything they handled and urged them to pray that she might yet be spared for twenty years. They retreated in umbrage, leaving her wheezing painfully and plotting to keep them from her wealth.

This exercise raised her from the depression that had seeped into her thoughts. Her spirits had sunk at the prospect of fruitless misery, of pain, of desperate, shallow breaths, of blood rising in her throat. She dreaded sleep lest she wake suddenly, foully with the hot, thick fluid that was redundant in her veins bubbling from her lips. If there had been a chance to defeat the disease, she could have borne any torment, scorning the effort it involved, but knowing herself to be moribund made her suffering futile. She felt that nature was drawing her down into an anonymous pit of affliction, depriving her of dignity and self as her father had done by disregarding her because of her sex. Sickness and her sire's belief that women were alike weak and foolish had cheated her of the life her bold spirit could have grasped, but she had not been defeated and she would not let death snatch from her the power to succour a friend.

She could have been a devoted daughter, a triumphant, earthy wife, a sarcastic, tigerish mother, but these were not to be and her love, disguised but clear to its recipient, had flooded out upon Philobeth. It hurt her that Philobeth was losing Frederick. She wanted her friend to have what she had not had herself. The refusal to pursue a rich man exasperated her. She thought that Philobeth had retired from battle out of false pride. It was not what she would have done herself, but she accepted that their characters differed and that her own was, perhaps, less fine. With all her heart, she wanted to give Philobeth independence by leaving her the whole of her means, but her father thwarted her desire.

Summoning her lawyers and then more for a second and third opinion, she laid before them her wish to overrule Mr Graham's will. Their answers were the same. The will must stand. She could not control her capital or leave it away from her cousins until she was thirty years of age or a married woman. The sombre men in satin neck-cloths, delivering their conclusions in low tones, were gruff with their clerks when they left the manor, and told their wives of the waste of beauty; but none could help her. She decided to help herself.

'I've been thinking about brown.' Philobeth was sitting on the day-bed in Mahala's room, her knees drawn up and her shoes kicked onto the floor.

'We must all think of something,' said Mahala.

Philobeth stretched out her legs and gazed into the sunlight that was throwing the pattern of the window-tracery onto the wall. A curtain of the four-poster had been pulled so that Mahala's face was shaded where she lay, but the room was bright.

'Papa's suggested that I submit a painting at the Royal Academy exhibition next year. We ladies can exhibit even though we can't join. Explain that if you can.'

'How does this lead us to brown?' Mahala's voice had become softer and sibilant with breathlessness.

'It would mean I'd have to obey their code absolutely if my work was to be chosen. I do now to some extent, of course, but it doesn't satisfy me. I want to get away from it, not move closer. Papa recommended a landscape but the Academy says the tone of landscapes must be brown. When were landscapes ever brown? It says colours must be muted and all outlines firm, but I look outside now and my eyes are dazzled and distant objects blurred. I must paint what I see, but I must also sell. I'll have to fend for myself one day.'

The implications of her solitude subdued them both. Mahala moved her head on the pillow. Her pallor, emphasized by her livid cheeks, made her eyes startlingly dark. She had not told Philobeth about her hope of changing her father's will for fear of causing argument or disappointment, and she declined from day to day in a fever of anxiety that the plan she was forming for her friend's advantage would miscarry.

Philobeth drew in air audibly as if steeling herself for an effort against depression. 'I don't see the world as brown,' she said. 'Black, certainly, but not brown. I can't even treat my canvases with asphaltum now. Whatever colour you use on it has its vitality drained away. If I see a rose as scarlet, surely that's how I should paint it – and not in a composition making either an S or a triangle.'

'I can't advise you on triangles,' said Mahala, 'but I've always preferred scarlet to pink.'

Philobeth picked up the book that was lying in her lap and opened it at a marker. 'Ruskin says that we should "trust nature and forsake all else".' She ran her finger down the page. 'He says we should – where is it? – we should "go to Nature in all singleness of heart, and walk with her labouriously and trustingly." That seems to mean scarlet.'

Mahala closed her eyes, tiredly, then looked at the canopy of the bed that imprisoned her. 'My cousins,' she said, 'tell me that my illness is decreed by God. Carmody says it's an effect of Nature and men will find a cure one day. I prefer to blame Nature, even though I walk with her labouriously. Disapproving of God would take more strength than I can summon.'

She sounded exhausted and Philobeth, who was learning the habits of the sick-room, did not reply. In a moment, she heard the slight change in breathing that marked the light sleep of an invalid. Mahala rarely slept all night unless she were drugged, but she fell in and out of dozes and was often so drowsy she could hardly testify to having woken.

Philobeth turned on her side and watched the shadowed bed. Her lithe body, curled like a cat, gave the impression of an indolence that her mind never experienced. She had not recovered from the news that Carmody had given her. In the hurry of her spirits and the egocentricity of youth, she had wanted to cry out that Mahala, who had always been a fixed point in her world, could not die, could not leave her. She had not done so, recognizing and rejecting her selfishness even as it electrified her, but summoning such strength of will had made her shudder enough to put out her hand to Carmody for support.

It had bewildered her that Mahala had seemed unchanged when they next met. She had found herself speaking in self-consciously gentle tones, skirting the subject that was most in her mind but Mahala, holding a cloth to her mouth, complained that she would die of boredom if she were raised to the sainthood prematurely, and harried her into their old intimacy. They accepted the truth of what was to come and, in the freedom this gave them, the love between the women flourished and showed itself in poignant care for each other's comfort. There was an intensity of feeling between them as they waited for their parting that was, at times, a strange elation. They were not embarrassed by the ugliness of the disease that Mahala would go to any lengths to hide from all but Philobeth and Carmody. An inexpressible tenderness filled her movements as Philobeth placed her friend's sputum-dish within reach or helped her to the close-stool and, forever after, when she smelt the sweat of the sick-bed, she also caught the scent of the hayfields that had hung on the summer air.

Carmody would come and sit with them and as they whispered together, Mahala's husky softness and Philobeth's low cadences made him think of the wind stirring ripe barley that rustles and murmurs in dry invitation to the reaper.

The slow afternoon filled the room with the quietness that is made to seem like silence by sounds that are just within hearing. Lying with her palm beneath her cheek, striped by sunlight, Philobeth was aware of the gardener's boy crossing the gravel drive, pulling the cart that held his watering-cans; somewhere deep within the house a door opened and shut and, far across the grounds, a peacock that used to eat from Mahala's hand screeched and spread its tail in the opulent shade of the Kashmir Garden.

Mahala opened her eyes. She felt rested. The hush that surrounded her was made peaceful and protective by her knowledge that Philobeth watched over her. She was afraid that she was putting her friend's good health at risk but, in her weakness, could not find the force that she would need to drive such affection away. All her determination was used for shaping her scheme to make Philobeth her heiress, and none was left for insisting on separation. The most that she could do was continue to cover her face so that her breath should not poison her dearest companion; she could not even refuse to allow Philobeth near her for, increasingly, she craved a loving touch.

'Are you still thinking of Paris?' she asked, as if she had not been asleep.

Philobeth, used to these sudden resumptions of conversation but deep in her own thoughts, stirred a little, flexing her feet, as she drew her mind back to her work. 'I'm thinking of it,' she said, turning onto her back. 'It interests me that the French paint oils out of doors; but I don't know. When – when the time comes, I'll make a decision.'

Moving imperceptibly, the sun reached the edge of Mahala's pillow, making her black hair shine against the white linen as if it were absorbing the spark that was fading from the flesh. Philobeth stood up, her own hair dishevelled, and went to adjust the bed-curtain.

'Frederick came to see me yesterday,' Mahala said. 'In the morning, before you arrived.'

'Oh?' Philobeth pulled the hangings into position and ran her fingers down them. 'You didn't say.'

'I don't know why. I was tired.'

Philobeth would not ask for details. She walked over to a mirror and began pinning up a braid that had come loose. There had been days when Frederick had liked to see her hair about her shoulders; she put them behind her as she did the coiled plait.

Mahala did not volunteer an account of what they had said. They were old friends and Frederick had come to show sympathy and offer any help she might require, but his treatment of Philobeth put difficulties in the way of an unargumentative visit. Knowing how complete an invalid Mahala had become, Frederick had not expected her to probe him for his intentions towards Philobeth and Ellen. He felt that he had come, bearing fruit and flowers, to deliver himself into the hands of an inquisitor. His natural courtesy was against him. He could not tell a dying woman to mind her own business – particularly one who would take no notice if he did – but his guilt made him resent the investigation into his private affairs. Even had he wished to be open, he could not have explained himself to his own satisfaction. He lived in a fog of shame and desire, unable to reason or decide how his confusion should end. He strode angrily about her chamber, his riding-boots increasingly loud upon the oak floor, picking up and setting down her trinkets, as he frowned at the neighbour he had come to soothe. The housekeeper, who had tried to stay in the room for respectability's sake but been banished by her mistress, had been alarmed by the sound of a raised voice and gone in to find Frederick apparently brandishing a pomade jar at a flushed Mahala. 'For all the world,' she told the servants' hall, 'as if he'd strike my lady dead.'

Mahala did not for a moment harbour any suspicion that his agitation meant her harm, nor was she one to hold a man's passion against him, but his reaction to her questioning persuaded her that Philobeth's prospect of becoming Mrs North was indeed bleak. It had been necessary to her plans to discover this and, though she grieved for her friend's first hopes, she believed the interview had been worth the fatigue and fever it caused her.

'He asked after you,' she said, remembering his attempts at normal conversation before her questions had been flung at his head.

Philobeth pushed the last pin into place. 'I wonder that he'd draw attention to himself in that way,' she said. 'It makes it plain that he no longer visits me.' She turned back to the bed. 'Of course, there may come a time when he calls at the house and I'm gone.'

There was acid in her voice and Mahala, whose weakness had made her less intuitive, took this to mean a relinquishment of yearning. She would have handed Frederick to Philobeth, tied in a ribbon, if she could but, as she could not, it encouraged her to think that her friend was coming to terms with her loss.

Philobeth again sat down on the day-bed, smoothing her skirts beneath her and leaving her fingers tucked under her legs. 'And I notice that he's been in no hurry to come to you,' she said. 'He should take a leaf from Carmody's book.'

It was on the tip of Mahala's tongue to retort that the obligations of neighbour and doctor were hardly similar but, under the circumstances, she was glad of Philobeth's changing attitude to Carmody, and she abandoned Frederick's character to its own devices. 'Ah,' she said, 'so Carmody isn't merely a gossip-monger and neglecter of his principal patient?'

Philobeth removed her hands from her legs and clasped them in front of her. She flushed, remembering how she had leant against him when he had told her of Mahala's turn for the worse. Her mounting colour interested her watcher greatly. 'I admit,' she said at last, 'that I was prejudiced against him. He does improve with knowing. I'd say that my opinion of him has altered materially.'

Carmody did not arrive at Combehays that day until the evening had ripened to a rich, full dusk. The air was soft and warm. On the road through the meadow, where weary reapers were slowly walking home, it was fragrant with mown hay, and in Mahala's drive the scent of eglantine was almost palpable, so that he paused as he reached it as if he were passing through a web.

Mahala was alone when he went into her room. The window was still open and her bed-curtains were pushed back to let the violet light fall onto her pillows. It pleased him that she smiled as he came in. He sat beside her, leaning forward in his chair to take her wrist and lay his hand upon her brow. Her pulse was rapid but she was not unusually feverish, and he thought that her excitement was caused by something other than illness.

'How have you been?' he asked.

'I'm well. I've had Philobeth here. We were talking of you.'

His fingers were resting on her upturned arm and she felt their pressure increase slightly. 'Oh?' he said. 'It makes your heart beat charmingly. I hope that was the object of the exercise.'

'It isn't my heart that concerns me.'

She was watching him as she had watched Philobeth earlier and it raised a tremor of anticipation in him.

'These must be deep matters,' he said, 'if they prevent you offering me wine.'

'Are you too idle to help yourself? You know where it is by now.'

He rose and went to the chest-of-drawers where a decanter of his favourite port had been placed. Filling a glass, he brought both it and the decanter back to the bed. 'I have a feeling,' he said, setting the decanter carefully on the floor as he sat down, 'that I may need to prescribe a second dose.'

The smile that had welcomed him enlivened her face again. There was mischief in it, but her eyes were more serious. 'I think you may. I want to usurp a little of your authority. I want to diagnose your condition.'

'How will you do that?'

'You've asked me personal questions,' she said. 'I need to do the same to you. As you see, I'm in no position to spread the tale round the market-place.'

'You can ask. I don't promise to answer.'

She smoothed the sheet in front of her. The skin on her thin hands was almost as white as the linen. 'I believe,' she said, her voice low and breathless, 'that you and I share a love of Philobeth.'

For a moment he said nothing. He had hardly admitted the nature of his infatuation to himself, and to reveal it would be a commitment he was unsure he wanted to make. He had not yet made his way in the world, and the thought of the financial burden of a family caused him to deny his emotions for an instant but, as he contemplated saying 'No', he seemed to be enveloped by her presence. The pit of his stomach tightened. He felt the pressure of her weight against him as he told her of Mahala, the velvet of her sleeve, her hair brushing his lips as she bowed her head.

'Yes,' he said. 'I love her.'

Mahala relaxed. Her most unorthodox inquiry was still before her, but she knew him to value the comfort and opportunities of wealth, and his admission reassured her.

The sun was setting behind the hills. Its last flush of crimson stained her coverlet and reddened the walls of the quiet room.

'You know the terms of my father's will,' she said. 'If I die before I'm thirty years old or married, all my fortune will go to my cousins. I can't alter that.'

'Yes, I know.'

'I want to leave my money to Philobeth. I want to see

her happy – to protect her from poverty.' The strain of what she was saying made her need to wait to regain her breath. 'I'm twenty-six,' she went on, faintly, 'and will never be twenty-seven. I can't help her by living. It isn't in my power.'

The sorrow of her death gripped him. He covered her hand with his. 'God forgive me,' he said. 'I would have saved you if I could.'

Her frail fingers linked with his. It was the most intimate touch she had given a man and all she would ever know of carnal love. She, who could have rejoiced in a lover, rested her weak hand in his and the room was full of unspoken longing, of lost dreams, of generosity and trust.

'Would you have Philobeth for your wife?'

'Yes.' He could barely speak for pity. 'I'll care for her. Don't be afraid.'

'I can care for you both.' She hesitated. 'Consider what I say. Don't answer me at once.' She moved her hand within his. 'Marry me. I won't be here for long. Be my husband and make both my friends safe. Marry me.'

Chapter Seven

Mahala and Carmody were married by Special Licence in the private chapel of Combehays Manor the following week. Philobeth and the housekeeper acted as witnesses, the former having been told of the wedding being arranged to deprive Mahala's cousins of their inheritance, but not of the bridegroom's intentions towards herself.

Mr Graham had not stipulated that Mahala should have her family's approval of her betrothed, believing that any man with sufficient courage and firmness of purpose to marry his daughter was fit to manage his estate, and deserved the reward. The couple did not, therefore, think it necessary to inform her relations until after they were legally husband and wife when Carmody, writing at Mahala's dictation, sent each of the Grahams a wedding favour and assured them that their congratulations would be well received.

Frederick heard of the wedding the day after it had occurred. The grocer's man, making a delivery at Combehays, had the news from the kitchen staff and passed it on to the under-cook at Holcombe House, where he was instantly invited in for refreshment. Frederick's butler, who was not ashamed to admit to a love of gossip as great as that of his underlings, dispatched the most inquisitive housemaid to Combe-hays for details, and himself related the tale to Frederick at dinner.

The information had a gratifying effect. It was no exaggeration to say that Frederick was astounded. Since the night of the wreck he had been absorbed by his own intrigues, and having had no warning of what was afoot at Combehays made him realize how much he had lost contact with his friends. It gave him a pang to think that Philobeth had known of the affair without telling him, and it did not ease his discomfort to be aware that the estrangement was of his own making. He was expected at Mythe that evening, but he sent a message saying he was detained on business and stayed at home, brooding long into the night.

The following morning he rode over to Chantry to call on Philobeth. He had felt the lack of her company before now, but the awkwardness of trying to resume their old amity while still bewitched by Ellen had prevented him approaching her. Grasping the excuse of Mahala's marriage, he tied his horse to the garden gate as he always used to do and rang the bell, only to be told that Philobeth was not in.

Slater, wiping her hands on her apron, was in two minds how to treat him. His rank counted for nothing in her eyes when weighed against the unhappiness he had caused her girl, and she was as capable of scold-ing him as she was Philobeth. It would have given her satisfaction to tell him what she thought of his behaviour, but she suspected this visit meant that he was coming to his senses and she would not scare away any man Philobeth loved. She could not tell him where Philobeth was walking but she was able to give him more circumstances of the wedding than were known in the servants' halls, and he went away more startled than he had arrived.

He chose not to ride straight back to Holcombe. An hour spent in the lanes did not bring him Philobeth, who was sketching in Mahala's garden, but it carried his thoughts an unexpected distance. Slater, having given him the benefit of the doubt, had talked to him in her old open manner and, after asking him not to pass it on, had told him that Mahala, despising her family, had married to 'put their noses out of joint'. He was taken aback and, as he turned off the road and his horse's hooves fell softly on the turf track into the hills, he wondered why.

His experience of the Grahams on the few occasions they had met at Combehays made him glad that they were to be disinherited. He acknowledged the usefulness of the arrangement to both Mahala and Carmody, and yet the doctor's action left a wretched taste in his mouth. It seemed unmanly to gain a dying woman's wealth in this way; but no sooner had he reached that conclusion than he reproved himself, for was he not carried on the shoulders of his ancestors? His money had come to him through the deaths of relations, and if Carmody gained his from a wife instead of a grandfather, the difference was mere accident. It occurred to him that much of his restlessness was caused by secretly believing that his own position was unmanly, and the thought was a revelation to him. He had never realized what had always been plain to Philobeth – that he was more suited to making a fortune than possessing one. His character was formed for struggle and endeavour, but he had never exerted this quality except to oppose the Corn Laws. It irked him that Philobeth did not appreciate what strength of mind

94

had been required to withstand the united disapproval of his class on this matter, but she lived amongst men who used their talents and he saw why she might complain of him.

With such painful reflections to occupy him, he could not call at Combehays that day, but the following afternoon found him under its stone porch asking to pay his respects to the newly-weds. The maid, a younger sister of one of his own, had not recovered from the excitement and giggled as she told him that only the mistress was at home but that if he would wait in the drawing-room, she would see if Miss – if Mrs Carmody would receive him. It was only when it was too late for him to make his excuses that she leant towards him like a conspirator and revealed that Mahala's cousins were also waiting.

'They d'want to see the mistress,' she said, 'but they're not allowed – master's orders.'

She announced this prohibition with the flourish of one impressed by masculine power but Frederick, knowing Mahala too well to picture her submissive, thought what a convenient ploy her marriage had been. He was still smarting from their last interview. Although he knew that she had deliberately provoked him and would bear no grudge, it rankled that he had allowed himself to lose his temper with an invalid. Recently his nature seemed to have been manifesting all its worst aspects and, as he considered this, it did not lessen his gloom to discover that he was to be closeted with the Grahams.

Percival and Clifford Graham occupied the drawing-room in the kind of silence in which a cough or scraping of a chair is deemed an affront and causes acute embarrassment to a nervous perpetrator. Frederick was not nervous. Greeting the men coolly, he crossed to the seat he usually took to talk with Mahala. From it he could see both the divan where he had first noticed Philobeth and the chaise-longue where Mahala had always lain. It wrenched at his heart to think that those days were gone. From what he had learned, it was likely that Mahala would now remain upstairs and this room would never ring with her wicked laugh again. He thought of her shrewd mischief and, looking at the men she had outwitted, privately congratulated her for her boldness.

The Grahams had taken attitudes that demonstrated they were not there for pleasure. Mahala had once said that it was a shame not to scandalize them for the poor things enjoyed it so. Middle-aged and corpulent, the brothers shared the manner of those who refuse frivolities with the expressions of men sucking lemons, and it was plain that they would milk their outrage to the last drop. With one step Mahala had transformed herself into family legend, ensuring that her disloyalty would be denounced at Graham dinner-tables for generations to come; not a will would be drawn up nor marriage settlement made without a shake of the head and 'Ah, if we had cousin Mahala's money—' and daughters yet unborn would whisper of the doctor who had suffered a love their parents could not understand.

The clock struck the quarter and Percival, seated stiffly in an upright chair carved with Goanese dancing girls, drew his watch from his waistcoat pocket and consulted it with raised eyebrows. 'We've been sitting here,' he said, 'for an hour and a half.'

Clifford, who was not sitting at all, preferring to stand with an elbow on the mantelpiece, occasionally strolling over to a portrait and sighing, tapped his knuckles impatiently on the marble. The overmantel was a Georgian addition and he had long coveted it for the worth of its stone. 'It's no more than I expected,' he said. 'I've no doubt the slight's deliberate.'

Percival shut his watch and tucked it back into place. 'You put it in a nutshell. We're to be deprived of civil treatment as well as our inheritance.' He pursed his lips. 'I've half a mind to go up. Who is this Carmody to forbid us our cousin?'

'He's the master here,' Frederick spoke with a calm that hid his disgust, 'and has the right to say his wife can't be seen. Mrs Carmody may not be strong enough for visitors.'

The brothers turned towards him as if they had not previously noticed that he was in the room. Both were men of independent means and tyrannized freely over wives and servants, but an authoritative voice left them nonplussed. Opposition from the strong-willed caused them to huff and strut and, ultimately, be defeated. They could not learn from their mistakes and, because Mahala was female, had never accepted that her resistance to their correction was permanent. Even now they would not admit that she had escaped them.

'Sir,' said Percival coldly, 'you're right that Miss Graham is not a well woman. Her constitution and her judgement have been weakened by her illness. Her family must decide if she was fit to make a choice that injures them so severely.'

Frederick crossed his legs and leant back in his chair. 'I visited Mrs Carmody regularly before her wedding,' he said. 'Her mind was always perfectly clear.'

Clifford glanced at his brother nervously. Although

they had hoped to find a way to have the marriage declared void, neither had been certain of their ground, and Frederick's statement shook their confidence. They did not relish the thought of crossing swords with Mahala, however debilitated she might be, and being watched with a steady, sardonic gaze did not strengthen them for the dispute to come.

Frederick felt a deepening melancholy. The emptiness of the men disturbed him. It seemed that he looked into a darkness that also held his own life. The room was dead without Mahala and he longed to gather Philobeth onto his lap, pressing her to him as he would cling to a raft on the open sea. He was suppressing this rising bleakness when the maid reappeared and said that the mistress would see him. Percival made an impatient movement in his chair but a look from Frederick prevented him standing up.

In the hall, Frederick was telling the girl that a man-servant should be posted at the stairs when the front door opened and Carmody came in. He had been called to a case of scarlet fever and had walked forward a few paces, checking the contents of his bag before he noticed Frederick. An awkwardness came over him. His envy of Frederick's wealth and closeness to Philobeth had always put him at a disadvantage when they met and now he was conscious that his marriage must seem pure self-seeking.

'Carmody.' Frederick offered his hand. 'I'm making my wedding visit. I was just going up to see your wife.'

The doctor took his hand. Frederick's voice was friendly but Carmody's readiness to bridle up at his financial superiors made him suspect it was not genuine. He did not yet feel in possession of his new fortune and was sensitive to imagined offence. 'Mrs

Carmody will be glad you came.' He recognized the pomposity as he spoke and made an effort to smile. 'Mahala's tired but she's braved the events remarkably well.'

'She is brave. I wish you could both have a happier future.'

Carmody did not know what to say. He was not as certain as Mahala that Frederick was no longer interested in Philobeth and, his happiness depending upon robbing Frederick of a wife, it was difficult for him to frame a reply.

Seeing his discomfort, Frederick went on, 'Your cousins-in-law are in the drawing-room. When I see Mahala, I think I'm an old enough friend to tell her how heartily I approve of her marriage.'

Frederick's tryst with Ellen had been rearranged for that day and he turned his horse in the direction of Mythe as he rode out of Combehays. Mahala had been more gentle than he had ever known, and her softness had been peculiarly upsetting. It seemed that she had ruled a decisive line beneath her life and, replete with success, was quietly waiting to die. Her changed manner, with its acknowledgement that death was inevitable, was another sorrow to add to the revelations and anxieties of the past three days. He needed comfort.

It was a drowsy afternoon. The stubble in the shorn meadows was pale yellow tinged with the young green of the aftermath. A shepherd had fallen asleep in the shade of an elm and his dog watched as Frederick rode slowly by. The heat and stillness were oppressive. The need for Philobeth that had come to Frederick in Mahala's drawing-room had not left him but, as he neared Mythe, it was overlaid by a desire for Ellen that made him restive. It occurred to him that he was hungry for tainted meat and, though he could not justify the thought, it left him with a disquiet that was more than simply his guilt over Philobeth.

He knew that he was bewitched by Ellen. Looking back over the time they had spent together, he could remember little of what they had said. There must have been conversation but he recalled only a voluptuous languor that enfolded him in her company. He became a lotus-eater in her presence. Once behind the cold stone walls of Mythe, in rooms that were always darkened, always scented, his understanding seemed suspended. He surrendered to a seductive tantalizing of his senses. Away from her, he had begun to see that she was a temptress, deliberately luring him towards a promise that, having made, he would keep. He did not hold this against her. A woman must make her way in the world and he was used to being sought after for his wealth, yet a recognition of something repellent in her disposition was stirring beneath his enthralment.

She had not been so forward as to say that she loved him but she had been careful to make him believe it, and there were ways of being immodest that, while amounting to nothing when put into words, cast a shadow over innocent behaviour. All her movements were calculated to entice him. As she clasped her hands behind her neck and arched her back to stretch, as she curled amongst the cushions of a couch, rubbing her face against their velvet, as she exclaimed drowsily at the uncoiling of her hair, he accepted that she knew the effect of her body. He did not disapprove of carnality in women but its use as a trap was distasteful and made him suspect its sincerity. There

was none of the unselfconscious sensuality of Philobeth in Ellen. The gratification she gave to his eyes,
with its suggestion of what more could be had, was
measured and false as a token of love, yet still he gave
himself up to it. He was not suited to celibacy. He had
had several amorous encounters whilst travelling
Europe after leaving Oxford, but their illusory glamour
did not hide their essentially sordid nature. The
physical pleasure they afforded him made them painful to renounce, but his character was not base and he
chose uneasy abstinence over the spiritual dangers
of licentiousness. Ellen roused his desires as she
smothered his conscience, and he could not shake
himself free.

He reached Mythe as a landau was issuing from the
stable-yard. Handing over his horse, he walked to
the front, irritated that he would have to greet his grandmother's visitors. The great oak door, reputed to hold
shot from a Cromwellian musket, was standing open
and he went into the dim hall to find Mrs North talking
to Sir John Packard and his sister, Mrs Wilbraham, as
they came slowly out of the blue sitting-room. It was
not a happy meeting. The animosity Sir John felt for
Frederick's political opinions was of a kind that could
not be set aside for the sake of keeping up a civil front,
and there was a stiffening about both men as they saw
each other. They nodded without speaking and Sir
John, unable to cut Frederick completely in his grandmother's house but rigid with the effort of this gesture,
stood apart, affecting to busy himself with putting on
his gloves. A thin, choleric man, he had been handsome in his youth, but sixty years of viewing the world
with tight lips had given his face a staring expression
that was not improved by his mutton-chop whiskers.

Mrs North and her female visitor were engrossed in an animated conversation on the unsuitably facetious tone of the curate at St Anne's and Frederick did not go forward to interrupt. He glanced beyond them as they stood frowning and inclining their heads in the doorway but no delicate form remained in the Blue Room, and the thought that somewhere in the depths of the house she awaited him gave him a shiver of anticipation.

The two women moved a few steps into the hall and saw Frederick. He bowed and Mrs North, touching her friend's wrist, gave her a brief, knowing look. Mrs Wilbraham raised her eyebrows a fraction then, gathering her skirts preparatory to entering the carriage, crossed the hall towards the porch. Frederick moved aside for her but instead of going out, she stopped beside him.

'Sir,' she said, sharply, 'are you aware of the price of corn?'

'It remains high.' He had not expected a direct attack and spoke as abruptly as she had done.

'But for how long?' She let her skirts fall back to the floor. 'We've had bad harvests for two years but this one's set to be good. What will become of us then?'

Frederick looked at the full-fed woman before him. He had never considered himself a democrat, but his realization that he was ashamed of his inheritance, and his revulsion for the greed of his class made him question the beliefs he had been taught from the cradle. He thought of the Irish, whose starvation had finally ended the Corn Laws, and wondered how Mrs Wilbraham would fare on an emigrant ship.

'You will continue to wear silks, ma'am,' he said, suddenly too weary to let her sex protect her from bluntness, 'and I'll buy hunters, but our farm-hands may eat a little better.'

She raised her chin as if he had struck her, and the old lace at her throat quivered. Her mouth worked, pursing in and out, then, with an angry twist of her shoulders, she strode towards the waiting carriage. At the door she turned so that Sir John, who had been following as he looked indignantly at the offender, was hard pressed not to collide with her.

'You, sir,' she said, pointing a black kid finger at Frederick, 'are a sore disappointment to your grandmother.'

He bowed again and, leaving Mrs North to take leave of her guests, went along a stone-flagged passage in search of Ellen. This scene, coming after the sadness of his visit to Mahala, ruffled his spirits and increased the need to be comforted that he had felt on his ride.

She was not to be found in the boudoir and he walked on down four steps, worn into hollows, and around two corners to the small parlour she had made her own. Going in, he saw her, as he had expected, lying on an ottoman, her head raised on tasselled cushions, a book cast negligently aside. She wore a gown of shot silk and its soft, opalescent greens made her look more than ever like the mermaid he had often called her. There was stained glass in the windows and the sun filtering through the blues, the purples and reds fell upon her as if she lay beneath the waves. He knew the effect was deliberate and today, in his disordered temper, her parted lips and the lift of her breast as she saw him were not as captivating as they had been.

Sitting by her in the low plush chair whose shape

made him lounge more than he wished to, he gazed at her fluid lines. His manner did not satisfy her.

She turned further towards him, her hand sliding beneath her cheek. 'Are you troubled by something?' she said.

He let out a heavy breath that was partly a laugh. 'I met Mrs Wilbraham in the hall,' he said. 'She rattled my politics in my face.'

'What business is that of hers? Women should think of other things.'

'I've heard her husband's been speculating in railway shares. If he has, the price of corn may well be very important to her.'

'Corn?' She extended one arm languidly and let the muted light play upon her rings. 'What has corn to do with politics?'

Receiving no answer, she did not press him but went on contentedly tilting her hand. He watched the heavy, old-fashioned rings – the rubies set in clusters of hearts and flowers, the moss-agate that looked too heavy for the fragile hand, the pearls surrounding a knot of hair – and contrasted what she had said with the conversation he would have had with Philobeth. He could not imagine Philobeth thinking that women should stay within their sphere nor forgetting what he had told her of his political storms.

'I could have done without meeting her,' he said. 'I've just come from Combehays.'

Ellen drew her hand back to her side. Her eyes fixed on him with interest. 'We've heard the story,' she said. 'What an extraordinary thing. A dying woman! What a prize for Carmody. Did you see him?'

'Yes.' He was taken aback by the unadulterated approval in her voice.

'Was he crowing? They say Miss Graham won't live till winter. There'll be no more sixpenny patients for him then.' She saw the hardening of Frederick's expression and, realizing that excitement had made her speak without thinking, altered her tone. 'Come,' she said, 'he's an ambitious man. If a fortune's offered to him, shouldn't he take it?'

He shrugged tiredly. 'Who am I to say he shouldn't? But you must remember that his wife has been my neighbour and friend for many years. I don't look forward to her death.'

With a lithe movement, Ellen sat up and put her hand on his. 'Forgive me. I've never met her. It makes me thoughtless.'

He clasped her hand, feeling the rings indent his flesh. Her skin was cool and smooth. 'Of—' he began, but a knock at the door prevented him from going on.

She called out for the person to enter. A young maid came in and, seeing Frederick, curtsied uncertainly.

'Yes, Susan?' Ellen spoke gently to impress Frederick.

The girl was shy in the presence of a gentleman and pleated a fold of her wide apron between finger and thumb. She was employed to do laundry-work but had become familiar with Ellen when she had been summoned upstairs to deal with an ink stain.

' 'Tis my sister, Miss. Her little one's come at last. Her man undid the locks and opened the doors like you said, to let out the pain, and a bravely boy come an hour since.'

'I'm so glad. Tell her I'll come to see her in a day or two.'

'Miss, he were born with a caul and if you d'still want un—'

Ellen stood up. An eager light shone in her eyes. 'I'll buy it,' she said. 'Don't let her sell to anyone else. Make her keep it for me. Tell her I'll give her a coral to protect the child from evil.'

As the girl left, Ellen turned to Frederick, her face glowing. 'Now I shall never drown,' she said. 'I have nightmares of the sea. My face,' she shuddered, 'stares at me through the water. But now I shall never drown.'

An unhappiness that was like a physical pain gripped Frederick. The beguilement that Ellen cast over him when she appeared to be passive was broken as she displayed the poverty of her mind. Disappointment at her folly, and so with his own, flooded through him.

'I'll have it set in a locket,' she said, too triumphant to notice his silence. 'I don't even need to wear it. As the child's face was covered against birth, mine will be covered against death and no harm will come to me.'

Chapter Eight

Having delayed his visit three times, Mr Alleyn arrived unannounced in late June, causing Slater to scold and threaten to be unable to feed him even as she forcibly took his parcels from his hands. He had come in a gust of good humour generated by a successful run of commissions and had been as prodigal of his fees as always. For an evening the parlour was an Aladdin's Cave as boxes were unpacked and straw and silver paper were strewn upon the floor. He had brought crates of art materials, a portfolio of historical costumes sketched in the British Museum, a Delftware punchbowl, a folding silver fruit knife with 'Ph.A.' engraved on its tortoiseshell case, a toast-rack with lion's-paw feet that had made him laugh, lengths of ruby silk figured in black velvet, novels, gold and turquoise pendant ear-rings and, for Slater, a black fringed mantle to be laid in lavender as too good to wear.

Philobeth had not seen him since Christmas and as they sat into the night – he in his chintz dressing-gown, she wrapped in the shawl he had brought – cracking nuts and being unabashed by Slater's sudden appearances, she felt a luxurious security that she knew to be false. She remembered how she had longed to have him there to comfort her for Frederick's loss and, though she accepted that she was the stronger of the two, she allowed herself a few hours of pretence that she could lean on him. He teased her a little about her admirer but she merely smiled and shook her head and he, being full of news, swept on to fresh tales of who had said what to whom.

It was the next morning, as she was showing him her work, that she mentioned the change there had been in her relations with Frederick. She told him lightly, with satirical comments on the faithlessness of lovers and fathers, and he did not guess what it cost her to speak in that manner. He abused Frederick soundly as a fool but, not understanding how deeply his daughter was hurt, gave most of his attention to the drawings with which she was distracting him. It was his way to disguise any seriousness he felt and he chaffed her with being a member of the Pre-Raphaelite Brotherhood, but he was startled by the intensity of her vision and impressed by the flowering of her talent. He did not share the prejudice against women painting in oils and an examination of her vivid canvases, as she stood large-eyed beside him, made him take her hand with pride and agree readily that she must study abroad. They consulted together and it was decided that he would write certain letters and, after Mahala's death, Philobeth would go to Paris.

The days passed and Frederick did not go back to Mythe. He was ashamed of his infatuation for Ellen and the light it shed on his cast of mind. Although he blamed himself for succumbing to her peculiar attractions, he did not give himself credit for the chivalrous impulse that had made him vulnerable to her supposed helplessness. He acknowledged his desire but not his protectiveness and, despite believing that he had awoken from his drugged sleep, he dared not approach her for fear his worst nature would cause his eyes to close again. Dissatisfaction with his way of living, sorrow for Mahala and guilt for his estrangement from Philobeth confused and darkened his thoughts so that he could not see his path forward. He wanted Philobeth but he felt unclean, and an impression of entanglement and unfinished business with Ellen kept him solitary and morose.

Late one afternoon, some three days after Mr Alleyn had arrived, Frederick was riding slowly back from Dorchester, debating with himself whether he should make a detour to avoid Mythe as he had done that morning. He had been attending a meeting of the Hospital Board and the contrast between his own predicament and the misfortunes of the patients discussed had had a salutary effect on him. The imagination that had made him understand the suffering caused by costly bread also obliged him to admit that it is more comfortable to be unhappy while having money than to lie in a charity ward wondering where the rent will come from. He gave his melancholy no importance, admitting, as he did, how much of it was well deserved but still he drifted on, making no plans for a new direction.

The day was hot with an intermittent breeze that saved it from being condemned as threatening to thunder. In fields of red clover, bees were loud amongst the blossoms, filling the air with a slumberous drone. Frederick's horse moved lazily, occasionally stretching forth its neck and shaking its head in a rattle of harness as flies troubled it. Sympathizing with its sloth, he did not urge it to walk briskly, content to amble through lanes that were dry and overgrown with summer. He rode with slack reins, keeping to the edge where shade was thrown by the flourishing hedgerows. At the side of an old wall – once the high boundary of a cherished garden, now crumbling beneath its weight of ivy – in the unbroken shadow that was more dense and cool than the play of light beneath the bushes, he stopped to rest, and heard another traveller in the silence of the heavy afternoon.

The sound disturbed him. It was only the faint roll of wheels drawn by a single pony, but his heart increased its beat and he pulled up his own horse from the grass it had been nuzzling. He could not explain his agitation. The country was so quiet that the noise he was listening for had carried from a point he could not see but he was convinced that he would find Philobeth if he followed it and he pressed his horse into a quicker pace than it had used that day.

She was watering her pony when he reached her. The river ran close to the road, and a rutted track, made by generations of drivers using it for the same purpose, led down to where the bank sloped into a shallow bay. She looked round as he approached but did not smile and he sat for a moment before dismounting to go to her. 'I heard you from Glover's Piece,' he said. 'I felt sure it was you.'

'It's the last Wednesday in the month.' She turned to face him. 'I always hire the trap to go to market. You know that.'

He was abashed. The memory of her habits had persuaded him that she was the traveller but had been too deeply buried to give him the reason for his conviction. Her few regular occupations used to be at

his finger-ends and that he had forgotten one emphasized how much he had neglected her. He could not
think what to say and Philobeth, misinterpreting his
silence, hardened the heart that had leapt at the sight of
him.

'I heard that Mr Alleyn was here,' he said at last. 'I
hoped to call on him.'

'I don't know that he'll welcome you.'

Frederick flushed. The accusation was plain and
understanding that his conduct had been related to her
father added to his discomfort. She was watching him
with a straight, cold gaze. He had had his fill of side-
long glances and the downward sweep of lashes and,
despite the embarrassment they caused him, he liked
her direct eyes. Her sharpness cut him, but he felt it
paring the confusion from his mind. Inwardly he
abased himself, accepting fully that he had been wrong
to be distracted by tawdry charms. In his new self-
awareness, he believed he was unworthy of Philobeth
and though unworthiness rarely prevents a man offering himself, he was perplexed by how to proceed.

Philobeth waited for him to speak with a mounting
dread that she would give herself away. She stood
steadfast and resistant, but a voice within her cried 'I
love him!' and all her will was necessary to hide her
want. Her need of him was bitter to her. It would have
satisfied her pride to have been able to tear her
yearning from her and cast it aside, but even now, after
so long a separation, she knew that she would take him
if he had the courage to ask.

The breeze had died and the shade of the overhang-
ing willows did not ease the heavy heat. Water rippled
over stones and amongst the fleshy stems of brook-
lime. The pony's flank quivered and it lifted its head,

111

disturbing the swallows that darted amongst the mayfly.

As each wordless moment passed it became more difficult for either to speak. Each was held in a private misery that blinded them to the other's pain. His mouth dry, Frederick sought to overcome his shame and reveal his true, if tarnished, love. Delay and indecision had been so much a part of his courtship of her that the one question whose simplicity would bind him to her seemed impossible to say. Guilt hampered his tongue and before he could loosen it, she stepped forward restlessly, her skirts trailing in a clump of plants at the water's edge. She looked down at what had caught her and seeing forget-me-nots, she raised her arms abruptly and, putting out her foot, crushed a spray beneath her sole.

Turning to Frederick, she showed him a face that was all anger and hurt. 'Don't call on my father,' she said. 'Don't come to my house. I've told him that you and I are nothing to each other. There's a sea between us. Do you remember it? We met it on a night when you feared for my reputation. What of my reputation now? What of my name after the liberties you've taken?' She swayed a little, locking her hands. 'There I'm wrong.' Her voice was strained. 'You never took them. I gave them to you just as I gave you my love and trust. What have you to reproach yourself for? Any man would have done the same. I behaved freely. Ask the world if I've got my deserts. But I thought you were better, God help me, I thought you were better than you are.'

He could not reply. His throat was full and he had no defence for what he had done. He started forward to take her hand but she moved away, dry-eyed and desperate with the accumulated anguish of the past months. The wreck, the hanging, the impending death of her friend pressed themselves upon her betrayal by Frederick, making all the world dark to her.

'Don't touch me,' she said. 'You're going to Mythe and you'd touch me?'

He stepped back, shaken by her violence. She struggled to control herself and when she next spoke, her words had lost their wildness. 'Mr North,' she said. 'An unwise – an unfortunate intimacy has grown between us. Now it must end. Soon there will be no Miss Graham to speak for me and I must leave. Not only for my sake – your future wife would wish it so. I've arranged to study in Paris and until I go, I must ask you not to approach me or cause me harm in any way.'

Chapter Nine

At Mythe the long afternoon passed slowly. July had brought out the lilies, and Ellen moved amongst them on the flagstoned paths, drawing her white hands over their waxy petals, her face serene and her thoughts in chaos. She snapped off a stem and, sap dripping onto her gown, tapped the bloom absent-mindedly against her chin as she strolled towards the bench at the corner of the terrace. A stone cupola had been raised above it on Doric pillars, and she sat in the shade it afforded, gently shredding the flower until her mind was calm and her decision made.

By early evening she had dined and was in her bed-room. Her preparations were complete. Mrs North had been sneezing and Ellen's soft persuasions had convinced her that she was too unwell to be up. A tray of invalid food had been taken to her chamber and now she lay against her pillows, feebly ordering potions and wondering if Carmody should be called.

It was not Ellen's intention to have a doctor sent for, particularly one whose immediate future seemed set to eclipse her own, and she had privately discussed Mrs North's condition with the housekeeper, steering her into agreement that the old lady's disorder would answer better to a good night's sleep than the excitement of a visit. She wanted the house quiet and clear of any demands that might be made for her presence. A belief that Miss Farebrother had retired early was essential to her, for although the action she was to take, while wholly indecent in its essence, was only mildly improper in appearance, she wanted to avoid the speculation it would cause if it were known. Had she been sure of a successful outcome, she would have snapped her fingers at gossip but if she failed, derision in the eyes of servants and the bilious sympathy of Mrs North would have been unendurable to her. She wished she had darkness to cover her movements.

It was four weeks since she had last seen Frederick. He was slipping from her grasp. Mrs North had sent a dozen invitations and when these failed to bring him, Ellen had written herself, a pretty note asking why she was forsaken, but apologies were all that came from Holcombe House. She could not think what had caused this desertion. Mrs North had dispatched her maid to Frederick's kitchen with instructions to solve the mystery, but all she could discover was that he had not again taken up with the female artist.

Ellen sat at her dressing-table gazing into the mirror on its damask cloth. She could not fault her reflection. There seemed no reason for Frederick to have cooled. He had seemed wholly hers. Anxiety and frustrated greed had grown in her over their month of separation until she could bear the suspense no longer. She felt no liking for him, but rank and wealth had been so nearly within her reach that it was impossible for her to give him up. It was not that she feared penury. She did not doubt that she could insinuate herself so far into Mrs North's affections that she would be made her heir, but waiting for the necessary death would be tiresome.

The months spent at Mythe had made her impatient for the power and luxury of wealth, and a husband of means would bring her these more quickly than a promise in a will.

The set-backs she had encountered in the past years had not shaken her confidence in herself. It did not occur to her that she would not dominate whoever she chose to marry. The arrogance that burned behind her alluring eyes made her sure that she would be mistress of her husband's income and caused the bewilderment she suffered over Frederick's absence. Why did he not come and how dare he thwart her ambitions? Her self-absorption prevented her understanding why those around her did not always fit themselves to her desires, and this narrowness of outlook kept her from feeling any guilt over the actions she took to satisfy her wants. She knew without question that she was justified in all she did, and though a fear of water now possessed her – water that invaded her dreams and surged at the edges of her hearing – she would not hesitate to press another face beneath the waves. Contempt for humanity protected her and tonight she intended to bring one of its weak members to heel.

She had dressed herself with care. The costume she had chosen was not suited to the walk she was to take but it was as Frederick liked to see her. She meant to go to Holcombe House to throw her broken heart upon his mercy. She would be tremulous, enticing, irresistible to one of his nature. Smoothing her palms over her tight waist, she contemplated her image in the glass. Pale shoulders rose out of a deep green glacé silk chosen to make him call her his naiad once again. The sleeves were a mere gesture but the night was warm and bathed her in its soft air as she sat anticipating the triumph of one bold move.

A sensation of fevered expectation began to suffuse her. An intoxicating certainty of success brought colour to her skin and made her breathing fast and shallow. A moth drifted in through her open window, its brown wings beating silently in the quiet room. It fluttered indecisively about her head before the scent of her sugared cordial drew it to the cup left half empty at her side. She watched its ungainly teetering on the thin gold rim and its sudden slide into the sticky liquid. It floundered blindly and, in a moment, she took a closed ivory fan and lifted the drowning creature from the cup, placing it before her on the cloth. It lay still, then, as it revived, dragging its sodden body inch by inch, she raised the fan and resting the ivory upon the moth's palpitating back, she pressed down.

As the dusk began to deepen, Frederick was in his dressing-room at Holcombe House changing his evening clothes for an outfit more suitable for roaming the country. The alteration was not really necessary and, as he stood at the long window that overlooked the lake tying his cravat, he admitted to himself that he was deliberately delaying setting out. He felt as nervous as a boy. The depression that had gripped him during the last weeks had not lifted, but he had come to a decision that required a venturesome spirit and tonight was to mark a new departure in his life.

He was going to call upon the Alleyns. There had been no contact between himself and Philobeth since she had told him to do her no more harm, and no civil messages had passed between the men. Alone in the vast house that was meant for a family, he brooded on his faults and yearned to undo the error he had made. Away from Ellen's influence, he saw more clearly how he had become enslaved. Without using them as an excuse, he allowed the finer feelings that had made the manner of their meeting so potent for him. The vulnerability that had seemed so captivating held no attraction now that his eyes had opened to the scheming it masked. He compared Philobeth's willingness to scorn the appearance of impropriety for his sake with Ellen's careful cultivation of surfaces, and it disgusted him that he could have mistaken Ellen's thirst for material gain with the purity of Philobeth's love.

He could not claim to have been pure in thought himself, and the loathing this knowledge aroused had driven him from Philobeth when she had commanded him to go. Shame at his unworthiness had made him retreat to grieve for what he had lost but, as the days passed, it occurred to him that he was behaving with the lack of determination she had always criticized. The notion grew into a certainty, and he altered his opinion of what he should do. Renunciation was set aside. He would confess his delusion and renew his addresses to Philobeth, offering her his heart and name. She might not accept; the lure of Paris and the fame he did not doubt she deserved might be stronger than the appeal of a flawed lover, but he could not stand by and watch her leave unchallenged.

A knock disturbed him and a man-servant entered. 'Miss Farebrother has called, sir,' he said. 'She's waiting downstairs.'

Frederick was startled. She was the last person he wanted to see; it aggravated him that she should have thrust herself upon him when his absence from Mythe must have made his indifference plain. A foreboding of an unsavoury scene crept into his mind. 'Damnation!' he said, making the final adjustment to his cravat. 'Is Mrs North with her?'

'No, sir. She came alone and on foot.'

Frederick considered his position. The time and method she had chosen for the visit reinforced his suspicion that she had come on uncomfortably personal business. He wondered whether she had slipped from the house without his grandmother being aware of it, or if there had been collusion between them. The annoyance of her arrival on this particular night tempted him to send down that he was not at home. Knowing this to be untrue, she might take such offence that she would not approach him again, but he entertained the idea for only an instant before he set it aside as the procrastination Philobeth despised. It was better to make it plain once and for all that he was not Ellen's bondsman, and this could only be done honourably face to face.

The concept of honour occupied him as he went downstairs. He could accept a woman hunting a good match from the same ambition that drove a man to try to rise in his career, but only if she were open about her lack of affection. The pretence of love disgusted him. He recalled his brief experience of the *demimonde* and thought that there was more virtue in a courtesan or the meanest woman of the street than in the lady who awaited him.

She was sitting in the hall when he came down. Hearing his step, she stood up, her light cloak falling around her in artful folds. He could not help admiring how well she judged the look of tentative hope that she assumed.

'Will you come into the drawing-room, Miss Fare-brother,' he said. 'You shouldn't have been left in the hall.'

Aware that he had stung her with his greeting as Philobeth had stung him with her 'Mr North', he led her into one of the formal apartments that were never used for friendly gatherings. She was not surprised by his reserve. Her knowledge of the difference between American and English manners was not great enough for her to anticipate how people would behave in every circumstance and she assumed he was acting as a gentleman should in front of his servants. Her cloak was taken from her and, when they were alone, she stood before him with all the bashful consciousness of a girl who cannot hide her love.

'You'll think it strange that I'm here,' she said.

'Not at all.' There was an edge to his voice that seemed to make the remark more than mere politeness, but she could not interpret it.

'Have I interrupted you?' she asked. 'Do you have guests?'

'No-one but yourself.'

Now that she was with him, she was unsure how to proceed. She was confident of her powers when he had relaxed and was drowning in her as he had done so often before, but she was not on home ground and felt the need of scented darkness. It was easier to throw out lures whilst curled upon velvet than when standing uninvited in a reception room. She thought of the young heir in Virginia who had let her be driven out like a dog, and the husband in Boston who had talked of love but submitted to his wife. Desire for revenge focussed itself upon Frederick, bringing a heightened colour into her already blushing face.

Frederick waited for her opening move. He did not ask her to sit down nor offer her refreshment. The room was unlit, but its long windows let in enough twilight for him not to send for candles until he should need a diversionary tactic. He observed her as she stood clasping her hands together. There was a seductive glamour about her that he could now see dispassionately. She was bewitching in a way that was both ethereal and earthy but, having broken free of her charm, he noticed small vulgarities that pointed to her opinion of men. The oil on the love-lock that fell over her bare shoulder was too sweet and beckoning; her gown was so low that it showed the crease between arm and body; her stays were so tight that her half-exposed breasts rose and fell in a constant stir of rapid breathing. He could not deny that she was arousing, but the deliberateness of this appeal to base instinct, coupled with her campaign to fascinate him, was repellent in effect. She had relied absolutely upon her carnal attractions and he felt degraded by her inability to understand that he was more than a source of wealth and a voluptuary. In the past months, they had spent hour after hour in the hushed conversation of the infatuated, yet she had not credited him with the wisdom to uncover her deceit. He watched her twisting her heavy rings so that their stones were hidden in her palms and thought of the hand that Philobeth had stretched out to touch her in the carriage – a hand that Ellen had never grasped in gratitude.

Ellen was summoning the appearance of unconscious sensuality that suited her so well. It filled her like wine being poured into a glass. 'I couldn't stay away,' she said. 'I could bear it no longer.' She turned her head, lifting her fingers to her mouth as if she was shocked that rash words had escaped her. 'I know what you'll think of me,' she went on, the foreign drawl in her voice soft and winning with its trace of fear. 'In my country perhaps I'd be found less guilty. We're more open there.'

'Are you guilty?'

She turned back to him, moving a step nearer. 'Yes,' she said, proudly. 'Yes, I am. Guilty of the truest feelings a woman can possess. I can't hide them from you. I will not. The world may condemn me but there's no disgrace in my admission.'

'To what do you admit?'

She could not ignore the coldness in his question. It might be that he disapproved of women taking an active part in lovemaking, but she dared not retreat and risk a continued separation. 'I admit,' she said, as though her words were born of tortured emotion, 'that from the night of the wreck, from the time you gave me my life, it has not been mine but yours.'

'Miss Alleyn was more instrumental in saving you than I.'

The flatness of his response coupled with the use of her rival's name enraged her. 'For pity's sake,' she cried, forcing her fury to sound like anguish, 'am I a housemaid come to ask for work? You've braided my hair; you've put fruit into my mouth.'

He flushed. He could not deny these intimacies and the shame that was so pervasive in his life kept him silent.

Seeing him hesitate, she moved closer. 'God help me,' she said, 'have I been deceived? I came to you holding out my love. Have mercy on me!'

She sank down to kneel before him. He had reached out to raise her before he realized what he was about and she leant against his breast, her head on his shoulder, breathing with a tremor that made her shudder in his arms. Her body was both firm and yielding, the scent of her skin was warm. Had he embraced her he would have been lost, but his entrapment hardened his heart.

He pushed her away. 'Madam,' he said, 'I've been wrong to visit my grandmother's house so often since you've been there. It may have given rise to false expectations.'

She was shaking with passion. The desire to hurt him almost overwhelmed her, but she clung to her purpose as she had clung to a spar in the violent sea. Wealth and ease were all around her and could be hers if this wretched man would only say the words. He was no longer open to persuasion but he was honourable in his way and, if he could be convinced that he had gone so far that he must marry her, she believed that he would do his duty. It did not matter to her that he would do it with reluctance. Riches were her right; the bitterness of one who delivered her into her proper station would be nothing in her eyes.

'False?' she said. 'Yes, you may well use that word to me. Your whole acquaintance knows in what condition you found me; they know how freely you've treated me since. If you leave me now, after such liberties, I'm ruined. Will you compromise me then talk of false expectations?'

Until this moment, his anger had been cold and controlled. Her accusation made him aggressive. The turn her hypocrisy had taken revolted him more than her pretence of love. Philobeth had justly reproached him for sullying her name, and immediately condemned herself for crying against what she had welcomed. This woman had offered herself to him with a cunning that had almost succeeded in its vile intent, yet could still stand brazenly before him as a victim of his loose conduct. His urge to strike her was so strong that he kept his hand tightly clenched on the bell-rope as he rang to have her shown out.

'You should go on the stage, Miss Farebrother,' he said. 'You have a remarkable talent for impersonating a character that isn't your own.'

'What?' She was too alarmed to recognize the insult of being compared to an actress. Fear that he knew who she was took away her voice.

'You portray yourself as an innocent,' he went on, his fingers white upon the rope. 'You and I both know that you are not. I haven't asked you to be my wife nor said or done any word or action that could be held against me in law. I won't compare you to a doxy; I will tell you to leave my house and never enter it again.'

When she had gone, he poured a glass of brandy to steady himself and found that the decanter rattled on the rim of the glass. He had retreated to his study and paced about the room as he tried to subdue his temper enough to decide what he should do. The vehemence of the interview with Ellen had so disturbed him that, at first, he did not realize that she no longer posed him a problem. It went against the grain of his romantic nature to speak with such brutal disrespect, but now that he had done so, his entanglement was at an end. He had given orders that she was not to be admitted to his house and it was unlikely that she would continue to pursue him through his grandmother's invitations. If she did not confide in her benefactress, Mrs North would eventually insist that he visit, but he could not imagine that Ellen would be there when he called.

His agitation subsided as it broke upon him that he had escaped the consequences of his foolishness, but he felt unfit to lay his heart before Philobeth. The argument, with its reminders of his indiscretions, made it seem repugnant to try to win another woman at once yet, having made up his mind to it, he did not want to be deterred. He imagined Philobeth sitting at her desk making the arrangements that would take her away from England; he saw himself knocking at her door one day too late. And what if Ellen had been seen coming to his home at this hour and Philobeth was told? It was imperative that he should explain before she could be wounded by the news and it occurred to him that, however distasteful the events of the evening had been, they might form a useful path into the profession of his love. The decisiveness of his breach with Ellen would be admirable to one of Philobeth's temperament and if it was followed by the admission of his folly perhaps he might begin to reawaken her tenderness.

Taking his stick from its lair behind the bookcase, he left the house by the french windows. The dusk had deepened but the Alleyns kept late hours and the time of his call would not affect their decision whether to let him in. He was not yet calm enough to prevent snatches of the meeting with Ellen intruding on his thoughts. Spurts of anger increased his pulse as the image of her leapt unbidden into his mind. Distracted in this way, he could not adequately make love to Philobeth and he decided to walk for a while before presenting himself at the cottage in Chantry.

He went down the stone steps into the rose garden that his mother had made, where lavender-lined beds of Portlands and Albas were grey in the diminishing light. Opening his knife, he cut one perfect bloom with two sprigs of leaves and tucked them into his waistcoat. The scent, rich and exquisite, enveloped him as he walked on into the park. The poignant sweetness of the flower that can only be savoured after an absence, appealed to his fancy as a symbol of his desertion of Philobeth. He had grown accustomed to her love and cast the rose aside for having no fragrance, but the air was still perfumed by a musk he had not breathed.

The night was soft and still. The surface of the lake was unmarked by ripples. Amongst the reeds, frogs croaked as he walked by but the carp that nosed beneath the lily-pads had sunk into the depths and did not disturb the restful waters. A bat flitted past him and he raised his stick involuntarily, its silver head gleaming dully, before he recognized the movement and heard the creature's high-pitched voice.

He thought he saw a figure as he left the park. Turning to look at the copse he had passed, he noticed nothing but the heavy summer foliage hanging motionless and black above the withering ferns. He was unconcerned. A deer must have stirred in its grazing and would be silently watching him as he stood. He went on, out of the iron gate and into the fields, choosing a track that would bring him into a lane that circled back towards Chantry.

There were small noises amongst the corn, rustlings that were here and there and never quite where he was walking. The wheat was changing from blue-green to gold and, though its colour was as indistinguishable as the dark spread of poppies, yet it had an air of fragile immaturity as it waited for ripeness beneath the warm night sky.

He climbed a stile into the lane, disturbing rabbits that scattered into brambles beside an old brick shed. Chantry was no more than a mile away and he started towards it with purpose in his step. The exercise and the quiet dusk had made him master of himself again. His thoughts were on Philobeth and he felt a growing confidence that eventually, when he had proved himself sincere, she would be his. It was not that he believed himself to have such merit that she would be unable to resist his desire but that she was so strong and true that having once given her love, she could not take it away.

'North!'

A stone spun past him as the voice shouted his name. He turned abruptly and had only time to see Barlow coming to him at a run before the man reached him and they were grappling together, stumbling from the rutted road to the rough grass of the verge. Frederick could feel Barlow's breath on his face and the sour smell said that he had been drinking, but the strength of his grip showed that it was not enough to incapacitate him. The suddenness of the attack had put Frederick at a disadvantage but he was used to acting with authority amongst men and after his initial shocked falling back, he gathered himself to have the better of the fight.

There was no mistaking the seriousness of his situation. The assault was meant in earnest. There was a hatred in Barlow's eyes that blotted out all intelligence and humanity. They wrestled on the long grass, their hands locked on each other's arms, struggling to keep their own footing as they tried to kick the other's feet from beneath him. Barlow grabbed at Frederick's cravat, twisting it tight, and in the instant his concentration was on that, Frederick wrapped his leg behind Barlow's knee and jerked so that they fell as one with Barlow beneath. The fall made Barlow lose his hold on the cravat and Frederick lunged at his wrists, pinning him down. They were breathing in gasps and they stared at each other with a primitive violence that was animal in its intensity.

Barlow lay with the stones of the road cutting into his back, looking up at the man who had become the one focus of his malevolence. Since the humiliation of his mock hanging, he had descended into an obsession that was almost madness. Growing solitary and too unreliable for the meanest work, he fed his blame of Frederick until he could not settle at night without poaching from his fields or lurking in his grounds, watching for some chance to cause him injury. He had no plan, but now that he had begun an assault there was no idea in his mind but murder.

With one quick movement, he raised his head and spat into Frederick's face. As Frederick recoiled, Barlow thrust his arms up and rolled over, staggering to his feet. He swung out his fist at Frederick as he got up, but Frederick, wiping the saliva with his sleeve, ducked aside and, clasping Barlow's wrist, pulled himself upright. They closed together, swaying from side to side of the lane as they clawed at each other in an effort to pull their opponent off balance. As they wheeled about, Frederick saw the stick he had dropped lying in the grass, but it was not near enough to reach and he did not think of getting out his knife.

Suddenly, Barlow's head darted forward and he sank his teeth into Frederick's neck at the same time as he dropped his hold to gouge his thumbs into Frederick's eyes. It was his instinct to protect his sight

128

but, feeling his body freer, Frederick grasped Barlow's groin and wrenched. Barlow shrieked and fell back. Frederick ran for his stick but he had lost his bearings and as he searched, he saw Barlow limping towards him. He grabbed a handful of dust and pebbles from the road and flung them in Barlow's face. It gave him an instant to find the stick and he turned, holding it before him, to see Barlow pouncing forward with a rabbit wire taut between his hands. Frederick raised the stick sharply to block the garrot and its end caught Barlow on the chin. There was a second when Barlow stood blankly rigid, then he folded upon himself, hitting the ground like a dead-weight and lying still.

Frederick sank down onto the verge, the stick resting across his knees. His shirt was torn at the throat and a seam of his coat was gaping. He put his fingers to his neck and when they came away red, he untied the cravat he had arranged with such care and folded it over the bite. His hands were slippery with sweat and he sat open-mouthed, drawing in air painfully, as he recovered from the abrupt changes of the night. Stars were beginning to show and he stared up at the sky as if puzzled by its peacefulness.

He wanted to stretch out on the grass and give himself up to exhaustion but he rose into a crouch and straightened slowly. Now that the attack was at an end, he could feel bruises forming. A pang beneath his ribs made him retch dryly and he felt an urgent need to make water but he went to kneel beside Barlow to see what damage had been done.

Barlow lay on his back. He was breathing, but there was no sight in his eyes and when Frederick said his name in a croaking voice, he did not respond. Frederick felt no pity. As he gazed at the unconscious figure he seemed to see the pale features of the girl whose face Philobeth had drawn in Holden's barn. She had lain more motionless than this. A surge of the anger he had felt for Ellen went through him as he considered what to do. However foul this man might be, help must be fetched. He stood up again, holding his side, and began to walk towards the nearest house.

There was silence in the lane. Frederick had turned the corner and his footsteps died away. Barlow lay like a dead man, the rise and fall of his chest imperceptible in the darkening night. Nothing moved between the hedgerows; no bird cried; no wind passed over the wheat.

A shadow came forward from the stile. Ellen went to Barlow with a gliding step, both surreptitious and decided. Her lips were parted and her face engorged with an unholy joy. She stood over the body but she did not see it as human. Sinister in self-absorption, she felt a fevered triumph and heard the blood beating in her veins.

She had followed Frederick from the park. Her loathing of him for thwarting her greed had been too violent to let her return to Mythe. She had lingered outside, prowling and desperate, unable to leave the property she believed to be hers. Seeing him enter the garden, she had stalked him, delirious with hate. Her hunger to be rich would not let her give him up. She did not think that argument would bring her what she coveted but she could not withdraw from the hunt until she had slaked the bitterness that seethed in her.

The rose made her dangerous. She guessed it was for a woman and who that woman was. The need for vengeance, that had been turbulent, grew cold and implacable. She would not see another usurp her place. Neither conscience nor fear of retribution troubled her. Her pursuit was unrelenting. Despite her apparent languor, she had great physical vitality and her walk was lithe and threatening in its energy as she slid from darkness to darkness in Frederick's wake.

She had not known what she would do. The unexpectedness of the assault raised her to ecstasy. She was not cast down by the outcome of the fight. The defencelessness of the injured man offered her a more piquant revenge upon Frederick than she had dreamed possible. With deliberation she lowered herself onto her knees beside Barlow. He did not stir and his breathing was low. She looked from side to side. No-one watched. She covered his mouth with her hand and pressed.

Chapter Ten

'But did North know the man was dead when he left him?'

From beyond the wall of the stable-yard, the sound of the garden party came drifting in billows of conversation and the yapping of the lap-dogs that Mrs Moran took wherever she went. A group of gentlemen stood at the door of a loose-box, ostensibly admiring a litter of retrievers. Wilbraham, their host, had offered them this excuse to escape the frivolities on the lawn and they had accepted it with the same dry eagerness that met the brandy-and-sodas awaiting them on the rain-barrel. They had an air of having been freed from boredom. The subject that was on everyone's lips was also on theirs, but their opinion of their intellects was too high for them not to believe that they were in more serious company.

It was Newman who spoke. He had been in Hampshire until the previous evening, spending a fortnight with a sister, and had missed news that had electrified the county two days before.

Sir John Packard sniffed. 'He says he did not. Ran to a farmhouse apparently, waking all and sundry, demanding assistance for a wounded man. Says he left him unconscious but,' he tapped the fob on his watch-chain, 'who's to say? No-one about. He comes on a poacher—'

There was a pause as they thought of this. Wilbraham took a biscuit from his pocket and tossed it onto the straw. The nursing bitch stretched out her neck to reach it. Wilbraham turned back to the men. 'Now, I've no patience with poachers,' he said. There was a general murmur of agreement. 'They're damnable scoundrels,' he went on, 'and I'd see every last one of them in irons but we can't kill 'em for all that.'

Corbett drew on his cigar and let out the smoke between his teeth. 'Not if we're North,' he said.

The bluntness of the statement transfixed them. Its implications made them shy away from direct assent.

'They say,' said Wilbraham, 'that this Barlow's been a thorn in his side for some time. North turned him off and the man took a grudge against him. Took to sleeping in one of his barns and calling him all names in the beer-houses. Best off without that sort.'

'I daresay North thought so.' Sir John spoke reflectively, and again there was an avoidance of his meaning.

'Why was the man turned off?' Newman asked.

'There was some story of a girl,' Wilbraham said.

Corbett gave a snorting laugh. 'Ah,' he said, 'North's always had an eye for a filly. Finds 'em everywhere – in a paint box, stretched out on a beach.'

Sir John stared at him with distaste but Percival Graham, who had been prodding the contents of his tobacco pouch, looked up. 'He was forever at my cousin's when she lived alone,' he said. 'I found him there myself and he was short – very short – in his remarks when I tried to protect her interests. Now, he's close with Carmody.'

'Aye,' said Sir John, 'apothecaries and bakers are about his level. We'll have a good harvest, gentlemen. What price our corn?'

'By God,' Wilbraham slapped his hand on the loose-box door, 'my wife said as much to him at Mythe. You were there, Sir John. And the language he used wasn't fit to be heard. He as good as told her she was a Rackrent. Starving the labouring men, he said. I'd a mind to call him out.'

'He isn't,' said Graham, 'one of us.'

There was a sound of giggling and two girls, who had forgotten that they had just had their hair put up, ran into the stable-yard with one of Wilbraham's daughters. Seeing the men, they fell silent and retreated to the lawn.

'I hear he had a powerful dislike of poachers,' said Newman, thoughtfully, 'and if there was a girl—'

Sir John was smoothing his fob with his thumb. 'I think,' he said, 'I do think we must give this matter more consideration.'

It was not only those least involved who were pondering Barlow's death. At Holcombe, Frederick could not turn his thoughts from it. When he had left his assailant unconscious in the lane, he had had no suspicion that the man was dying. The shock of returning, after rousing the farm and sending for Carmody, to find a corpse had been severe and sickening. There was no sign of Ellen and Frederick had no reason to think that it was not his blow that had killed Barlow. He did not blame himself, for he had done no more than fight in self-defence, but the act of killing, of hurrying a soul to judgement, was too momentous not to inspire awe.

He had not seen Philobeth that night. There had

been hours of waiting for Carmody, of transporting the body to a disused dairy house that stood nearby on Combehays land, of explanations and discussions before he had been driven back to Holcombe by one of Mahala's grooms. Carmody, arriving the next day to make a further examination of the injuries Frederick had dismissed before, had found him grim and aching in mind and limbs. It had been the doctor's orders, as he changed the dressing on his patient's neck, that there were to be several days of rest and Frederick, believing that he could not go to Philobeth with blood on his hands, agreed.

His rest that day consisted only of not leaving the house. The morning was occupied by Carmody and two embarrassed constables, whose apologies for carrying out their duty of following up a crime made their interview tiring for all concerned. By the afternoon, news of the assault had spread and the Rector began a procession of neighbours calling to make enquiries. There had been no looking askance at Frederick the night before and there was none now. Barlow's history was well known in the valley and it was taken for granted that his obsessive hatred of Frederick had at last turned into violence. The shame-faced farmer, who had been awakened by Frederick's knocking, had admitted, as he and his men had carried hurdles to the lane, that he had been meaning to send word that Barlow had taken to sleeping in the old shed since he lost his lodgings. Frederick was assured that he had had a lucky escape and, though no-one said 'good riddance', Mahala pointed out through Carmody that, by dying, Barlow had saved himself from a lifetime's transportation.

Frederick found the constant conversation irritating

but it had the effect of distracting him from the brooding melancholy that might otherwise have settled on him once more. As he sat in his chair, wincing as any rash movement reminded him of his wounds, repeating the tale of the attack, the savagery of Ellen's self-seeking and Barlow's rage sank into his thoughts and lost the raw quality its recency possessed. He had known that both man and woman were depraved, yet the abrupt revelation of how unprincipled they were pierced him so that he needed to have his attention called to the relating of bare fact. The repetition of how Barlow had attacked him was a reminder of his innocence in this unintentional taking of life and acted as a support as he recovered from the shock.

He had no visitors in the evening and, as he lay in bed with his bruises throbbing, he looked back over the day and realized that he had had no message from the Alleyns. Was his separation from Philobeth so complete that she would not be concerned by such an incident as this? Was she so horrified that he had killed a man that she would not even send a note in her father's name? It was possible that word of the fight had not reached them but fatigue and disappointment at the delaying of his plans made him favour a darker view. The confidence in her forgiveness, that had blossomed in him as he had walked through the fields, withered as he thought of his changed condition. He would still lay siege to her but he was not sure of the outcome.

His pessimism was misplaced. Mahala had summoned Philobeth that morning so that she could have the story and the latest bulletin on Frederick's health from, as she put it, 'the horse's mouth'. Although she still hoped Philobeth would marry Carmody, Mahala realized that events so startling as a brawl and death involving an old lover would be bound to be agitating. If this sentiment was partly prompted by a feeling of possessiveness towards her husband and a pretence that there need be no new Mrs Carmody, Mahala did not lose sleep over it. She could no longer sit up but she was not yet so enfeebled that she could not laugh at herself.

Philobeth was as stricken as her friend had expected. The final sundering of her relations with Frederick had cost her dearly. She valued herself too highly to regret her decisive rejection of him at their last meeting but she bitterly regretted its necessity. Her love would not die despite her efforts to stifle it and the self-discipline that let her appear to carry on her normal life without pain could not survive hearing of the danger he had been in. She was able to control herself at Combehays but her defences were down and she had to lean against an oak on her way home to subdue her trembling before she reached the house.

She found herself in a quandary. Her first reaction had been to half rise from her seat to go to him, but the fear that she would not be welcome or that he would assume too much from her interest prevented her from standing. A vision of Ellen tending to his wounds tormented her. She had no doubt that she had the right to care for him and her certainty, in the face of his philandering and her repudiation of him, was frightening. She wanted to maintain her independence but her love rose within her, clamouring to be heard. Its intensity forced her to admit what she already knew – that the past, present and future of her love were as one in their strength. Her heart was steadfast. It was not her constancy but what action she should take that made her hesitate. If her way to him was not barred by Ellen, the susceptibility of the sick-bed might lead to a renewal of their old intimacy, and what would come of that? Should she abandon her plans for the favour of a man she could not trust? It was ridiculous to think so, yet he was her Frederick and he was hurt.

Walking on slowly, she decided to postpone her decision for an hour until she had calmed herself a little. She thought, with a wry annoyance, that she should not have to make a resolution on a serious matter in such weather as this. The air was balmy, the sky was blue without being dazzling, the heat soothed without oppressing. It was a morning for deciding between a hammock and an arbour, for suggesting, from a comfortable position, that a stroll might be pleasant later – much later – in the day.

She entered her garden by the back gate and looked about for her father. He was sitting in a wicker chair beneath an elm, wearing a wide-brimmed straw hat and loose linen jacket that gave him the raffish manner of a solicitor indulging in amateur theatricals. The country did not suit him unless he was hard at work upon a landscape or surrounded by the same people he moved amongst in London, and he was happily anticipating August in Yorkshire. He had been invited to shoot grouse by a man whose daughters he was to paint and, though he would not go out with the guns, he looked forward to the tea-table scandal of the ladies.

As Philobeth approached him over the lawn, he saw that she was rolling her sunshade back and forth along her shoulder and knew she was distressed. The expression on her handsome face was serious and he could not help thinking that she would have found life easier if she had been as empty-headed as the girls whose portraits were ordered. He had suggested that she come north with him, saying that even if his patron's guests would be unable to accept she was an artist, the change of scenery would do her good, but she had declined to leave Mahala.

He moved his book and glass onto the ground and she sat on the stout rustic table where they had been.

'Is she worse?' he asked.

'Who?' Philobeth was momentarily puzzled. 'Oh! No. That wasn't why.'

'Something has upset you.'

She laid her parasol down on the grass and leant back on her hands. It touched her that he had noticed, but the fact that she was both touched and surprised showed how much they were strangers to each other. It had not occurred to her to go to him for advice, but she was anxious for sympathy. She told him what she had heard and he did not fail her.

'My dear!' he said. 'My dear!'

He put the fingers of one hand to the place where his brows met and squeezed his eyes shut as he did when his head ached from close work. It was his boast that he had never needed spectacles but at such times he looked as though he habitually wore pince-nez. Frederick's treatment of Philobeth had naturally decreased the proud father's respect for him but, nevertheless, the situation was apalling.

'My dear, I hardly know what to say.' He took her hand. 'And Mahala sent to tell you. That was thoughtful of her. And her husband involved, of course. Well, we must be thankful it turned out as it did. It could so easily have been the other way. A sudden attack at night! It won't affect you as it would have once but, still, you must feel it. Indeed, you must.'

'I do.'

Her voice betrayed her but his imagination was running too fast for him to notice it. 'The same man that caused the girl's death. To have blamed North and stalked him like a cat— And finally, retribution at the hands of the one he cursed. A powerful scene. It would sell.'

Philobeth bent for her sunshade and stood up. I must beware what task I set myself, she thought. I might do it too well. I wanted him to believe that Frederick means little to me and he does. 'I'll go and rest,' she said. 'It's been a tiring morning.'

The hall door was propped open with the shoe-scraper and she walked in wearily. She was hardly inside when Slater appeared in the passage, holding a knife and a half-pared apple. 'You'll be wanting tea,' she said and Philobeth, interpreting this as a command, followed her into the kitchen. The makings of a tart were spread out on the table and Philobeth sat on a stool beside it. She could tell from Slater's movements that the news had already reached her and was glad that she did not need to astonish another member of her household. She received her tea in silence, unafraid that her nurse would jar her feelings as her father had done.

Slater set the sugar-box back on the dresser and resumed her peeling. 'Mrs Carmody'll have told you,' she said.

'Yes.'

'That little scullery-maid of hers – the one with the yellow hair – she brought me over these apples as we've no decent ones left ourselves. She told me.'

'With what exaggerations, I wonder?'

Slater glanced at her severely. 'That one's got too

140

much sense to bring tarradiddles here. She won't be in the scullery long. She put two and two together and got the same answer as I did.'

Philobeth was idly moving the rolling-pin backwards and forwards. She did not like to think of Frederick as a subject of speculation for anyone but herself. It was inevitable that such a shocking episode would be discussed by all and sundry; she did not feel compelled to accept it gracefully. 'Was there a question?' she said. 'It seemed straightforward to me.'

Slater laid the last pared apple on the chopping-block and began to slice. It was not her way to show tenderness in words or tone, but hidden within her was a warm satisfaction that she had a gift to give her injured girl. Philobeth had told her that she had refused Frederick permission to call on them again and she had been waiting grimly to see if he would come. She knew Philobeth too well to believe that she wanted his absence and she intended to measure his worth by the degree of meekness with which he obeyed the decree. The detail of the night's events that had been too insignificant for Carmody to pass on to his wife, but which had been picked up by the sharpness of a serving-maid, was making her secretly rejoice.

'Well, missy,' she said, 'the fight was straightforward enough, but what was he doing there to be fought with?'

It was not an aspect of the affair that Philobeth had given any consideration. 'Mahala says Barlow was sleeping in that old shed. Perhaps Frederick had gone to send him on his way.'

Slater pointed the knife at her triumphantly. 'He was dressed for visiting,' she said, 'with a posy in his waistcoat-pocket. And where would he be visiting

141

along that path? Here. Yes, that made you sit up. He was coming here.'

The familiarity of old retainers might have its dis-advantages to those with an interest in privacy and position but they are balanced by the flow of infor-mation it encourages. It seemed to Philobeth, as she sat repeating the version of the assault that she had had at Combehays, that her doubts over what she should do sloughed away when she heard that Frederick had been coming to her. She did not touble to reflect that the conclusion drawn by Slater and the maid might be wrong. Retrospective fear for his safety had opened the sluice-gates on her love and the slightest excuse was needed to send it swirling out towards its object.

She knew at once that she would go to him. Thoughts of what might follow their meeting were set aside. She neither drew a line through her plans nor determined to uphold them. In the release of her pent-up spirit, she existed only in the present. A trance-like glory infused her. She felt herself loved and, in the re-generation of her hope, she scorned to dwell on the neglect that had caused her misery. Her understanding of his cruelty did not diminish, but she was not petty and could accept the foolishness inherent in human nature. If she were to be united with him, she would tell him plainly what he had done and then hold her peace. Certainly, today she would not spoil her joy with grievances.

Alone in her room she looked at herself in the glass. Slater, mixing pastry with pursed lips that did not deceive her nursling in the least, had challenged Philobeth with suddenly having roses in her cheeks. The mirror did not deny it. There was a glow beneath her skin and in her eyes that had not been there these four months. Her body felt freer, her walk was more supple. She would go to her lover glad and without reserve. Brushing her heavy, dark hair, she remembered how he had put her braid to his lips when it had uncoiled one sultry afternoon in Combehays Wood.

She did not tell her father what she was about to do. No mention was made to him of where Frederick had been going. She did not want to be chaffed upon her prospects nor display an expectation that might be dashed. Letting him rove over the assault, discussing its criminality and the gothic possibilities of its portrayal in paint, she answered with an absent-mindedness that he put down to the heat.

When they had lunched and Mr Alleyn had spread a handkerchief over his face and fallen asleep under the elm, she left the house to walk to Holcombe. She sent no message before her nor made any change in her appearance, trusting to Frederick's change of heart to make her welcome. In the hush of somnolent meadows, where cattle stood like stone beneath unmoving trees, she walked in bliss, treasuring an hour that she knew was divorced from the reality of life. She avoided the lane where the death had been and the old dairy where the body lay, preferring quiet paths with gentler memories. The way was lonely and, wanting solitude, it did not please her to see the farmer standing at a gate, talking with his men. He hailed her as she passed. Her heart was beating with the fervour of her thoughts; she believed her intentions were written in her eyes but she turned and went to hear that Frederick North had been arrested for the murder of an unarmed man.

Chapter Eleven

The news of Barlow's death reached Mythe within hours of its occurrence. Unaware that one of the inhabitants of the house had a fuller knowledge of the killing than he did himself, Frederick had sent a servant with a note giving a clear and sober version of the ambush and assault. Despite his dislike of his grandmother, he did not want her to suffer from hearing the exaggerated accounts of desperate deeds that would be bound to circulate as reports spread.

The servant did not confine himself to delivering the letter. It would have been more than flesh and blood could stand to keep such choice intelligence to himself and he regaled the wakening kitchen with a dramatic and galvanizing rendition of the happenings in the lane. So it was that Ellen received the tidings as her curtains were being opened, a little late, by a flushed and excited maid.

Ellen had not slept. The strange ecstasy that had overtaken her when she had seen Barlow lying defenceless in the lane had not subsided until dawn had begun to break. She had not stayed to see the body found. The temptation to remain and declare that she had seen Frederick kill a harmless man had been strong but she was afraid that her own secrets would be uncovered if she were prominent in court. She had slipped away, confident that she had destroyed Frederick as surely as he had injured her. None of her thoughts were for Barlow. It did not enter her consciousness that he had been a living being with as much right to walk the earth as she. Guilt did not touch her. It was not simply that Barlow had been a stranger that kept her conscience clear. Her inability to understand that those around her had ambitions and desires as real as her own robbed them of their humanity and protected her from doubt. She could not believe in the pleasure or pain of anyone except herself and when her hands had closed over Barlow's nose and mouth, it had been no harder for her than telling a lie to gain her ends. It was true that, twice in the early hours, she had felt a brief nausea as the single weak convulsion he had made had seemed to be again beneath her palms; his tremor had made her fear that he would revive to overcome her and she attributed her sickness to this alarm.

Elation had carried her across dark paths to Mythe. She entered the house without difficulty and reached her room exultant with success but, as morning began to lighten the sky, her mood changed. The ordinary demands of life brought by the coming day dampened her euphoria. It would soon be necessary to play her normal part until news should come from Holcombe. She must ready herself to be shocked. Frederick had told her that she should go on the stage and it filled her with childish glee to be preparing to show astonishment at his downfall. She was proud of her talent for passing herself off as a gentlewoman. He had accused her of impersonating a character not her own and it amused her to think how near he had been to the truth.

Her only problem in maintaining her role was in deciding whether her reaction should be the distress of one whose heart was to be broken by her lover's fate or tempered by a cooling towards him.

Tiredness had started to affect her. She wanted to order her curtains shut again and sleep through the morning but it seemed unwise to draw attention to herself by unusual behaviour. Impulse prompted all her most extreme actions and so far it had only been good fortune that had kept her from discovery but having committed a crime, she covered her tracks as best she could. She wished that she had not been seen by the servants at Holcombe. It would be prudent to have her presence there discussed as seldom as possible, and she determined not to tell Mrs North of her excursion unless the old woman heard of it from some other source. Shame over her rejection or the desire not to cause her benefactress more agitation on the day she received troubling news would be enough to excuse her silence. It was a mark of how completely she had fallen into the life of a lady that she could imagine that her secretive absence from the house had not been noticed by anyone at Mythe and was not being wondered at behind the green-baize door.

She was leaning against her pillows, trying to rouse herself with the coffee that was always brought to her before she dressed when the maid came back to ask her to go at once to Mrs North. Frederick's note had been carried in with the tea-tray and its recipient was, the girl said, 'in a rare taking'.

Wrapping herself in a loose robe, Ellen went expectantly to knock at the door of Mrs North's room. The events she had set in motion were beginning and the anticipation of her revenge was too sweet for her to be hindered by exhaustion.

Mrs North was sitting up in bed with the letter spread out on her lap. The maid's description had led Ellen to think she would have to dry tears but the principal expression on the face that looked at her from beneath a frilled cap was a bewildered irritation. She crossed the room and sat on the edge of the coverlet as Mrs North waved the closely-written pages at her. It struck her that Frederick might have mentioned her visit and the first suggestion of fear for her own safety made her catch her breath but she reminded herself that he had not known that she had followed him. I must have sleep, she thought, or I'll quake at shadows.

'Susan said you needed me.' She put her hand under one of Mrs North's. 'Have you had bad news?'

Mrs North squeezed the fingers clasping hers. Neither woman removed her rings at night and there was a scraping of gold against gold. A page of the letter slipped free and, letting go of Ellen to snatch it up, she thrust both sheets into the hand she had dropped. 'Read this,' she said. 'Read it. You'll never believe—'

She shook her head helplessly, pulling a shawl more closely about her shoulders despite the warmth of the morning. She had not decided how to react to the killing and wanted to be guided by Ellen. If it had been possible, she would have preferred to close her eyes to the whole matter but she knew it would be in the mouths of all her acquaintance; she would need an opinion. Her lack of interest in Frederick as an individual made her angry that he had burdened her with a potential scandal. She had no sympathy for his physical hurts, nor did it occur to her that he might be suffering in spirit from the outcome of the night. Her imagination was not strong and, knowing him to be safe, she was unable to accept that he had been in danger. The episode seemed designed to give her annoyance yet she had a vague consciousness that she ought to feel differently and it puzzled her. Frederick was, after all, a North. Perhaps she should give his action her full approval for that reason. Her father had set man-traps about the estate and would have thought nothing of the death of a poacher. Wealth and position must have its rights. Yes, it would be best to defend him. If only he were not so unsatisfactory—

As Mrs North struggled towards thinking she should be glad that her grandson was unharmed, Ellen read the letter. Mrs North had been right in telling her that it contained something she would not believe, but the subject of her incredulity was not what the old woman would expect. It astounded her that Frederick was free. Her confidence that his arrest would follow the discovery of Barlow had been complete, yet he was able to write of the death without the slightest suggestion of being threatened by the law. He admitted openly that he had killed a man. Surely even in this land of privileges for rank a murder would not be winked at? She began to shudder, the pages quivering in her grip. Had she been seen? Was Frederick safe because the authorities were coming for her? Her throat constricted as if a noose were already around it. The pride she felt in her daring did not lessen but retreated to the recesses of her mind as a childlike denial of blame came forward. She almost cried aloud 'It wasn't me! I wasn't there!' All the pity for affliction that should have been expended on those around her was concentrated on herself and magnified her fears. The absence of guilt for her viciousness was balanced by a horror of her own death. She could not endure the thought of punishment.

A second reading of the letter did not quiet her apprehension but gave her time to control her panic. She was shivering so much that she was afraid Mrs North would be suspicious but the old lady was not one to notice distress in others. The effort to control her body calmed her and she told herself fiercely that she had not been watched. There were no witnesses to her crime. Frederick had not mentioned her visit to him and was making no secret of his part in the killing. Her presence at Holcombe that evening might never be mentioned. If she was discreet, who would ever connect her with such violence? She made her decision. The problem of how to react was solved. She must be gentle and loving in her attitude to Frederick, tremulous in her grief for his wounds, grateful that he was alive. No-one should guess that she wished him harm and, even though he escaped her revenge, all would be well.

Mrs North had been staring vacantly at a walnut commode that had been in the house since she was a girl. Seeing from the corner of her eye that Ellen was folding the letter, she looked piteously into her face. 'What shall we do?' she asked.

It seemed a curious question for a grandmother to ask, but its timidity and its dismissal of Frederick's plight was reassuring to Ellen. A devoted relative hurrying to Holcombe, demanding every detail of the night and searching for reasons to exonerate her boy, was the last thing that she wanted.

'My dear Mrs North,' she said, 'please try to think of yourself. The shock— May I send for your drops to calm you?'

Mrs North relaxed. It seemed that it would be acceptable to avoid the initial scandal by retreating into ill-health. At her age it was natural that such a report should affect her badly. If she could keep to her bed today, word of the assault would have spread before she could be asked of it and she would gain a clearer notion of how the world viewed the affair. She liked Ellen's softly-voiced concern: an old woman should have her comforts.

'There are some on the wash-stand,' she said. 'In a little water, Ellie dear.'

Ellen filled a glass from the jug beside the bed and carried it to the flask of eau-de-cologne. Mrs North's recent habit of using the familiar form of her name annoyed her. It showed a promising fondness that must be fostered but it robbed her of dignity. The irritation of hearing it again, in circumstances when she should be admired for her self-control, made her put the glass down clumsily, catching her wrist on the stand. The coldness of the marble against her skin made her draw in her breath and shiver once more.

This time Mrs North was watching her eagerly and noticed her falter. 'What is it?' she asked, plaintively. 'Are you unwell? Is it the chill I had last night?'

Ellen had almost forgotten she had already persuaded Mrs North that she was ailing. The convenience of it helped her to compose herself. She poured a measure of cologne into the water and brought the glass back to the bed. Mrs North reached out to take it but Ellen put an arm round her shoulders and held the rim to her lips.

'Let me,' she said. 'You're the one who must take care. I'm just alarmed for Frederick.' She tilted the glass and Mrs North drank with the pathetic air of one whose health depends on such mixtures. 'Won't you stay in bed today?' Ellen asked as she set the empty glass back on the bedside table. 'I don't want to have to worry about you as well. We could go to Holcombe tomorrow if you've recovered, but you won't get strong if you don't rest.'

Mrs North let out a perfumed sigh. 'You're right,' she said, 'of course. I'd like to order the carriage but, for you, I'll stay.'

The swiftness of events after Sir John Packard said that Barlow's death should be given more consideration startled the group that had taken their brandy-and-sodas in Wilbraham's stable-yard. Although they agreed that North, as Graham had stated, was not 'one of us', the more timid amongst them were dismayed that their censure should lead to a warrant for arrest. They were unanimous in condemning Frederick's character but he was, after all, a landowner and if a man could not protect his own property, where would it end? Fear that they had been wrong caused them to close ranks behind Sir John, exchanging grim-faced tales of Frederick's betrayal of his class and building mental barricades against doubt. Before Sir John, in his capacity as the longest-serving and most domineering of the J.P.s present, had driven away to gather the necessary documents and reinforcements for the arrest, his fellow conspirators were already convincing themselves that Frederick was not only debauched but the son of a tradesman. As news of what was to occur spread through the garden party, rumours began of Frederick's violent hatred of poachers and it became a known fact that Barlow had stolen North's wench. The men of the stable-yard grew reserved and severe, shaking their heads at questioners and saying that they knew when they must do their duty.

Sir John's expedition caused him to miss the admirable outdoor luncheon that Mrs Wilbraham had provided for her guests but he was not fond of his stomach and he had a much more satisfying occupation on hand. He executed it with every possible dispatch, and so it was that as Philobeth walked across the meadows to her lover, she was already too late.

Jackson, the farmer who had been roused by Frederick after the assault and who now hailed Philobeth, had been feeling guilty for not warning Frederick that Barlow was lurking in his fields, and had just been up to Holcombe with a present of cream as an apology. He had arrived at the house to find its staff in a state of confusion and near-hysteria. The butler, who had been born in the coachman's quarters and lived all his days under the Norths, had been white and shaking as he described how his master had been taken away by soldiers from Dorchester.

''E said,' Jackson told Philobeth, 'as how Sir John Packard and Mr Caine from Peverell come riding down the drive with the military and their horses all a-sweating as if there'd been a cavalry charge, though they come up to the house soft enough. And they marched into the hall saying "Fetch your master. Sharp!" as if Boney 'ad landed. Well, what could 'e do? 'E fetched un. And you never saw two gentlemen look at each other more black than Sir John and Mr North when Sir John says why 'e's there. They argues it back and forth but Sir John's got a paper with 'is name on and after a while Mr North tells 'is man to send for 'is lawyer and they all starts to go off. Sir John says to the sergeant "Ent you a-going to chain un?" and Mr

North 'e gives a kind of a laugh and says to the soldiers "My men, I ent no fox to be a-hunted. I'll ride with ee companionable", and so they goes.'

As she listened, Philobeth felt the blood drain from her face. A sensation of sinking and dizziness made her lean against the gate; and Jackson, fussily anxious, took her by the elbow with a grip that could have supported a bullock. He was a soft-hearted, loquacious man, always ready to do a neighbour a good turn or pass on gossip he thought would be interesting. He had called to Philobeth because he had assumed she was going to Holcombe and he wanted to share the astounding news whilst saving her a journey. Like all the inhabitants of the valley, he knew of the unusual intimacy between Philobeth and Frederick, and of its cooling since the advent of the woman from the sea, but his nature was too convivial to make him slight her on that account. That she was not quite a lady in his eyes, was plain from the way he felt able to shout to her across a meadow and this narrowing of the division between them made it easier for him to talk to her freely. He thought her 'a fine piece' and had not wanted her to walk on in the heat of the afternoon in ignorance of what had happened, but he had not expected her to turn pale and faint. Never having been touched by love himself, he could not anticipate that a woman could be deeply affected by even the most serious tidings of a man who was out of her reach. He understood fondness and merrymaking, clumsy flirtations and the pique of disappointed hopes, but pallor for an old admirer was beyond him. Keeping his grasp on her arm, he stood by helplessly as Philobeth recovered herself.

'But this can't be true,' she said, her low voice husky

with the shallow breath of shock. 'Not murder. Every-one knows what Barlow was like.'

Seeing her raise her head and flex her hand on the bar of the gate, Jackson felt it safe to let her go. 'There now,' he said, 'so they do. 'Twill all come right.'

It was his instinct, when faced with an agitated woman, to soothe her without regard for the truth. Having brought about this unforeseen reaction, he was keen to give what comfort he could, but it was not a situation that lent itself to a cheerful outlook.

'Something must be done,' she said, looking about her as if she could not comprehend why the landscape should be peaceful, 'but – oh, at the moment, I cannot think.'

'Will ee come back to the house, Miss Alleyn,' Jackson asked, 'and take a drop o' tea? 'Tis a powerful warm day for thinking.'

She nodded absently and took his arm to cross the field. The terror that had overcome her was subsiding into a slow beat of fear that she believed would be with her until it became mourning or relief. This can't be, she thought, there was no suggestion of this. Yes, he has killed a man but it can't be called murder, to defend yourself from attack. Frederick, Frederick.

'There's more behind this,' she said, suddenly. 'Who arraigned him?'

They had been walking in silence and her ve-hemence made Jackson start. 'That I can't say,' he pressed her arm to him, thinking that she might grow weak again. ' 'Twas Sir John and Mr Caine come with the soldiers, like I said.'

'So you did. I'm sorry, my mind isn't clear.'

They had come to a stile and they climbed it to pass through a tunnel of brambles into a lane. To their right, the narrow road turned a sharp corner and led down, past a thicket and three meadows, to the place where Barlow had called Frederick's name. To their left, a hundred yards away, stood the long, creeper-hung farmhouse to which Frederick had limped for help for his assailant. To the surprise of them both a carriage with a liveried coachman was drawn up outside the house.

'Now, who—?' asked Jackson.

'It's Mrs North's,' Philobeth said, recognizing it as they approached. Her feelings misgave her. She did not want to open herself to the scorn and incivility that had been all that she had ever received from Frederick's grandmother, but the old woman's presence there made the killing and arrest more real, and if there was information to be had, she meant to have it. Her thoughts were too stricken and confused for her to have any idea of how she could aid Frederick and, for that reason, she was sure she must trawl for any clue that could assist him. She did not believe in Fate and so was spared railing against the cruelty it had shown but she was aghast that life had taken such a turn and was prepared to undergo far worse trials than being insulted by Mrs North, if it would throw light on the affair. The astuteness of a servant-girl had caught up an unconsidered trifle from the account of the fight and cast Philobeth into a mood of blissful reconciliation. Was it impossible that some small detail, lying undiscovered, might not be the key to the mystery that was Frederick's arrest?

Jackson was about to make his usual turn into the yard when he checked himself and led Philobeth up the rosemary-bordered path to the front door. The family was not used to visitors who expected such a formal entrance, and it was necessary for him to kick the warped wood to make it scrape back across the flagstones. Once inside, he took her through a passage and into the wide room that was both kitchen and parlour.

She walked behind him, thinking of Mrs North. The spiteful attitude of the old woman towards her, with its inherent lack of concern for what would make her grandson happy, did not incline her to expect to meet genuine grief. The family name, that would have been blighted by an alliance with a professional artist, would be equally harmed by its representative being condemned as a felon, and this consideration might be causing anxiety, but Philobeth was too much of a realist to think that her sympathies would be needed. She was so absorbed in resentment on Frederick's behalf against his grandmother that she gave no thought to the domestic arrangements at Mythe. When Jackson stepped aside to let her enter the kitchen, she looked for Mrs North – and found Ellen.

The two women had not met since the night of the wreck. Indeed, they could be said never to have met at all, for Ellen had not been more than semi-conscious during the time they were together. Philobeth's remembrance of her was of a bruised, defiled body on a dark shore, a shadowed face in the swaying light of a lantern in the carriage and, although her eye for essential form had told her that the victim was beautiful, she had not anticipated the loveliness that was standing beside the hearth. Even in the midst of her grief for Frederick, she felt a pang of jealousy as she admitted that the delicate face before her was truly one to make men forget their loves.

Ellen glanced at the newcomers without interest.

Philobeth realized with a wry amusement that this striking creature, who owed her life to the woman she now looked at blankly, did not recognize her. Of course it was not to be expected that she would. She had not thought it necessary to seek out her saviour to thank her, and it was unlikely that Frederick had ever shown her the likeness that Philobeth had given him when the weather between them was fair. So many of my days, Philobeth thought, have been given up to the sorrow she had caused that it seems as if we have lived as sisters. Well, sisters, I have heard, can live as strangers.

There was an exclamation from the other side of the fireplace and, turning her gaze from Ellen, Philobeth noticed Mrs North sitting in the great, high-backed armchair that was Jackson's exclusive property. Leaning against its blue-and-white checked cover, a ham suspended above her head, Mrs North looked uneasy and out of place, but there were no particular signs of agitation about her. She did not greet Philobeth, but the tightening of her knuckles on her ebony stick made it plain that she was not pleased to see her.

As her husband touched his brow to the ladies, Mrs Jackson came forward and moved a chair a few inches as an invitation to Philobeth. She had been answering her visitors' questions about the night before last and was given the impression that all her answers were either lies or stubborn stupidity. Reinforcements in the shape of Jackson and Miss Alleyn, and the diversion of finding the two rivals for her landlord's affection in her own house, were a relief to her harassed spirit. Thinking that her guests were known to each other, she did not introduce them but Philobeth, wondering how Ellen would react, went and proffered her hand. She said her name as Ellen put her gloveless fingers coldly into hers, and the sudden vicious clenching it produced astonished her. The rush of strength died as swiftly as the hatred that had flared in the lambent eyes, but not without her heavy rings leaving indentations in Philobeth's flesh. The episode was over so quickly that if her skin had not been marked, Philobeth could hardly have said that it had happened. It seemed that she had looked upon a tranquil lake and, momentarily, seen a darkness rise from its waters. The animosity was shocking, but it confirmed that Frederick had returned to his first love.

Taking the chair that had been moved for her, Philobeth sat quietly listening to Jackson give Mrs North the news of Frederick's arrest. It had not occurred to his grandmother that Frederick would suffer more than the disapproval of his peers, and the tidings made her drop her stick to clutch at her chest. Philobeth did not judge her symptoms to be serious and was able to give her attention to Ellen. Just as loathing had burnt briefly in the calm beauty of Ellen's face when she had heard Philobeth's name, so now a queer elation shone for an instant before passivity slid back into its place. The expression was so bizarre in its timing that Philobeth could not immediately pin-point its nature but, as Ellen reached into Mrs North's bag and bent over her companion with a phial of salts, she realized that it had been triumph.

There seemed no reason for it. She was too generous herself to believe that even a woman shunned by her former lover could glory in his degradation and shame. Nevertheless, she began to observe Ellen with a scepticism that would have done Mahala credit.

The salts had their effect and Mrs Jackson improved

upon it by passing glasses of sloe gin amongst the company. The medicinal qualities of the pungent liquor restored Mrs North to herself and she was able to interrogate Jackson, with Ellen standing serenely at her side in case of further anxiousness. Neither lady had yet addressed Philobeth and, though she had a sensation that Ellen was scrutinizing her despite looking elsewhere, she continued to watch and listen with a mind made alert and receptive by her fears.

Jackson told Mrs North nothing that he had not related to Philobeth and the conversation, hampered by the differences in rank and amiability amongst the participants, turned to conjecture and wonderment. In the course of exclaiming against Barlow's character, Mrs Jackson ventured a theory that was derided by her husband. Barlow, she said, was the kind of ne'er-do-well that made many enemies and it was as likely as not that a father or sweetheart of a girl he had wronged had chanced upon him lying in the lane and finished him off.

'And a good job of work 'twould 'ave been,' she announced, 'if Mr North weren't called for un.'

'You know nought about it,' said Jackson. 'The master caught un a crack. What more do ee want? The parson watching?'

Already unnerved by the reception her original report had had from the ladies, and unaware that suspicion and disparagement were natural to Mrs North in talking to working people, Mrs Jackson did not defend her idea, but she was a woman of lively, if uneducated, imagination and was not completely suppressed. 'Well, then,' she said, 'do you go and ask Dr Carmody to raise up Barlow's eyelids. A murderer's face is printed on a dead man's eyes, sure as eggs, an' when Mr North's picture's not there, that'll show it weren't no intended killing.'

'By God,' said Jackson, 'your 'ead's as full o' notions as a hive is o' bees. If—'

'What do you mean?' Ellen's voice cut through Jackson's with an authority that held an indefinable element, silencing both husband and wife. Her expression was blank but it seemed to Philobeth that the blankness was a mask.

As Mrs Jackson did not speak, Philobeth answered for her. 'It's believed here,' she said, 'that Providence likes to bring murderers to justice. The last image a man sees as he meets a violent death remains portrayed on his eyes and thus the culprit can be discovered.'

Ellen stared at her and Philobeth, who had seen her receive the news of the arrest with no response but the instant's strange rejoicing, marvelled to witness the colour sink from her face until it was ashen.

'Horrible!' Ellen said, her voice high and piercing. 'Horrible! Hateful! Who could believe such a thing? Why did you tell me?'

'Because,' said Philobeth, 'you asked.'

'It's foul!' Ellen leant against the side of Mrs North's chair. 'Foul! I'll have none of it!'

At Combehays the following afternoon, two doves from the cote on the far side of the lake settled on the sill of Mahala's window and began to peck the seed that lay there with darting movements of their ruffled necks. Carmody paused in his reading to gaze at them, and think how the sun made their whiteness more like a dazzling absence of vision than an image. A door opened nearby and the birds rose up in a hysterical beating of wings. When they and their shadows had gone from the room, Carmody turned back to his wife.

Mahala was lying flat in the bed. She had developed a habit of drawing short, hissing breaths through her teeth in an effort to prevent herself coughing, and she was breathing in this way now. Carmody found his place in the book and went on reading aloud in gentle, soothing tones.

> ' "A heap of withered boughs was piled,
> Of juniper and rowan wild,
> Mingled with shivers from the oak,
> Rent by the lightning's recent stroke." '

He liked to read to her and it pleased her that he liked it. The act gave her the attention and warmth of conversation without the exertion of speaking, and comforted them both. Since the night of Frederick's attack she had been talking more than had become usual for her and Carmody was glad to see her rest. The excitement, the discussion with Philobeth and the nervous strain of knowing that a friend had been in danger, had exhausted her small reserves of strength. She had not yet been told of Frederick's arrest and if Carmody had not been sure that one of the servants would let the news slip, he would have kept it from her forever. He dreaded the effect it would have on her weakened frame.

Already he regretted having had to tell her of the assault. They had arranged that he should sleep in a room several doors from hers, beside the back stairs, so that he was near enough to reach her quickly in the night if he were needed yet far enough to be summoned to patients without disturbing her; he had attended Barlow and returned before she had known he was gone. He had found that rumours had reached her through her maid by seven the next morning and so had been forced to give her a full account, but the increase in her temperature and pulse had warned him that she must be kept as calm as possible.

He knew that she was very near to her death and that all his care could only push away the evil hour by days, but his regret made her last weeks precious to him. When he had agreed to marry her, he had been amused by her brazen outwitting of her despised relations and astonished by the generosity and cunning of her plan. He had always liked her: they shared the same humour and the same pragmatism that had enabled her to make the proposal and him to accept, but he had not expected the bond that had grown between them.

Her diseased condition drew out his tenderness. He was not repulsed by the indignities of the sick-bed, and her imprisonment made it easier for him to live in harmony with her than if she had been free to exercise her independence. It flattered him that she asked for his company. He was moved by the way her eyes softened when she awoke and found him in her chamber. The position he had thought to fill while she lived had been physician in residence; he had not thought to be master of the house and fortune that the law had made his when he gave her his name, but she had brushed aside his embarrassment, encouraging him to ready himself to take control of the estate and teasing him over the better cut of clothes he had worn since his first tentative use of her money. 'Ah,' she would say, 'you'll ruin us with tailors' bills, and me with not a shoe to my foot.' He had only distressed her once. On a languorous evening, when the June air was sweet with roses, he had bent to kiss her and she, who had always allowed him near, had cried 'Don't die for me!' and, turning away, had covered her mouth with her hands and wept.

She opened her eyes and one of her thin hands came from beneath the sheet, clutching a linen handkerchief. He stopped again and saw the look of concentration on her face that meant she was trying not to cough. She was rigid for a moment and then the need passed and she relaxed.

'Do you want me to go on,' he asked, 'or would you rather sleep?'

'Do you want to,' she countered in her low whisper, 'or are you tired?'

'"Since to your home A destined errant-knight I come",' he said, '"Doomed, doubtless, for achievement bold" – I'm prepared to read all evening.'

'Oh,' she put the handkerchief to the corner of her lips and smiled, 'if this isn't cold enough for you, read me one of your dreary journals. Entertain me with purges and Peruvian bark.'

'They should never be read to a layman. They'd make you think you were ill.'

She raised her eyebrows. 'Well,' she said, 'then we must avoid them. We don't want me a prey to fancies.'

He did not resume reading immediately and she stared up at the canopy of her bed.

'Edward?' There was a change in her tone.

He put the book down on his knee. 'Yes?'

She hesitated. 'You will be kind to Philobeth?' she said.

He leant forward. 'Now why,' he asked, mildly, 'should you think I wouldn't be kind?'

163

She stirred painfully on the pillow. 'For no reason. Just that sometimes the world seems dark.'

He ran the back of his finger softly down her cheek. 'It will be lighter for you soon,' he said, 'and then it will be dark here for your friends.'

She turned her face to press against his hand. Her eyes were filled with a longing for what she could not have. She did not fear death, but she mourned the days she would not see. It pained her that all she could give this man must be served to him upon a bier; she grieved that he had never known her body except as a wasted thing of drugs and suffering; she wanted ripeness and fertility; she wanted to grow old. 'Bring Philobeth,' she said, 'bring her to my house and live for me.'

'It was extraordinary. I hardly know whether I should have allowed it. Unusual requests can take you off your guard.' Carmody succeeded in lighting his cigar and waved it distractedly at Philobeth. 'I had no reason to refuse. It didn't seem like ghoulish curiosity. She said it was to set Mrs North's mind at rest.'

They were in a small boudoir of blue silk hangings on the first floor that Carmody used as his sitting-room. It was early evening and, since the weather was fine and she was restless, Philobeth was calling at Combehays for the second time that day. Mahala was sleeping and her husband was glad to talk to Philobeth until she woke. The pair now had secrets. It had been agreed between them that Frederick's arrest should be kept from Mahala until the following afternoon, when they hoped that she might have recovered a little from hearing of the assault. Carmody thought it proper for a man to conceal harmful information from his wife but

Philobeth, despite admitting its necessity, loathed the deceit involved in leaving the shocking news out of her conversation with her friend.

Nor was this the only deception she was practising. Throughout their discussion of the attack, Philobeth had hidden both her belief that Frederick had been coming to her and her joyful acceptance that her love for him had not decreased. She had not wanted Mahala to expend any of her waning energy on persuasions against trusting a man who had once been fickle, and her silence was valuable in the light of the horror that was Frederick's arrest. Her fears for his safety were so great that she did not feel she could have endured them if she had not needed to pretend for her friend's sake that she was suffering less than she was. The anxiety that would eat into Mahala's strength if she knew the true state of Philobeth's emotions was too dangerous to her health to be risked. It harrowed her to come to this decision. The realization that they could no longer share every thought and hope made the imminence of their parting more real and terrible than all the previous manifestations of Mahala's illness. To be unable to receive grave news with acerbic comment meant that Mahala was already partly dead, and sorrow for the failing of that bold heart was like a knife lodged in Philobeth's side.

'Miss Farebrother,' said Philobeth, dryly, 'is a curiosity in herself. In what way was viewing the corpse supposed to help Mrs North?'

Carmody looked embarrassed. 'I can't tell you,' he said. 'It seemed clear enough at the time, but when I try to recall her reasons they dissolve at a touch. She has a strangely compelling manner. I felt almost panic-stricken at the thought of not giving her what she wanted and now I don't know why. I was swept along by the strength of her wishes.'

They were silent for a moment as Philobeth thought of another man's entrapment and Carmody puzzled over how he had been beguiled into pandering to morbid sensation-seeking. He remembered how uncomfortable he had been when Philobeth had walked into the barn where he was examining Mary Taylor and announced that she intended to sketch the dead girl. Looking back he felt that, however unsuitable it was that a woman could undertake such an action with composure, there had been a purity about it that was missing from Ellen's behaviour. He would go further. There had been a depravity in Ellen's conduct. He could not explain himself but there was more behind her request than the satisfaction of Gothick eccentricity.

His afternoon, already complicated by rising affection for Mahala, had been interrupted by a summons to attend Miss Farebrother. He had gone down into the hall, expecting to be told that Mrs North was in need of attention following the arrest of her grandson, and was taken aback to discover Ellen, in a state of what he could only describe as vehement confidence, asking to be taken to see Barlow's body. She had had an air of being perfectly sure that he would not refuse and, indeed, he had fallen in with her desires as if he were mesmerized. For the hour he had been with her, it had seemed perfectly reasonable that Mrs North would be unable to accept that Frederick had killed a man unless her companion could vouch for there being a corpse. Initially, he had even admired the self-sacrifice with which the young woman was acting, but once in the dairy house, where Barlow lay wrapped in linen upon a marble shelf, a revulsion for what was afoot had begun to creep over him.

'I regret having let her,' he said. 'I should have said "No".'

Philobeth shrugged. 'I gather she has a habit of making people say "Yes",' she said. 'I've no experience of it myself but I hear she's talented that way.'

'I wonder what she was in America. She has the appearance of a gentlewoman, but I find it difficult to believe a lady wouldn't have been more affected by the presence of violent death.'

'I'm surprised if she was unmoved. Yesterday an old wives' tale made her beside herself.'

Carmody knocked the ash from his cigar. 'She was affected,' he said, 'but not—' he grimaced, half-ashamed at his prudishness, 'not in a respectable manner. I've never seen the like. She insisted on looking at the face; if Mrs North wanted confirmation that it was Barlow, I suppose that was necessary, although how would Miss Farebrother have recognized him? But when I'd uncovered it—' He paused, recalling his distaste.

'Is it—' Philobeth asked. 'Is there decay?'

He shook his head. 'No, the dairy's cool. The face is well preserved. There are the wounds made by North's rings, but even so it's not terrible for a woman to see. It's what she did.' He inhaled and let out the smoke in a downward stream. 'She didn't just look. She opened his eyes. I was too shocked to prevent her. She opened his eyes and stared into them and I'll swear – she laughed.'

Chapter Twelve

Mahala died the following week. She had haemorrhaged the Thursday before and had been afraid that death would come with blood in her mouth, but her last days were peaceful. Her extreme weakness acted as a sedative and she drifted from recognition of her friends into oblivion more calmly than she had lived. Her courage did not fail her, and she crossed the bar holding the hands of Philobeth and Carmody, smiling faintly at something they could not see.

When life was gone and Mahala's nurse was laying out the body, Philobeth wandered into the garden. Later, she would go back to the room where she would never again be greeted with love and irony. She would sit beside her friend, who would be dressed in the white satin grave-clothes she had chosen to look, she had said, her best for visitors, and wait for the fact of death to register upon her heart as well as her intellect. Now, she walked stiffly, without purpose, her hands clasped before her, to the stone bench beside the lake, and Carmody, gazing aimlessly through the window as he paused on the stairs, saw her sitting as still and upright as an effigy with swans gliding silently on the shining water.

She could not think; she had no emotion. The

knowledge that Mahala was gone hovered on the edge of her mind as if it were a faint memory of a tale she had heard long ago. Her numbed spirit was dimly aware that soon she must fall into the gulf of inconsolable sorrow that is the recognition of loss, but as these first moments passed, she merely sat, dazed and unseeing.

It was almost noon and, although cooler than it had been, was bright with the sun. Sheep were grazing on the hillside across the lake and Philobeth stared at them sightlessly. Two bullfinches, their colouring as exotic as Mahala's name and temperament, fluttered suddenly from a small willow at the water's edge. Without meaning to, she turned her head towards them and, as she moved, tears that she had not realized were in her eyes wet her passive face. Images of Mahala began to crowd her thoughts. Unconnected and vibrant, they sprang into being from a forgotten store of unimportant incident: the curve of her throat as she laughed one rainy September day, the stretch of her hand as she had reached for a shuttlecock they had knocked into this lake as girls, the rueful tug of her mare's ear on the evening she had admitted she was too tired to ride, her stance as she considered herself in her grandmother's blue brocade gown.

'I am the Queen of Sheba,' said Philobeth and was startled to find Carmody at her side. He looked puzzled. 'Mahala said it once,' she told him. '"I am the Queen of Sheba and there is none to compare with me."'

'She had a way of speaking the truth.' He went a pace forward and stood watching the swans. A slow arc had taken them to deep water where their reflections were as perfect as themselves. 'You shouldn't sit here without shade,' he said.

'Oh,' she shook her head, 'I can't care.'

He looked over his shoulder at her. 'She would have cared if you caused yourself harm. She would have remarked on it.'

Against her will, Philobeth smiled. 'I think she would,' she said.

She got up and they began to walk back to the house. There was an unnatural hush in the grounds. No gardener's boy wheeled a barrow across the gravel, no laundry maid set down creaking baskets in the courtyards. For Philobeth, there was an emptiness before her more vast than the eternity that had claimed her friend, but she took Carmody's arm and, with resolution, passed inside.

When night came, Carmody was prowling round the house. He carried a candle in his hand, but the small flame merely emphasized the darkness of the silent rooms. Weariness weighed upon him, but he could not keep still and he roamed the corridors, the hall, bedrooms swathed in dust-sheets, the schoolroom with its blackboard and pair of globes. He stood in the doorway of an attic where his light fell upon a broken hoop, snapped years before by an irate Mr Graham and retrieved from the rubbish heap by a young Mahala he had never known. Opening his wife's wardrobes, he stroked riding-habits and ball-gowns he had never seen her wear. He trailed his fingers along tables and cabinets, unsure if he wanted to mark his possession or touch where she had touched.

Combehays was his. He was a rich man, but he felt no triumph. Mahala was dead and suddenly it seemed intolerable that he should benefit from her absence. He had never understood why men threw prudence to the winds for women's love but tonight, standing on the stairs down which she had been carried to their wedding, he thought he would exchange all his lands for the fragile body and robust soul that had been his for so short a time.

He turned to take the passage to the chapel. She had not wanted to be buried in the vault and was to be laid outside the walls, where he would place a broken column at her head and order new and intricate railings about the consecrated ground. Until then her coffin, sumptuous in scarlet velvet, would rest on stools on brass memorials to earlier ladies of the house.

He pushed back the chapel door, his heart lurching at the scraping of its latch, and was met by brilliance. Three-branched candles burned on every surface, dazzling eyes accustomed to the dark, glinting on the ormolu fittings of the casket. There was light and the sharp scent of rosemary. Two red-eyed maids were kneeling in the servants' pew. One looked round at his entrance and began to rise, but he shook his head and she subsided. He put his hand to his breast – he had not expected such an ache within it.

Stepping backwards with care, he pulled the door to and, once again in darkness, laid his brow upon its wood. This was not what she had wanted of him. She had summoned him to be her husband to confound her family and protect the friend she loved, and if, as he suspected, there had grown to be another complicating love, she had not let it tarnish her intended gift to Philobeth. She had liked to see him enjoy her wealth. He would not linger here. He would go to his room and raise a glass to her name and he would write to Miss Alleyn, commissioning a portrait of Mrs Edward Carmody.

*   *   *

It was to Frederick's advantage that he had had his purse about him on the day of his arrest. He had wondered, as he was escorted from Holcombe by the contingent of soldiers, whether the malice of his accusers would have him shackled and thrown amongst the felons, but he found to his relief that his money was allowed to be as eloquent as any other's. Previous experience of the gaol, when he had visited malefactors from his estates, had taught him that an acceptable standard of comfort could be obtained for little outlay and, on his arrival, he immediately set about procuring what luxuries were to be had. He was not intimidated by his situation and his coolness, coupled with the disorientation caused to the prison officers by having a magistrate in their charge, pro-tected him from insult. His gaolers did not venture to take away his clothes, and he was able to hire a debtor as a personal servant. Food was brought to him from that same inn where he had attended the dinner in honour of Sir James Lasdun's thirty years upon the Bench, and he ate it in his private room.

Physically he was content but, in the short term, it was not corporeal matters that concerned him. His innocence, honour and the ultimate preservation of his neck were of far greater consequence, and he dis-covered, as he passed long hours in thought, that the last of the three was of the least importance. It was not that he was tired of life – he would infinitely prefer to live – but if he were offered his freedom in exchange for a confession of guilt, he would choose to die proclaiming the truth.

The realization surprised him. He had not suspected that he had such virtue, and he regarded this sure and settled conviction with the same amused interest with which he would have watched a wildcat in a drawing-room.

His amusement did not include his difficulties in communicating with the world he had left behind. To his fury and dismay, he was forbidden to write letters and it was not until four days after his incarceration that his lawyer was able to gain admittance to see him. He had no desire to be sacrificed for the sake of a rogue like Barlow, and the obstacles being placed in the way of his defence engendered a grim and bitter anger that strengthened his determination not to be cast down.

He greeted his lawyer in his cell, which he believed to offer more privacy than the prisoners' visiting rooms, and Mr Knowles, stepping through the doorway with no appearance of finding his task unusual, noticed a change in his client that he mentally marked to North's credit.

'I'm glad to find you well, sir,' said Knowles, in the dry voice that had drawn out many a family secret. 'I see you're not despondent.'

Frederick closed the door and offered Knowles the chair he had placed by the small table, taking the stool on the other side himself. 'I'm afraid I can offer you very little hospitality,' he said, 'but The King's Arms has sent quite a reasonable brandy.'

'Thank you, no.' Knowles took a pocket-book and pencil from his frock-coat and put them before him. 'I didn't bring a clerk,' he said, 'and must be my own secretary. Naturally all my men are entirely to be trusted, but sometimes a client prefers complete discretion.'

Frederick smiled. 'As my supposed crime is to be shouted in court and from the roof-tops – and will, no doubt, feature on ballad-sheets – discretion hardly seems to apply, but I appreciate your sensitivity.'

Knowles inclined his head. His eyes had become pinched at the outer corners from years of staring in concentration, making him look as shrewd as he was. The legal affairs of the Norths had been in his family's care for three generations and their details were better known to him than to the two surviving bearers of that name. He was, as yet, unsure of the circumstances of Barlow's death but he thought it unlikely that Frederick had been the aggressor, and considered it improper that a gentleman should be inconvenienced by remand for such a case.

In the interval between receiving news of the arrest and gaining entry to the gaol, he had himself been to Holcombe to question the servants, to Jackson's farm and to Combehays for Carmody's description of his part in the events. He had, with a handkerchief held to his nose, viewed the corpse, that was now in some need of burial, and sent an employee, who had an easy way of conversation, to make inquiries at the ale-houses Barlow had used. The information he had gathered would have made him contemptuous of the charge had it not been for learning that Frederick had gone out on the night of the death in the throes of suppressed rage after manhandling a gentlewoman. His application to Miss Farebrother to be allowed an interview to ascertain whether Frederick had indeed used intemperate language, treated her with violence and cast her from the house without means to return to Mythe had not been granted. He intended to persist until it was.

It had also been mentioned to him at the hotel where he was in the habit of taking a chop in the company of other men of business, that Frederick had an extra-ordinary dislike of poachers. He had not been aware of this himself and it was a prejudice so common amongst landowners that it must be unaccountably strong to be remarked upon. He was inclined to think that it was merely a rumour that had sprung up to fit itself to the alleged crime but if it were not, it was a possibility that, meeting Barlow in the act of laying a trap, whilst being himself in an inflamed state of mind, had provoked Frederick into an assault.

He asked Frederick to relate the course of the attack and listened quietly, noting that his client began his tale at the moment of being accosted in the lane, and made no mention of Miss Farebrother. 'It seems curious,' he said, when Frederick had finished, 'that if you were to be charged with a felony, it should be murder and not manslaughter.'

Again, Frederick smiled. 'I think,' he said, 'that my accusers believe I may as well be hanged for a sheep as a lamb.'

Alone in his cell that night, Frederick did not find it so easy to appear sanguine. The locked door oppressed him. The confidence in his bearing since he had entered the gaol was born of outrage and a refusal to seem cowed, rather than a secure belief in his eventual release. The combination of darkness and solitude encouraged a sombre turn in his thoughts.

The injustice of his arrest had cleared his mind of the awe natural to the taking of life. While in these straits he was not prepared to torment himself for Barlow's sake and was able to set aside the solemnity that had beset him when he had not known he was a suspect. There was a sourness in discovering that he was hated enough by his peers to be falsely accused. He could not believe that they were sincerely convinced he had killed in cold blood, nor that there was a conspiracy to be rid of a politically troublesome neighbour by callous and calculated means. It was more likely that one vicious spirit had guided weaker men into asserting a belief that they were now secretly ashamed to hold, and this was frightening, for cowards will stubbornly maintain a false opinion rather than admit that they were wrong. Knowles had told him of the declaration that he had a particular spite against poachers and he pictured timid faces nodding approval as the whisper of his enmity soothed their fears.

It might be that his life must end. He raged against the waste of years this must entail but he scorned to tremble at the scaffold. The stain of felony must not tarnish his name and he would defend his character with as much vigour as he had defended his person from Barlow, but he would not do so from terror of the rope. An energy had risen in him when he had heard the charges read and it had not lessened since. His mind was alert, seeking to and fro for arguments in his favour, upholding his courage, rejecting despair. He thought of Philobeth's impatient assertions that he did not use his talents to the full. Would it please her that crisis had revealed a strength that she had always said was there?

He yearned to have her near. In the few days since he had set out to humble himself before her, alive with love for her and revulsion for the woman who had beguiled him, he had dwelt upon his betrayal and cursed himself for his stupidity. The scene with Ellen at Holcombe had left him, like the slaking of lust, with a dull repugnance for having ever needed her. He had heard from Knowles that his butler had heard him call Miss Farebrother a 'doxy' and two housemaids, dispatched to gather rose-heads to scent water, had been overcome by the urge to pry and had witnessed the entire interview from the flowerbed outside the far window. Before he had encountered Barlow, an exaggerated tale of how he had knocked a lady to the floor had been circulating his household.

It seemed that Ellen would have her revenge. She would never be his wife, but nor would Philobeth. Even if he were freed, how could he ask her to forgive not only neglect and disloyalty but scandal and suspicion? Clarity of thought and decisiveness of action had come to him too late.

He sat up from lying on his bed and reached for the candle he had bought. Lighting it, he went to the table and set it down. He was not yet allowed to send letters but Knowles had persuaded the Governor to allow him pen and paper, and what he had to write would be well begun now. He could not offer his hand to the woman he loved but he could offer his sorrow and the truth of his heart.

'My dearest Philobeth', he wrote.

Chapter Thirteen

'I couldn't bear to have you know.'

Ellen laid her head in Mrs North's lap as she had done during the weeks when they had waited in triumph for the sound of Frederick's horse upon the drive. They were again in the Scarlet Boudoir – one in a wing-chair, one artfully arranged across a long stool – but the atmosphere in the stifling, perfumed room had none of the expectation it used to hold.

'How could I tell you?' Ellen pressed her cheek into Mrs North's skirts. 'That morning? The morning you learnt of the death? And then you were so ill. How could I burden you?'

'He struck you?'

Ellen drew her knees closer to her body, curling like a child against the stiff gown. 'I will not say so.' Her voice broke. 'He pushed me and I sank down. I'll admit no more.'

She could feel the old woman trembling, but Mrs North had said so little while she recounted what had occurred between Frederick and herself at Holcombe that she could not judge whether it was through shock or anger, nor who might be the object of that anger. Her situation was not happy. The ecstasy that had carried her through the killing had lasted only until the first fear for her own safety had penetrated her exulting mind. Since she had read Frederick's letter and realized that her visit to his house was bound to come out, she had lived upon alternate waves of satisfaction in her cleverness and terror of discovery. It had cost her dearly to ask Carmody to show her the corpse, but the triumph she had felt in finding that her face was not upon Barlow's eyes had made her fear recede until she could not remember it. She believed that Philobeth had lied to her from spite and, not seeing that Philobeth's ignorance of the real murderer made this impossible, gave her credit for a spirited attempt at causing harm but derided her for trying to have the better of her superior in resourcefulness.

She would have felt herself safe had it not been for Mr Knowles. His initial request for an interview had been like a net cast about her. Her inability to believe she could do wrong made it difficult for her to assess what would count against her in this case and she was afraid to subject herself to the interrogation of a lawyer. A chance word that she knew to justify her hatred of Frederick's weakness might lead an alien mind into conjecture about her journey home. A lawyer would have experience of reading character and if he recognized her firmness – what then?

Knowles's note had been burnt by her and she did not mention it to Mrs North. She had not yet spoken of her walk to Holcombe, and none of Frederick's servants had reported it to their master's grandmother when the women had visited the house on the day of his arrest. Circumstance had worked to her benefit in recent months and she hoped that silence would discourage Knowles, keeping him from her door.

It did not. A second note came, and a third. She

replied to neither. On the fifth day of Frederick's imprisonment, Knowles called in person. Hearing the news of his arrival before it had reached Mrs North, she sent word that the ladies were not at home. Knowles presented his compliments, saying that he would return on Monday and await Miss Farebrother's convenience.

Since their meeting seemed unavoidable, Ellen considered her position. She was bewildered by the way the world tried to thwart her, but the effort needed to decide how she could convert a failure to marry Frederick into an advantage enlivened her and caused her confidence in her cunning to flourish once more. In sober moments she recognized that this mood had become a danger to her and she almost cringed from it as it approached. The temptation to hint at her successes was beginning to trouble her. If she had been on the brink of entering Holcombe as a wife, she could have endured the hiding of her talents, but life as Mrs North's cherished guest was too lowly to content her. She had grown used to being accepted as a lady and the achievement now seemed stale and unrewarding. It was necessary that she should have security and power and, as she had brooded upon her ills, the thought had come to her that she could still become mistress of Holcombe. Frederick had no children, the estate was not entailed, and Mrs North, in the days when Frederick had called at Mythe as a lover, had said that there were no close relatives to claim the generosity of the head of the family. When he hanged, who was more likely to be his heir than his grandmother? And if she could only retain her sympathy, who was more intimate with Mrs North and more suitable to be favoured by her? Since her first weeks at Mythe, she had kept in reserve her scheme to fasten herself onto the old woman's affections to guard against penury if she did not marry, and that secondary plan seemed set to bring her two fortunes at one blow.

Mrs North's hand was shaking as it stroked the lovely head upon her lap. A terror of life that had never before darkened her days had closed about her when she had heard of Frederick's arrest. She had lived undisturbed by trials other than those born of her own selfishness. Jealousies and imagined slights had hurt her more than the deaths of her husband and son, and she was unprepared for catastrophe. She had neither self-discipline nor mental stamina to help her bear hardships, and her instinct was to thrust unpleasantness from her as an infant will thrust away hated food. A whimpering resentment of Frederick for his notoriety kept her from being worried by any sympathy for him and her mind scrabbled frantically for ways to disassociate herself from his plight. The horror of scandal overwhelmed her. She could withstand the knowledge that her grandson had killed a man but not the bland eyes that would greet her as she entered a room, and the conversation abruptly stopped. It was imperative that she should have an unimpeachable reason for renouncing Frederick and, if she only had the courage to grasp it, Ellen was offering her one.

'My dear,' she said, 'it was rash of you to go to Holcombe alone. And to a man with such a temper.'

Both women were aware that Frederick's supposed ferocity had not made its appearance at the time of Ellen's secretive call, but neither mentioned it.

Encouraged by Mrs North's impersonal reference to her nearest living relation, Ellen let out a sigh that held a hint of a sob. 'I'd waited so long for him,' she said. 'I could wait no more. I thought my heart would break.'

'But alone, Ellen!'

'How could I ask you to take me? How could I face you if I failed? You've done so much for me. I'm friendless without you. And I'd believed him to be other than he was.'

Her words explained nothing, but a comfortable agreement was forming between the two without need of explicit statements. Discreetly, with small, irreproachable steps, they were putting a distance between themselves and the prisoner – one unconcerned and one jubilant that this would serve to underline his guilt.

'And he struck you?' Mrs North said again.

'I cannot say so. Don't press me. I was near to fainting. A touch would have made me fall.' There was a sweetness in Ellen's voice, a thrilling resonance that was the epitome of an injured woman's forgiveness.

Mrs North did not need to deceive herself into believing Frederick's violence: she was deceived. She twined her fingers into the hair that rippled across her lap. 'You must tell Mr Knowles,' she said, 'just what you've told me. Now!' She lifted a hand admonishingly as Ellen shook her head. 'I understand your reluctance, but we must all put duty before our personal preferences. There's no shame in visiting my grandson. I could have asked you to call on my behalf. Tell Knowles that. It'll satisfy him. And then you and I must be all in all to each other. We've both suffered a blow but we must be resolute and justice will be done.'

Philobeth did not wear black – Mahala had told her not to – but she found it necessary to wear the mourning colours of other times and lessening woe. She wore white, yellow, red and violet. The ruby silk, figured in black velvet, that her father had brought from London became an evening-gown, too rich and vivid for August nights in Chantry, and she would sit late in the window-seat or the arbour, watching clouds obscure the moon, brandishing its splendour like a challenge to any who would dare to say she did not grieve.

She could not endure the ordinariness of life. Her friend was dead, yet lamps still burned and laughter was still heard. She wanted darkness and desolation, rent garments and ashes on bowed heads. Weariness weighed upon her, making her limbs ache and her movements slow. A lethargy had sunk into her mind so that her thoughts were laboured and effort seemed impossible. She had no hope that Frederick would be saved. The Governor of the gaol had refused her requests to be allowed inside, and she had received no letter to console her. A note had come from Mr Knowles, reassuring her that Frederick was undaunted but still it felt to her that the two whom she most loved had been snatched from the face of the earth, to leave her lonely and forlorn.

Mr Alleyn did not know how to comfort her. He had always relied upon Slater to guide her through child-hood sorrows and he was as helpless in the face of misery as he had been with croup. An attempt to lure her back to work ended in nothing. Her paints were discarded before she had put a brush to canvas, and her palette left uncleaned. Standing waveringly in the background, hurt by his daughter's pain and wishing himself elsewhere, he watched Slater's unembarrassed concern with envy. Slater, sad that her nursling was wretched, offered solace in the shape of sudden flurries of face-patting and gown-straightening and the constant supply of milk puddings. Philobeth, too dejected to defend herself, took the onslaughts on her dress in good part and ate the puddings gravely, with the single complaint that she would soon be as stout as a pug.

The days passed and Philobeth, recognizing that her condition was profitless and would have been given short shrift by Mahala, struggled to raise herself from despondency without success. As she became more used to Mahala's death, her fears for Frederick increased in vigour; her inability to help him when he was in such danger was a frustration that made her want to scream aloud. Her days were tormented by images of the noose about his neck and her nights were broken by dreams in which Frederick hung from Mary's red silk scarf. The cruelty of their separation just as they were to be reunited seemed like a malignant Fate cleaving them apart. If she could have spoken to him or written to assure him of her love, it would have eased her, but he was allowed no communication with his friends, and the most that she could do was entrust his lawyer with her warmest wish for his release.

On an evening when there was a flicker of summer lightning in the sky, she was sitting alone in a window in the studio, leaning a flushed cheek against the glass. The newspaper that carried the report of the Coroner's Inquest, that had found Barlow to have been unlawfully killed, was lying discarded on the floor where she had let it slip after reading it yet again, searching for some clue that would prove Frederick innocent. The day had been long and the night before her, with its whispers of despair, made her sick at heart. She did not look round as the door opened and Slater, approaching with a letter in her hand, added a briskness to her step as if an increase in her own energy could fortify her suffering girl.

Slater stooped as she reached the window-seat, picking up the offending newspaper and holding it at arm's length. 'I should have thrown this away,' she said. 'What's the good of reading it over and over? If you don't ruin your eyes with the print, you'll do it with crying.'

Philobeth turned towards her, uncurling her legs to put her feet on the floor. 'There must be something I've missed,' she said. 'Some small thing lying unnoticed.'

'You know as well as I, that it was wicked minds that got up that charge.' Slater tucked the paper beneath her arm. 'You leave it to the lawyers to deal with such as they. That Knowles'll be one too many for them. I hear he's sent up to London for a man to speak at the trial.'

'A barrister?' Philobeth had been too convinced of a conspiracy to deprive Frederick of all defence to have expected this.

'That's right. What's the use of having money if you don't use it in times like these?'

'But how do you know?'

'I was just talking to one of his messengers. Didn't you see him going along the lane? He rode over with this.' She held out the letter and Philobeth, recognizing Frederick's writing, drew in her breath. 'I'll leave you to read it,' Slater said, putting it in Philobeth's hand and squeezing her fingers. 'You can tell me what's in it later.'

She went out, looking back for one satisfied glance as she left, and Philobeth, suddenly afraid that her hopes would not be realized and acting as she always did in moments of fear, broke the seal before she could hesitate.

'My dearest Philobeth,' she read, 'this is not the first letter I have written to you since I was brought to this place, nor the second nor the third. I cover each page with the story of my heart but I have no skill, and shame for the hurt I have done you hampers my pen. Have I begun wrongly? When we last met, you told me to call you Miss Alleyn, and who knows more than I that you have the right to withdraw the cherished privilege of using your name? But "Philobeth" is sweet to me, it comforts my hand to write it, my lips to speak it and if you say that you hold to your command, though I will submit in outward forms, I will carry it in my private thoughts as a remembrance of what I might have had.

'I have been foolish. I ask your forgiveness. If I were free, I would come to you to tell you of my love and offer you all that I have if you could overlook my fault, knowing that you of all women would not be influenced by any worldly thing I have to give. I am not free and I write only to tell you that while no man may say with honour that I am not innocent of the crime for which I am held, I am humble and contrite as I think of you. I was bedazzled, but now my sight is clear. There are deeds for which a rogue may not be punished by the law and I am guilty. Did your love die, as it should, when I cast it aside? I wager it did not and I say so not from arrogance or any belief that I am worthy of the smallest part of your affections, but from the value I put upon your steadfast Soul. Where you love, you will

186

not waver as I have done, your eye will not wander after jack-o'-lanterns. You may admit that your attachment has been to one who has not deserved it, you may build walls about your heart, but within those walls lie sentiments of truth and loyalty.

'It may be that I shall die. Do not be concerned for me for, though I condemn the injustice of my fate, I fear nothing but the continuance of your silence. Do not turn your face from me. Scorn my weakness, upbraid my betrayal but send me one word of pardon, I beseech you. Though we cannot meet, let us shake hands in spirit and I will put into your palm a devotion that is stronger from having faltered, truer from repenting its lapse.

Yours ever and always,
Frederick.'

Philobeth lay awake late that night, but the sleepless hours were far removed in character from those she had been enduring since the day of the arrest. Her grief allowed her some respite and let its darkness be riven by that same trance-like joy that had overtaken her when she had heard Frederick had been coming to her on the night of the attack. Reason protested that his danger was no less for telling her his love, but still gladness sang within her as she waited for the dawn.

In its first light, she sent him her word. There was no accusation in her letter, no bitterness or reproof. She accepted his love plainly and affirmed her own. Perhaps they would not meet again on earth but, in these initial hours of reassurance, she believed the years that parted them would be lived upon a sure foundation of trust and hope.

By the time she was called to breakfast, she was

more sober. A mystical union had less attraction than Frederick's release and her mind was once again hunting for the means to be of help. Mr Alleyn, rejoicing that even so unpromising an event as a near-proposal from an imprisoned lover had shaken his daughter from her lethargy, offered to carry her letter to Mr Knowles, taking her with him in the trap. Unable to bear such proximity to the gaol she could not enter, Philobeth declined a journey to Dorchester, but she was too restless to sit at home. It occurred to her that Carmody might not know that Frederick now had permission to communicate with his friends and she decided to walk to Combehays to tell him. He had already been questioned by Knowles but, despite his acquaintance with Frederick having been civil rather than warm, she felt sure he would write to the prisoner, for pity of his situation, and in doing so might reveal some half-forgotten detail that would strengthen the defence.

She did not take her usual route to Combehays. The path that wound through the manor's gardens had been her private way since she had been old enough to walk alone, but now it passed through Carmody land and she did not want to be judged presumptuous. She made a longer journey by road. To her left lay Holcombe's park; to her right, Combehays: the absence of their owners was a sadness that oppressed her steps. A rhododendron that Mr Graham had shipped back from Bombay had pushed its branches through the railings at her side. She touched its hard, glossy leaves and thought of the accidental nature of life. If a whim had not caused a nabob to bring his Indian wealth to this valley, she and Mahala would never have loved each other as sisters; if Barlow had not wanted the amusement of a virtuous girl, Frederick would not be in danger of his life; if a wave had not flung a lovely woman to the shore, there would have been no neglect or separation.

It took an effort of will to go through the gates onto the gravelled drive. She had not entered Combehays since the funeral and the knowledge that, from now on, Mahala would not be there to greet her made her want to turn back. The sensation of being an interloper, together with the dazing effect of grief, gave her the fancy that it was she who had died and was approaching the house as a phantom. Scenes that were as familiar to her as her own home – the clearing where a stone faun played his lichened pipes beneath a deodar tree, the glimpse of the lake through the azaleas, the granite urn beneath the eglantine – were as if they lay behind glass. The rights that love had given her over this place had vanished with the vanishing of her friend, and a new master gave a different aspect to his grounds. Change had come and must be endured.

She was shown into the drawing-room while Carmody was fetched from the desk where he was writing comments on the broken ribs he had set the day before. He found her standing in front of the empty hearth, pale and agitated.

'Coming here affects you,' he said. 'Let me give you some wine.'

'No.' She put her hand to her breast which rose and fell in rapid breaths. 'There seems to be no air. Will you – if you're not occupied – may I speak to you out of doors?'

He offered her his arm and led her through the hall into the garden. He was growing more used to being in possession of Combehays, but Philobeth calling to see only him made him more conscious of their altered states. Mahala had not thought to tell him not to wear mourning and he walked beside his guest in the dress of a widower. It had surprised him to find how much he needed the comfort of deep black and he was pleased to see that Philobeth had sidestepped his wife's instructions by wearing white. He approved Mahala's eagerness to keep a young woman from sombre attire that would depress her spirits, and yet he liked Philobeth's need to show her sorrow.

Time had hung heavily upon his hands since Mahala's death. He could not adjust to her absence. The emptiness of her room seemed to spread itself throughout the house. Twice, sitting late at his books, he had risen from his chair to see whether she was sleeping before he had remembered that she would sleep no more. He could not bring himself to order that the few belongings that he had seen her use in her last weeks be put away and her brushes, her favourite fan, her silver-topped scent bottles still lay on her cabinet, waiting to be carried to her bed. He, who had looked on marriage as a weakness in an ambitious man, had taken to the condition as one born to have a wife, and he now felt bereft and incomplete.

Mahala had married him to be of use to her friend. There was no disloyalty in yearning for the comfort of a second union so soon after the first. He had been asked to bring Philobeth to this house to live the life Mahala should have had and doing so seemed a natural continuance of what had gone before. Until Combehays had the mistress that Mahala and he had chosen, he seemed to drift in limbo, unable to proceed along an allotted path.

He had met Philobeth several times since Mahala's death, but none of the occasions had been suitable for sentiments other than grief. She had attended the funeral and he had wondered why her father had given her leave to come, deciding at last that it was the laxness of the artistic mind that prevented Mr Alleyn taking proper responsibility for his daughter's care. He was not averse to older women attending burials, but it was his belief that such services presented too great a strain upon the youthful female mind. A young woman's nature is yielding and she should be encouraged to give way, not to melancholy, but to the counsel of more experienced men. If he had the charge of her happiness, he would guide her away from the exhausting independence and long hours of work that her father allowed and let her enjoy the protection and leisure a lady should have.

He hoped that he did not let his disapproval of Mr Alleyn show. Since the funeral, whenever he had seen Philobeth her father had been present and he could tell that she felt a creditable affection that he did not wish to injure. He had no argument with Mr Alleyn's energetic pursuit of his profession; it was only as a family man that he thought his neighbour failed and, even here, he accepted that a man without a wife might forget what was best for a daughter. It was true that he had witnessed Mr Alleyn's attempts to cheer and soothe Philobeth during the visits he had paid to the cottage. Knowing her previous attachment to Frederick – another unfortunate lapse in parental wisdom – he had felt obliged to give her accounts of his role in the inquest and of his interview with Knowles. The whole subject of the killing and its consequences was one that he felt should be softened for her ears, and he dreaded the extra distress that might be caused her by callous or exaggerated tales. He was glad to hear Mr Alleyn try to rally her to take an optimistic view of the outcome of the trial for, though he was himself horrified that an act of self-defence should be so misinterpreted and fearful that the foolishness might extend to a verdict of guilty, he wanted her to be spared all unnecessary suffering.

The startling proposition that Mahala had put before him on the day she had asked him to marry her had become so much a part of his thinking that he barely remembered that Philobeth knew nothing of it. His hunger to have life brought back to his house made him shut his eyes to the possibility that she would not look on the addresses of a newly-bereaved man with the same reasonable attitude that Mahala would have had.

They walked together down a shady path that twisted through the shrubbery until it met the stream that ran out of the lake. She made no suggestion as to where they should go and he deliberately led her by a way that did not pass Mahala's grave. Of course, she would want to visit it in time but he felt that her sadness was still too raw to have the sight of the settling earth inflicted upon it. Her thoughts were on her friend as they passed through the gardens, where she had sketched and talked away the years, and she did not speak but allowed herself to be drawn gently in the direction he chose.

The roots of a beech writhed across the path as it turned on itself to wind aslant the steep slope to the waterside. She was too familiar with the best footholds to need assistance, nevertheless Carmody moved ahead of her, taking her hand and warning her to be careful, and she did not like to seem churlish by managing alone. Old husks littered the soil and she remembered how often she and Mahala had filled their skirts with nuts and eaten the sweet fruit with their childish legs dangling above the stream.

'Shall we sit down?' Carmody had brought her to the iron seat that looked towards the lake and was standing beside it inquiringly, still holding her hand.

'Yes.'

She took her fingers out of his and they sat side by side. The seat was placed on a small promontory that narrowed the channel and changed a slow-moving river into a cascade that fell into a brook. Upstream, the eye was led over the placid, lily-strewn reach that flowed beneath a graceful, balustraded bridge from the lake; downstream, the waters rippled over stones between fern-hung banks in romantic disarray; here, at the bench, serenity and wilderness met and mingled.

Philobeth spoke of Frederick. She did not reveal the contents of his letter nor the renewal of their love, as she would have done had Mahala been alive and strong. Her words, tempered by the melancholy of her walk to Combehays, were solemn and calm. The relent-lessness of unwelcome change, that had impressed itself on her as she had entered what was now the Carmody estate, drained her of the jubilation and opti-mism she had felt and gave the news that he could now send and receive correspondence a gravity it had not seemed to have the previous night. Then, an avenue had opened between them, making them closer than they had been for months, but now explaining that he could be reached by writing only emphasized that he was imprisoned. She was chilled by his captivity.

There was nothing in the way she spoke to alert

her companion to her true feelings. He listened to her gravely, flattered that she should have come at once to him in the belief that hearing from him would do Frederick good, but concerned that her tender heart should make her anxious for an outcome that was far from certain. Fearing the worst for the unfortunate prisoner, he wanted to shield her from the pain of losing another friend and, in his single-mindedness, it seemed that taking her beneath his wing was the answer to her cares. He could not prevent a hanging but he could so protect and cosset her that she felt safe and not alone.

'This is a heavy burden for you,' he said, when she had finished speaking.

'Oh, it isn't my freedom – my life – that's at risk,' she said, knowing that she lied.

Her compassion was sweet to him. He had watched her tending to Mahala and silently praised her womanly virtue of staunch, self-sacrificing love. Thinking of her as his own, it caused him pride that, in the midst of her grief, she could still put others before herself. 'It would mean much to me,' he said, his pulse quickening, 'if you would let – if you would do me the honour of letting me ease that burden.'

'Thank you.'

His manner of agreeing to write was curiously fervent but she was glad to have an ally and it was not until the words were out of her mouth that her tired mind suggested another interpretation of his request. She became conscious of an ardency in his eyes and a suspicion of his intention made her colour.

He turned further towards her on the seat, his body poised and taut as if he held himself in readiness for a sudden attack. The simplicity of her answer delighted him. It was as unaffected as Mahala's offer had been and something within him that had been frozen since her death seemed to thaw and flow warmly through his veins. He had an urge to clasp her to him and feel her heart beating against his.

'Miss Alleyn,' he said, 'Philobeth, we've seen such sorrow together. There's been no proper time for other sentiments but I cannot bear to restrain my affections any more. I must try to make you happy. You weren't made for misery. It isn't what Mahala wished. Marry me. I haven't spoken before, but you've known of my love. My dearest Beth, marry me.'

She sat transfixed. Contradictory emotions were loose within her and she stared at the sun glittering on the flashing waters as she waited for one to gain ascendency. She should not blame him; she was aware of the circumstances of his marriage and yet she could not think of him turning from Mahala so soon without needing to cry out that he was false. Disappointment with him, with life and with herself almost over-whelmed her and the exhaustion that had been sapping her strength returned in force. She wanted to find a refusal that would extricate them from this predicament with no-one's feelings injured, but all she could think was that Frederick had called her his Wild Hart and she preferred that name to 'Beth'.

'You confuse me,' she said. 'What wasn't what Mahala wished?'

There was a degree of withdrawal about her that made him wonder if he had been unwise to be so precipitate, but it was too late to go back. For an instant he saw how strange and improper Mahala's plan would seem to most who heard it and he was reluctant to explain to Philobeth the plot that had been devised out of love for her. He thought of protesting that Mahala had only wished her friend to be contented but the statement seemed to have a weakness that was foreign to both women, and he wanted the extent of Mahala's generosity to be known and understood. His hesitation was short and he told of Mahala's desires with a directness that would have brought out her slow smile.

Philobeth turned her face away. The ache that was now always within her became a pang that made her put her fist to her breast. She was bemused. There had been no suspicion in her mind that there had been more behind Mahala's proposal to Carmody than the thwarting of her family; she could not accept the truth of what he said without a sensation of betrayal. Reviewing the scenes of Mahala's last weeks, she felt excluded by the secret the Carmodys had shared. It touched her that her dear friend had been so concerned for her comfort that she had arranged this very situation, but saddened that Mahala's failing health had dulled her perception. If she could not have Frederick, she would have no-one. She had approved of the marital strategem but she herself could never come to an accommodation over marriage as Mahala had done – as, indeed, Mahala would have known if her wits had still been sharp.

She moved her feet restively on the husk-strewn ground, dislodging a stone that rolled into the stream. As she watched the ripples spread into the turbulence of the cascade, she remembered how she had stood at another river-bank and ordered Frederick not to come to her home. Was she to dismiss Carmody with as little consideration for the nature of his attachment? She had observed his constant sympathy for Mahala, whose suffering roused gentleness in one who did not seem to be essentially a gentle man, and admired him for it. If the love he claimed to feel was not the passion that love was for her, it did not mean he could not be hurt. She tried to regret the dejection she must cause but her sympathies were swamped by jealousy. Mahala had been hers; there should have been nothing hidden between them – nothing known to this man and not herself.

'Philobeth—' Carmody reached for her hand but she drew it back and stood up.

A wave of bitterness made her want to reject him cruelly but she recognized that the impulse was ignoble and forced herself to speak softly. 'I'm so sorry,' she said. 'So very sorry. Mahala was mistaken. Frederick and I – we remain pledged to each other.'

He got up from the seat. The shock of her assertion destroyed his expectations, but he was not one to surrender ambitions easily. He did not despise loyalty and could see that a woman might think it shameful to cast off an old lover in Frederick's circumstances. 'I cannot ask you to break your word,' he said, 'but I offer you my hand and heart should you need them. I won't press you but I will wait. I will be here. Tell me that I may wait and hope.'

His implication made a coldness spread over her skin. The sun still shone but she drew her shawl about her.

'I think,' she said, 'that, for both of us, there is no hope.'

Chapter Fourteen

A young woman receiving two declarations of love in as many days may be excused for being agitated. When one of those declarations is from a man imprisoned on a capital charge and the other from the widower of her closest friend, it is to be expected that she will suffer the grip of strong emotion. It was so with Philobeth. When she left Carmody she did not go home. The feelings that raged within her would have been too obvious to her old nurse for her to escape an inquisition: a distaste for what she had learnt made her want to keep it hidden.

She left Combehays by her familiar path with none of the scruples about making free with Carmody's demesne that had afflicted her earlier that morning but, instead of following it to Chantry, she cut across two meadows and onto Frederick's land. Passing through the deer-park, she climbed a low hill to a place that had been a favourite of hers as a child and again later when her intimacy with Frederick had given her the use of his grounds.

A cedar had been planted at the top of the rise and its lowest branches drooped to the earth in such a way that a comfortable seat could be had by anyone who wanted to enjoy the view. Philobeth, unladylike and reflective, had often sat dreaming with her back against the resinous trunk and her legs stretched along the widest bough: it was natural to her to come here to think of what had occurred.

She climbed onto the tree, letting one hand stroke the ridged bark while she threw off her hat with the other. Above her, through the dark green needles, the sky was streaked a milky blue, but in the valley, where the cloud ended, the sun shone with an unimpeded glare, draining the colour from the landscape. The circle of bare earth around the trunk had dried to a pale dust that coated the edges of the turf. Below the hill, the house, the lake and gardens all lay in perfect stillness, as if a general desertion had followed the loss of their master.

A possible theatre for her life lay before her. If Frederick were released she would be mistress of this estate, rich in love and property, wanted and secure whether or not she succeeded in her art; if he hanged, the years would be bleak, lived out with an endurance which would not shame her but which would render hollow whatever she achieved. It was inconceivable that she should take a third course and become a wife at Combehays. Had Mahala lived, she could easily have pictured herself accepting a home with her friend, but her love was not hers to give away and she could not marry without it.

Already she thought more kindly of Mahala's attempt to help her. How could the plan have been revealed? Mahala had known that they did not share the same absolute pragmatism and that she would have shied away from so worldly a scheme. It had all been arranged from love of her and, though it did not seem that Carmody's attachment to her was strong, she believed that he was convinced it was, and his agreeing to take part in Mahala's design had been prompted by no insincerity. It was plain that he revelled in wealth but she credited him with never having misled Mahala about his feelings for herself. She abandoned her envy of him as too petty to be countenanced and, in doing so, released a warmth within her that gave her more comfort than she had felt since the death. She opened her heart to the generosity and devotion Mahala had displayed and the knowledge that the last of her beloved friend's energies had been expended in her service filled her with a joy as powerful as if she had turned her head to find Mahala lounging beside her, languorous in body and sharp in mind.

She wished there was a method of wiping a conversation from the memory of its participants. Carmody had been coldly civil when she left him and though that was better than an open breach, it was a reserve that had not been between them before. She did not want to quarrel with him. It would please her to remain on good terms, for Mahala's sake. There was much to appreciate in his behaviour: his compassion as a husband, his grief as a widower, his willingness to aid Frederick, his puzzled disgust at Ellen's laughter when he showed her Barlow's corpse.

Allowing Ellen to view the body was itself an act of kindness that would have been refused by many men, who would not have thought the calming of an old woman enough to justify the trouble involved. Mrs North's supposed inability to believe that her grandson had killed a man unless her companion could vouch for the remains would have been dismissed with a curt message that it was so. It was repulsive to remember the turn the visit had taken. What could have possessed Ellen to touch the dead face and look into the eyes? And why the laughter? Had it been hysteria after what she had done, it would have been understandable, but Carmody had said it was not. It had been a laugh of satisfaction and relief.

Picturing the scene revolted her. The unused dairy, the wretched man lying wrapped upon the marble, Carmody uncovering the face. He had told her that there had been little decay and the skin had been soiled only with the marks of Frederick's rings, yet there must have been terror and awe in the presence of one who had lost his life in trying to take another's. She thought of Frederick pressing his hand upon his attacker's face and pitied him for the simple defence that was now called murder. Those innocent hands seemed to be before her and there was something about them that was wrong. She knew his hands as well as she knew her own. In a portfolio in her room there were drawings of them clasped and outstretched, beckoning, praying and resting quietly on a book. He wore no rings. As long as she had known him, he had worn no rings.

Another pair of hands sprang into her mind. Hands richly covered with rings. Ornate rings that would mark a man's face. Rings that gleamed in stormy moonlight – rings on fingers almost severed from the hands.

She sat forward, putting her own hand to her throat and breathing slowly to stave off the horror that threatened her. Was her hatred of Ellen so great that she could imagine her killing a man? It was natural that she should wish for another culprit to be found in Frederick's place but jealousy should not tempt her into squalid fantasies of her rival. She had heard that

Ellen had walked to Holcombe on the evening of the killing and had had high words with Frederick; she believed her to resent not becoming Frederick's wife and to have the character to want revenge if she were thwarted; she had seen her panic-stricken reaction at the farm when she was told that a murderer's image was printed on the victim's eyes, and, having seen, could explain why she had lifted Barlow's lids and laughed.

A shuddering took hold of her so that she gripped the branch for support but the pressure of her hand against the bark made her think of the wounds on Barlow's face and she snatched it away. She scorned herself for her fancies. There was no doubt that Barlow had died from the struggle with Frederick. It was whether the final blow had been accidental or deliberate that was in question. Frederick himself did not deny his part in the death, despite his insistence that he had left Barlow alive when he went for help.

She leant back against the trunk, still shaking with disgust at herself. Thinking back to the night of the killing, she wondered what it had been that had caused Frederick to behave with such unusual aggression towards Ellen. She discounted most of the rumours of his violence that evening, rumours that had him calling Ellen a whore and throwing her to the ground, but there must have been some incident for his own servants to spread such tales. Whatever it had been, it had not prevented him leaving the house soon afterwards to come to Chantry. He had cut a rose to bring to her – a man does not turn from striking one woman to cut a rose for another, nor does the gesture portray a murderous state of mind.

A swan appeared from behind the copse beside

Holcombe's lake and circled slowly before curving towards Combehays. She watched its graceful flight as it beat its long wings over the lane where Barlow had made his assault. The old shed where he had slept cast a short shadow onto the verge and she thought how easily he could have watched Frederick's approach without being seen himself, how easily another watcher, walking vengefully back to Mythe, could—

She stood up abruptly. Her head throbbed and her eyes were blurred. It is tiredness, she said under her breath, tiredness that makes me think this way. Too much has happened too suddenly. I'm not myself. I'll go home to sleep and when I wake this madness will have left me.

During the next week, she tried to free herself from her imaginings. Every day she wrote to Frederick and every day he wrote to her. She wanted to go to him but he could not endure the idea of her setting foot inside the gaol. 'I cannot command you,' he had written, 'nor would I on any matter if I had the power, but I entreat you not to come nor ask again. I have degraded myself in my treatment of you and I will not degrade you by a knowledge of this place. I would not have you taste this confined air. I would not have the shadow of these bars fall across your eyes. You were not born for locked doors.' They spoke frankly of their love without accusation or excuse for the past, nor false hopes for the future. An intense desire for his safety consumed her, a desire so strong it seemed to writhe within her, yet still her thoughts fled back to Ellen. Once she dreamt she stood beneath the gallows and saw Ellen's ringed hands push Frederick's face into the noose. Her struggles to rid herself of suspicions that were groundless and repugnant were vain and, at last, to exorcise the demon, she asked Frederick for an account of Ellen's call at Holcombe.

His answer did not set her mind at rest. He told her all that they had said and done and how it was being interpreted by servants, who had half seen and heard. She accepted his assertion that Ellen's vaunted love was a pretence and it seemed to her that a woman capable of such determination to catch a man that she would corner him in his own home to continue her lies, would be liable to react to an insulting refusal with extraordinary spite. But, still, she told herself, even had Ellen followed Frederick into the lane, pressing a hand over the mouth of an unconscious man was cold-blooded murder; was it possible that a young woman could do that?

She began to roam about Holcombe's grounds, asking gardeners, keepers and grooms if they had seen by what route Miss Farebrother had left the park. No-one could say. She questioned the farm-hands who worked the fields between Holcombe and Mythe, but the only glimpse of Ellen had been on a path a mile from where Barlow had died and the cowman, who had noticed her, could not remember the time. She wrote to Carmody, requesting a description of the marks on Barlow's face and confirmation that they had been made by rings. He replied that, although the thought that rings had caused them had immediately leapt into his mind, he could not be certain and he urged her not to dwell on the unhappy details of a wretched event.

Lack of corroboration for her suspicion only stimulated her to search further. The idea that had disgusted her was growing into a conviction and a frantic hunger for evidence would not let her rest. A fortnight after she had sat beneath the cedar, when she had lost all doubt of Ellen's guilt, she packed her sketching materials into a satchel and, declaring she would be gone all afternoon in search of the picturesque, set out for Mythe.

She was not fond of the time of year. She disliked parched meadows of yellowing grasses and the choking dust raised by carts in the arid lanes. The dry rustle of ripe barley did not charm her as the sway of the green shoots had done. Today, great clouds were piled in the sky, driving sudden shadows across the land and walkers passed from heat to shade, alternately loosening their collars and drawing their kerchieves closer. She left the road before she reached the village and made her way to the side of Mythe's gardens by a path beside the stream that fed Mrs North's ornamental pond. She remembered the layout of the grounds from the only time Frederick had brought her to visit his grandmother, when they had been sent to stroll about the lawns while their hostess decided whether she was well enough to receive them. It had not been a successful day and the memory of Mrs North's rudeness gave her the audacity to trespass now.

She entered by a door in the wall of the kitchen-garden and, hurrying through the neat beds, emerged behind the offices at the side of the house. Her hand was inside her satchel grasping the recipes that she was carrying from Slater to Mythe's cook. She had led Slater to believe that she would leave the papers with the lodge-keeper but they were her passport into the house, and she had no intention of letting the opportunity go by. It was true that she could have walked boldly up the drive on such an errand, but she did not want to run the risk of being ordered away before she had ascertained Ellen's movements on the night of the killing.

There was trepidation in her knock at the back door of a house where she was not only unacceptable as a guest of the mistress but hated by a woman capable of murder. It seemed to make the situation stranger to be admitted by a girl she had known slightly all her life and to answer the offer to take her to Mrs North with a declaration that she would rather sit in the kitchen. The ordinariness of her welcome made the evil that had come into their lives dreamlike and insubstantial and, as a chair was pulled back for her at the long, scrubbed table, it was hard to cling to the idea that Frederick was in gaol.

The room was quiet. Lunch was over and there was a pause before dinner needed to be started. The female servants had gathered around the table to drink tea before they started work again and there was a shifting in seats and general stiffening as a lady joined them. Philobeth was unsure how to open the conversation but a ginger cat, which had been lolling amongst the geraniums on the window-sill, jumped softly onto the flags and, stretching its front legs to an extreme, sauntered over to jump into her lap. The apologies that followed, the offers to remove it and her assurances that she did not mind opened the way to giving Slater's recipes to Mrs Groves. From there, it was a small step to discussing what was still on everyone's lips: Frederick and Barlow. The bell rang from the Scarlet Boudoir as they leant on their elbows with their cups between their raised hands and a maid left to answer it without interrupting the talk. No-one liked to say in Philobeth's presence that Frederick was guilty of a crime and, indeed, there was a sympathy for him based more upon his kind words and generous tips than a belief in his innocence.

'And Miss Farebrother was at Holcombe that very evening,' said Philobeth, stroking the cat's curling tail. 'What a mercy she didn't meet Barlow in the lanes.'

Several of the women, now quite at ease with their visitor, gave meaningful looks and half smiles.

'That one can take care of herself,' Mrs Groves said emphatically.

''Twould be a rare sight to see my lady troubled by the likes o' Barlow. 'Twould be "Oh, my man, I do so need ee to help I" and 'e be a-running after she, a-fetching and carrying.'

'She's not a favourite with you, Mrs Groves?'

'That she ent. As sly and secretive a minx as ever tried to feather 'er own nest.'

Susan, the young laundry-maid who had been befriended by Ellen, sat forward. ''Er ent never paid my sister for that caul her little one was born in. Us could've got two guineas for un down Weymouth and we ent never seen a penny.'

Mrs Groves gave a short laugh. ''Tis money going into her purse she likes, not going out. I'd bet a sovereign 'er's after getting into the mistress's will. 'Er's getting 'erself settled in right comfortable now that she ent going to be the new Mrs North. And what was she a-doing trampsing about the fields that night, throwing 'erself at the master like a hussy and not coming home till all hours? That ent no way for a lady to go on.'

Philobeth gripped the cat and it sank its claws into her gown. 'Was she late?' she asked, trying to keep her voice calm. 'Did someone see her return?'

There were half smiles again, but this time with more humour.

'Oh, yes,' Mrs Groves said, without disapproval. 'Daniel, as is a man-servant here, was a-courting Alice Lee from the dairy, yonder in the shrubbery, and they both saw Miss Farebrother passing nigh 'em round eleven that night. She come slipping through the dark like a deer and in through the scullery door. Weren't no mistaking 'er. Give 'em quite a turn.'

'Why? Was it their – absence from home?'

'No, bless ee, what the mistress don't see, won't grieve 'er. No, 'twas 'er appearance. Give 'em the shudders. Daniel says 'e once went to open a barn that was quiet as death outside but when 'e pulled back they doors 'twas all raging flame behind 'un. Said the minute 'e laid eyes on she, that barn come straight to 'is thoughts. 'Twas a marvel.'

'And was she—'

The door from the house opened and Ellen came in. The silence that fell was broken by the sound of the servants rising to their feet. Philobeth did not stand. She was momentarily disconcerted, but a rush of anger at what this creature had done gave her confidence.

Ellen stepped inside the room. She had not over-heard the conversation and was gratified by the fear she inspired and by Philobeth choosing to come to the tradesmen's entrance. 'Miss Alleyn,' she said, 'we were surprised to discover you had called. Would you care to tell Mrs North the reason for your visit?'

Philobeth was prepared. She had wanted to talk to Ellen alone in the hope that she could persuade her to condemn herself out of her own mouth and she saw her chance. 'Miss Farebrother,' she said, 'you see I have my sketching materials. I am, as you know, an artist and as such may say what would be impertinent in another. You have a face of striking beauty. I would appreciate permission to take a likeness.'

A warm satisfaction made Ellen raise her head as if she were already posing. If she could not brandish her cleverness in depriving Philobeth of Frederick, she could at least be seen in a position of superiority over her rival. To her there was no difference between an artist and a servant, and she felt that sitting for her portrait would be a form of triumph.

'I'm glad to do whatever I can for you,' she said. 'I understand you have your way to make in the world and if my face could affect your fortunes, I wouldn't hesitate to let it do so.'

Rather to her surprise, Philobeth was able to draw Ellen with a coolness she did not think she would possess in the circumstances, but the frustration she felt on her way home was so great that, at one point, she clenched her fists and groaned aloud. She was convinced that Ellen was guilty, but none of her questions had brought an answer that would support her belief if repeated to a more sceptical listener. Everything in Ellen's manner had made Philobeth's flesh creep – the gloating references to Frederick's misfortune, the preening comments on her fitness as the subject of an artist's brush, the self-congratulation for being so beloved by Mrs North, the assumed sadness for the sorrow the grandmother would feel when, no doubt, the full penalty of the law would be exacted – yet not a word could be singled out to suggest Frederick's innocence. There had been a revelling in her own genius in Ellen's demeanour that plainly revealed her wickedness, but an arrogant attitude is not evidence and Philobeth was heavy-hearted as she walked slowly back to Chantry.

She had mentioned to Ellen that her return to Mythe on the night of the killing had been seen to be late and Ellen, glancing at her side-long as she had used to do to Frederick, had agreed that she had needed to sit out in the evening air for a considerable time to recover from the treatment she had received at Holcombe. She had put it to Ellen that she would be required to recount her interview with Frederick in court and Ellen, her eyes gleaming, had said that nothing would make her depict his violence to her in an angry light. It seemed hopeless to expect her to give herself away and, for several days after the encounter, Philobeth was depressed by a sense of the futility of her efforts to help Frederick.

On the fourth morning, she berated herself for cowardice and put her theory in a letter to the gaol. Though she did not have the experience in interrogation to enable her to wrest a confession from a culprit, barristers did, and if she could persuade Frederick of Ellen's part in the death, he could put the matter in the hands of his defenders. His answer, manly as it was in its wish to protect her, was a bitter disappointment. 'My dearest,' he wrote, 'it warms my spirit to have you so nearly concerned for me, but do not pursue this, I beg you. I believe the woman to be a Jezebel yet I cannot, in fairness, accuse her of murder because she desired to be a rich man's wife. Sweetheart, I struck the blow and, though it was done to preserve my safety, I cannot deny it. Yes, Barlow was living when I left him on the ground but a man may die of injuries hours, weeks after he received them. Yes, on my return, his face was marked in a fashion it had not shown when I departed, but bruises came on my own limbs that were not there when the wretch fell. Do not distress yourself with vain searchings for some secret villain, but trust in God and the good sense of jurymen to set me free to clasp you in my arms. Let us not comb through what has been done but look forward to a reunion more joyous from its delay.'

She turned to Carmody. They had not met since she had refused him and she was reluctant to give him pain by parading her love of another man, but desperation drove her to seek some authoritative voice for her cause. He listened to her gravely, questioning her tale with a minuteness that encouraged her to think that she was winning his support, and then, pitying her for the effect her troubles had had on her imagination, advised her to find some quiet distraction to occupy her thoughts.

She turned to her father. He chaffed her at first, trusting that she was diverting herself with flights of fancy. It dismayed him to find that she was serious and he retreated into an insistence that her suspicions were a consequence of her bereavement and would fade as she recovered her strength. He offered again to take her with him to Yorkshire and when she would not go, strapped his trunk and left, glad and ashamed to be away from such sadness.

She turned to Slater, who believed her but was powerless to help.

The Assizes approached. The date of the trial drew on and Philobeth was in agony. Beneath a rigidly composed exterior, maintained to give weight to her story, a frenzied need to convince someone with influence tormented her day and night. She tried to feel the same confidence in the wisdom of a jury that Frederick professed, but the turmoil of the last months had left her too certain of life's cruelties to succeed. On the Tuesday before Frederick was due in court, she could bear her inaction no longer. Hiring a mare from the stables in Weston, she rode out towards Maiden Newton to plead her case with the J.P. most likely to be sympathetic.

She had not written ahead to ask for an appointment and, as she entered the drive of Thorne's house, she was disconcerted to see a number of vehicles with empty shafts lined around the circle of close-mown grass before the porch. In her single-mindedness, she had not expected her quarry to have other engagements and her courage misgave her at the thought of petitioning him amongst so many. She had continued towards the house as she wondered whether to return later and the sound of hooves brought a groom from the yard at her left. He offered to take her horse and, feeling herself committed, she handed over her reins and rang the bell.

'Is your master at home?' she asked when the door was opened, and instantly condemned herself for a question that was so obviously answered by the carriages waiting outside.

She was shown into the hall and given a seat beside a stuffed stag while the maid carried her name to Thorne. Now that she was inside and could hear the swell of masculine voices in the dining-room, she regretted her decision. Thorne was a long-standing friend of Frederick but she suspected that he would have been more amenable to persuasion if she had found him alone than surrounded by men.

The double doors between the hall and dining-room were standing open and she could see a corner of the table. A stout man with a calculating eye leant his chair

212

back on two legs to stare at her. For a moment she endured his gaze, then stood up and walked a few paces to be out of his sight.

'Alleyn? Is that the artist's model North took up with?'

Try as she would, she could not help hearing what was said and her face flushed at the inference that was being drawn.

'I believe her to be respectable.' Thorne's voice lacked the firmness to curb the others.

'Well, she was when she met him, eh? Before she got into line with farm-girls and mermaids. Gentlemen, our weaker sisters!'

'Sisters? I don't think North would have use for them.'

A gust of mirthless laughter made her turn to leave but as she did so Thorne came into the hall and closed the door behind him. She could tell that he had been drinking and, though not drunk, did not have his wits fully about him.

'Miss Alleyn,' he said. 'You find me in the midst of a bachelor party. My wife is away or you would have been better received.'

'Thank you. It was you I wished to see.' The difficulty of wording her suspicion so that he would act upon it stopped her.

'Are you here on a matter concerning North?' he asked, with the kindness for female frailty that was habitual to him.

Encouraged by his tone, she began to tell him of Ellen's guilt. His expression was guarded but he did not interrupt her as she spoke. When she had finished, he took her gloved hand in his. 'My dear Miss Alleyn,' he said, 'your eagerness to help your – to help

213

North does you credit, but you must leave these things to wiser heads. There's no substance in your tale; now, don't mistake me, I mean merely that your keen imagination has led you astray. There is nothing to connect the lady with this unfortunate death and I must warn you most seriously that if you continue to defame her character, the law will have its turn with you.'

Chapter Fifteen

'And you saw him strike her?'

'No, sir,' Mahala's housekeeper watched the barrister as if she had been washed out to sea and he was throwing her a rope. 'But 'twas in his hand and his arm raised. And shouting! If I hadn't gone in, I don't know what would've happened. And Miss Graham lying in bed like a sacrificial lamb.'

Before this biblical and inappropriate reference to Mahala was out of her mouth, Frederick's counsel had risen in an unfolding of robes. 'My Lord,' he said, 'need we have wonderings?'

The judge nodded and turned to the witness. 'Mrs Dawson, you must say only what occurred. Don't dwell on possibilities.'

The housekeeper curtsied nervously and Judge Brownlow, who was fond of his rank, acknowledged it with a smile.

Mr Dey approached her again. 'In all your years at Combehays, Mrs Dawson, in all your years attending your late mistress, whose death followed so swiftly upon this incident—'

Mr Hellier began to rise again but the judge stayed him and looked reprovingly at Dey, who bowed and continued.

'I say in all your years at Combehays, Mrs Dawson, had you seen anything like it?'

'Oh, no, sir. 'Twas shocking.'

The courtroom was stifling. There were no open windows and already, in the late morning, Philobeth found the smell of closely-packed human bodies overpowering. From her seat at the back of the spectators' benches, she had a clear view of Frederick as he stood in the prisoner's box. He was leaner than when she had seen him last, and there was a grimness in his face that had not been there before, but his health seemed good despite the weeks of confinement and he had an air of vigour and resolve that showed he was not despondent. A look had passed between them when he was brought in that would have dispelled every doubt of his love, had any lingered in her thoughts.

To be so near and yet unable to take his arm or say a word of comfort, knowing that the twelve men who sat listening to twisted evidence had the power to separate them forever, was a form of suffering more exquisite than anything she had experienced before. Mahala had not told her of the argument she had had with Frederick when trying to discover his intentions towards her friend and, not having heard of his brandishing the pomade-jar in his irritation, Philobeth was bewildered by Mrs Dawson's account. It appeared to her that the trial was going against him. Innocent actions were misinterpreted; innuendoes were made to sully his relations with Mary, Ellen and herself; a false assertion that he had a vicious dislike of poachers had risen from nowhere in the past weeks and was repeated in the court; a connection was made between his owning the freehold of The Swan and the mock hanging which

Barlow had received there. She was afraid. The most blameless life could seem depraved if treated in this way, and since the jury's decision must rest mainly on what they believed of his character, there was much to make her tremble.

After that first glance, Frederick tried not to look in her direction. Alone, he could maintain his composure, but the anguish in her eyes almost unmanned him. The strength of will that he had discovered in himself since his arrest would have let him go to the gallows with little more than contempt for those who sent him there, were there no-one to mourn him, but the misery Philobeth would suffer made the fight for his life doubly urgent. Like her, he thought his defence was failing. It hurt and exasperated him to hear his actions being moulded into a pattern of violence and debauchery, but part of him was able to look on wryly and admit that it was cleverly done.

When he did not think of Philobeth, he was able to watch the witnesses with a detached interest, amused to see how much embarrassment there was amongst the gentlemen who were called. Mahala's housekeeper and his two empty-headed maids, who had mistaken his behaviour with Ellen at Holcombe, had obviously wished themselves elsewhere, but gave their evidence with a consciousness of doing right. With the exception of Sir John Packard, the men of his own rank hedged their answers with ifs and buts, with excuses for their opinions and justifications of their dislike of him. Even Carmody, who clearly wanted to have Barlow's death known as an accident, was not able to swear to blows he had not seen, and plainly felt the awkwardness of his situation.

The difficulties of the witnesses told their own tale.

His political beliefs had made him an outsider amongst the gentry, but if an unlucky moment had not found Sir John in the company of others with a spite against him when the news of the assault broke, there would have been no arrest. Carmody and Sir John, with different intentions, had both met his eye as they were questioned, but regret for being involved had kept the rest looking everywhere but at him. He observed Sir John closely and, after considering all that he knew of the man and the nature of his digressions when answering, came to the conclusion that he did not even have the distinction of being pilloried for his stand upon the Corn Laws. There was a love of power and cruelty in Sir John's attitude that showed he had merely taken his opportunity to turn on one who had momentarily been the weakest in the herd. Frederick did not fear death, but he loathed dying for the sake of chance and malice.

In his cell that night he discussed the increasing possibility of an unwelcome verdict with a coolness that caused Knowles to tell his wife that if ever Sir John asked for his services, they would be refused. The iron that adversity had revealed in his client saddened him for he, too, was pessimistic, and Frederick's stoicism made the threatened dishonour more poignant. There was an unease involved in sitting with a man whose vitality, determination and intelligence would soon be extinguished with one jerk of a rope. The waste of talent, the theft of years pained Knowles more in this case than it had done since he was a youth and learning to harden himself to his profession. He found himself mentally urging their barrister on as another man might urge a horse he had backed towards the winning-post and he took an extra pint of port in the evenings as that man might when the favoured animal had lost.

'I think,' Frederick was saying, 'that we may take it as read that I'll be condemned.' He scrutinized Knowles for a reaction and, seeing none, smiled slightly. 'I have certain matters I don't wish to leave until after the verdict. When I'm officially a felon, I may find myself more constrained than I am at present. Obstacles may be placed between us and there's legal business of much importance to me that I want to have out of the way.'

'Speaking as your lawyer, I must applaud you but speaking as, I hope, a friend, I'll remind you that the die is not yet cast.'

Frederick put his hand to his throat. 'I feel a certain tightening that makes each breath precious. I'd prefer to have my affairs put in order as quickly as you can manage. It would relieve my mind.'

Knowles dipped his pen into the ink-pot and drew the nib carefully over the rim. 'You've only to tell me what must be written,' he said.

Frederick rubbed his thumb over his chin. An emptiness seemed to open in him as he prepared to give Philobeth the security after his death that he wanted to share with her throughout a long life. The finality of what he was doing made the cold air of the grave seep into his bones, and he needed a moment to shake off the fancy. 'I have no family to provide for,' he said.

Knowles inclined his head. Neither mentioned the craven disloyalty of Mrs North, who had refused all contact with her grandson since his incarceration, but the statement was understood.

'However, had I been free I would have taken a wife,

and as the lady is without reliable provision, it's my duty and desire to protect her from want.'

'A natural and admirable decision.'

'Therefore, I'd like you to draw up a contract passing all my possessions to Miss Philobeth Alleyn of Chantry.'

Knowles set down his pen. 'All?' he said.

'All. House, land, investments, spoons. All.'

Knowles gazed at him. There was a sound of marching feet in the corridor outside and a shouted order to be sharp. 'That would make Miss Alleyn a considerable heiress,' Knowles said.

'Heiress isn't quite the right word. It implies that she would come into her wealth after my death. I wish her to be its possessor before that event. Again, it's my intention to avoid any slip 'twixt cup and lip.'

'You put yourself in danger of slips. Suppose you're acquitted?'

'Then Miss Alleyn will become Mrs North and the property remains mine.'

'Sudden riches have been known to change a woman's matrimonial ideas.'

'I trust her sentiments for me.' Frederick leant towards the lawyer. 'Mr Knowles, I recognize the peculiarity of my direction, but it is a command and not a request. This may be the last thing I can do; I will have it done.'

'I could not go home for shame of – for shame.' Ellen's eyes were downcast and her fingers, soberly gloved in grey to match the rest of her demurely respectable attire, were gripping the edge of the witness box.

'For shame, Miss Farebrother, of having made a solitary and secret journey to accost an unmarried man in his home? For shame of having thrown yourself into his arms on the pretence of faintness?'

'No, sir.' Ellen raised her head and looked at Hellier with gentle sorrow. 'My walk to deliver my benefactress's message to her grandson was at her bidding and I was not afraid – then – to be alone. I believed that innocence would protect me from insult. I could not go home because there is a shame that comes from having been in the presence of – of one who acts disgracefully. It was necessary that I calm myself before I returned to Mrs North. She was confined to her bed and I dared not grieve her.'

Sympathetic murmurings in the courtroom made the judge gaze about him to quell them, but he was himself susceptible to the quiet loveliness of this young creature, whose curious history would have made her fascinating even without her beauty.

'Miss Farebrother,' he said, 'the law doesn't wish to make its demands more exacting than necessary. A chair can be brought for you if you require it.'

'Thank you, my lord, I can stand.' There was a tremulous quality to Ellen's voice that made her assertion seem courageous, but the quiver that affected it was not caused by the timidity the majority of the onlookers were attributing to her. She was aware that a modest woman was expected to quake at public questioning of such a nature, and so made no attempt to hide that she was shaking. It delighted her that her excitement was being interpreted as outraged virtue. Her triumph was absolute. When Knowles had first sent asking to interview her, she had dreaded being called to give evidence, but as the weeks passed and no suspicion was raised against her, she grew in confidence. Now, as she stood in court sensing the good

221

will of the spectators, seeing Frederick at her mercy and the hatred on Philobeth's face, she felt an exhilaration which was almost the ecstasy that had consumed her on the night of Barlow's death.

She had no consciousness of having killed; she had a fierce pride in having done the deed that was being called murder, but there was no realization of the awfulness of ending a man's life. Standing in that lane with Barlow on the ground before her, she had seen what harm she could achieve by closing her hands over his mouth, and she had taken her opportunity as simply and with as little thought for his humanity as if she had been gaining her object by putting out a candle. There were moments when she was puzzled by the importance given to the death and her mind swam, as though it were struggling to let in a concept it had not harboured before, but the moments were rare and could not survive her elation.

She had begun to feel that there was more to her superiority over mankind than simple worth. Acts that horrified others came easily to her and did not bring retribution. She had held a woman's face beneath the waves and been given Mythe; she had smothered Barlow and her enemies were punished. Her failures did not touch her except to fuel her need for revenge. She believed herself chosen to stand apart and above those who should serve her desires and, despite its satisfaction, it was a burden not to reveal what she had done. The temptation to astonish the unsuspecting with her cleverness had grown until it took all her self-control not to disclose her daring. She wanted Frederick to be blamed for Barlow's death, but she also wanted her audacity to be marvelled at and esteemed. It was not possible to have both this time.

'Let us be clear,' Hellier moved closer to Ellen, 'you assert that you – a lady not used to wandering the country in darkness – lingered alone until night had fallen merely to avoid causing anxiety to a woman most probably asleep?'

'Oh, no.' Ellen settled a soft, reproachful gaze upon him. 'Not only that. Twice I turned back to reason with North, to try to soothe him. He had been so violent, I was afraid for whoever he met next.'

In a small room at the back of the courthouse, Frederick stood, restlessly looking out of the small barred window at the yard beyond. He held no hope of release. The jury had retired an hour before, but he did not doubt that the interval before they pronounced him guilty would be short. Until now, even in his imprisonment, he had been North of Holcombe but there might only be minutes until he became a felon, condemned and debased in the eyes of men. The helplessness and stupidity of his position sickened him. He turned to Knowles, who was sitting uncomfortably on a high stool.

'I cannot say that I admire my counsel,' he said. 'The arguments could have been put better by a washerwoman.'

Knowles straightened a leg to support himself. 'He's been a great disappointment,' he agreed. 'I can't think why.'

'We all have days when we're not as able as on others. It's unfortunate when those days end in a rope.'

'My dear sir, we don't yet know—'

Frederick gave an impatient sigh that cut off the lawyer's protestations. 'Where,' he asked, 'in all this folly, was it made plain that I was not being tried for having struck the blow that killed the wretch, but for having intended to kill him? That was an eel which slipped through everyone's fingers.'

Knowles, who was acutely depressed by the turn the trial had taken, did not answer.

Frederick strode angrily across the room and back. 'It's a curious amusement,' he said, 'hearing your life cried down in such a manner, your every action seen through a squint, every word falling sour on the listener's ear. It's as well I'm not a juryman. After hearing my character, I'd readily call for death.'

There were voices outside in the passage. He went to peer through the grill in the door but could see nothing, and the voices faded. Waiting for the verdict was worse than his captivity. He wanted to beat and kick the wood until it splintered, to smash the furniture in the cell, to shout for justice – instead, he touched his brow to the door and thought of Ellen. All that had been said against him had been wounding but he believed that ignorance, not cruelty, had prompted every unfavourable witness except Sir John and Ellen. He was revising his opinion of Philobeth's extraordinary theory. Despite her behaviour to him, until he had seen her in court he had not imagined Ellen capable of more than the squalid love-lies of a woman with ambitions in the marriage market. Her deliberate and unashamed falsehoods, told in the knowledge that his life was in the balance, had shocked him, destroying what was left of his romantic illusions. He saw her mastery of projecting an appearance quite contrary to her nature and did not wonder that the jury, whose members cast him vindictive glances as she spoke, had been as bewitched as once he was himself. For a second, as she was leaving the courtroom, she had flashed at him a look of such jubilant hatred that though he did not yet accept Philobeth's conclusion, he found that it and Ellen's expression were entangling themselves in his mind.

There were sounds again, this time of purposeful feet and the rattling of keys. Frederick stepped back from the door. Knowles stood up, his face solemn. A prickling broke out on Frederick's skin and there was discomfort in his bowels but he showed no outward sign of fear. The feet stopped before the door; the lock was turned.

'You're certain,' Frederick said, 'that Miss Alleyn is safe?'

'My dear North, the documents are signed. Nothing can change them. I assure you I'll see to Miss Alleyn's interests.'

The door opened. A guard and officer of the court stood outside. 'Mr North, if you would come this way.'

Frederick walked between the men. His heart beat heavily and it was an effort to steady his breath. It occurred to him that this might be the last time that 'Mr' was attached to his name.

The verdict was given. The jury, confused by what they were to decide and disapproving of one who was violent to gentlewomen, pronounced him guilty. In the spectators' seats, Philobeth stifled a cry and clutched Slater's arm. The black cap was placed upon the judge's wig.

And so it has come, thought Frederick. I expected it. I told myself I did, yet even now it does not seem real. My life will end, and for what? Pointless, pointless. And my love watching me as if her soul were torn from her body. God help us, we have not deserved this.

The judge was speaking. He forced himself to attend. '— but you have been found guilty of murder and however – shall I say remarkable?' here Judge Brownlow's gaze passed slowly along the jurymen, who quailed or looked stubborn according to their disposition, 'that may be, it's incumbent upon me to say that you will be taken from here to the condemned cell to await execution. I tell you with confidence that the sentence of death will not be carried out. Clemency is within the gift of the law and it will operate in your case. You will not hang, but you are a man of vicious temperament and habit and must suffer in accordance to your crime. Therefore, I do not doubt, it will be ordered that you be transported upon the seas to such place as Her Majesty, by the advice of her Privy Council, shall think fit to direct and appoint, for the term of your natural life.'

'Good God! Knowles, prevent it!' Frederick stood in the corridor behind the courtroom. His hands were stretched before him as two guards, with the grace to look conscious, were fastening manacles about his wrists. Knowles was beside him, his face wan, unable to speak for horror. A clamour of voices dissecting the verdict came through the open door but the men seemed to stand in a private place of despair.

'I can die without fear.' Frederick tried to turn more towards Knowles, but a guard prevented him. 'Even though I'm innocent, I can endure the scaffold – but this! Refuse it for me. I will take death.'

Knowles, his professional calm deserting him in his sense of failure, gestured helplessly. 'I can do nothing. I—'

'Frederick!'

He twisted sharply as he heard Philobeth cry his name, pulling his hands out of the guard's grasp. One of the manacles fell open and swung from the chain that linked it to the other. He saw Philobeth run towards him with Slater, giving the impression of flurried confusion, impeding officials from passing through the doorway. A guard gripped his arm to pull him back but the other, with the murmur of 'Sweetheart,' persuaded him to let go.

Philobeth, her eyes wide and dry with terror, pressed herself unashamedly into his arms and he clasped her to him, the chain dragging against her hair. Beyond them, Knowles walked forward to meet the officers, who had succeeded in extricating themselves from Slater. He begged a moment's patience and, with anxious glances, they agreed, waiting in a speculative group inside the corridor.

Her nails sinking into his coat, Philobeth clutched Frederick's shoulders so tightly that the marks of her fingers were left on his skin. 'I will follow you,' she said, fiercely. 'I will find you, I swear. I will find some way to help you.'

He held her closely, lowering his face to rest against hers. Her braids smelled of the sandalwood casket where she kept her combs, and he breathed in the scent, storing it for the bleak years to come. She did not yet know what he had given her and it wrung his heart to think that she would not hesitate to start out across the world for him with no care for the hardships that would mean.

'No,' he said. 'My love, my Hart. I can't ask it. I won't have you suffer such a land.'

'I will come.' She raised her head and now her eyes were full. 'I will come,' she said again. 'There's no power will keep me from you. Neither Queen nor Court nor—'

'Madam. Enough.'

She turned to see a severe, black-whiskered man at her side. The guards moved nervously in his presence, reaching for the loose chain, aware of their neglect of duty. She did not recognize the Governor of the gaol but his tone, though not unkind, was firm and she knew that authority was to part them. Frederick released her and she stepped back, afraid to cause him harm by protests.

'I will come,' she said. 'Trust in me.'

Chapter Sixteen

Water slapped against the longboat, sending irregular showers of salt spray over the prisoners as they sat looking vacantly at the grey sea or staring ahead at their destination. In the past three days, the weather had turned cold and Frederick, lifting his face to the fresh, autumnal breeze, thought of a storm upon the Chesil and the ill wind that had brought him here.

He was not resigned to his fate. The commutation of his sentence from death to the transportation the judge had promised had been granted with unusual speed and it was not yet a fortnight since Philobeth had sworn to cross the oceans for his sake. The Queen's mercy did not comfort him. A numbness had settled in his mind as he lay in the condemned cell, contemplating the years of disgrace and degradation that were to be endured. At times, although he made no sound, a madman screamed within his skull, raving for justice and hopes that were gone. He laughed at himself in the watches of the night, wondering if any other poor wretch had yearned as he did to hear a scaffold being built. It was only when he was not alone that he could muster the appearance of the undaunted courage that had sustained him until his conviction and then, as true as it seemed to onlookers, it was no more than a veneer over his misery. The collapse of his spirit had filled him with contempt for his cowardice and it was with relief that he felt his fortitude rise as the waiting ended and the journey to Australia began.

His calves throbbed as he sat amongst the oarsmen. He had travelled to Portsmouth chained to five other unfortunates and the discomfort of being unable to shift the position of his feet without pulling the felons' legs from under them made the relative freedom of being loosed from his comrades to climb into the boat an intense relief. The shackle still locked about his ankle was too heavy for him to make a sudden dive for liberty with any chance of being able to swim and, although he would sincerely have preferred to hang than be transported, he would not willingly take his own life when the possibility of escape might remain.

He saw no opportunity now. His clothes and manner marked him out, making him an object of interest to the sailors, who watched him covetously while they rowed, as if calculating the price to be had from his belongings. It seemed that, to take advantage of an opening to slip away, he would need to be indistinguishable from the rest of the convicts and he did not doubt that the gaolers would soon see that he was. He did not relish being submerged into the dirty, ragged mass of prisoners – indeed, despite winning his fellow travellers' goodwill by treating them to hot rum when they had stopped to change horses, his fastidiousness was insulted by the rank smell of their bodies and he longed to be far from them – but if such disguise was useful, he would embrace it.

The boat slowly made headway against the wind, lifting and falling on the swell with lurches that had the felons slithering on the wet wood. A labourer, who had lived thirty-four years on the Somerset levels and had never laid eyes on the coast, twisted about and vomited painfully over the side, rinsing his mouth with water that made him gag again. He sank back into the boat, too lost in home- and sea-sickness to notice the spectacle before them.

They were drawing closer to the hulks and their attention, which had been divided between the harbour and abject introspection, was riveted upon the dreadful manifestations of the law that wallowed at anchor amongst the spurting waves. Old warships, obsolete and decrepit, lay in lines across the horizon. Decayed leviathans towered out of waters dark with scum and the draggling weeds of rotting timbers, their hulls mazed by outcrops of decks, eyries and lairs never dreamt of by naval architects. Ropes of bedding flapped between broken masts. A fetid stench of animal corruption was carried to them over the shifting refuse that eddied about the boat.

A desolation greater than their previous griefs gripped the convicts, who were never to set a free foot on England's soil again. The shoemaker from Taunton, his thin, sandy hair fluttering about ears reddened by the wind, began to whisper the Lord's Prayer in a monotonous undertone, reaching its end and returning to 'Our Father' in one ceaseless stream of supplication. An ageing weaver, already exhausted and humiliated by travelling in irons from Carlisle, sobbed aloud. Frederick himself felt a pang of hopelessness that left him forlorn and desperate for a safety that was past. The image of Philobeth declaring, with the savagery of a woman parted from her child, that she would follow him, came into his mind and, in the suddenness of extreme anger, his half-formed intention to escape became a resolution. He would not lie helpless and passive in the bowels of a transport-ship, pining for his love to seek him out. His behaviour to her in the past had run contrary to his belief that women should be able to rely upon their men, but now she should have no complaint. He would not leave these shores in chains. Somewhere in this hell there would be a means to break free. He would take it at whatever risk and return to her before she need set forth across the world. The brave and daring spirit that would send her to Australia would make her embrace the hazard of joining her fortunes to his. A change of name, a secret place, his wealth in her possession and there would be a life for them.

The longboat nosed against the side of the *Achilles*. Shouts were heard and answered. A ladder was thrown down and the order given for the felons to come aboard. As he climbed painfully up the swaying wooden rungs, his hands slipping on the slimy ropes, Frederick concentrated upon his rage. With every clumsy motion of his shackled foot, every glimpse of the sneering faces above, he intensified his fury at his situation, chilling it into a cold determination to be undefeated, crushing the fears that still beset him. When he stepped onto the deck, he was as much master of himself as he had been as a landowner, but he was careful to display neither arrogance nor a false meekness that would bring peculiar cruelties upon his head.

There had been a form of privacy in prison and on the coach to Portsmouth: there was none here. On the road, people had stared as they stood in inn-yards, easing their legs as the horses were harnessed, but no-one had approached them. As they arrived on the deck, staggering on the rolling planks, the new transportees were mobbed by old hands. Convicts surrounded them, asking this, asking that and all the while, under cover of their jostling and flow of conversation, patting the pockets of the strangers, sliding their fingers into coats and under shirts, filching coins, combs, penknives and any article not grasped by its owner. Anticipating such theft, Frederick had secreted money, small toiletries, needles and thread in a bag slung on a cord about his neck and hung next to his skin. He had no confidence that this forethought would preserve his ownership for more than hours once on ship, but it was worth the attempt. He stood with his back against the bulwarks, one arm crossed over his chest and the other guarding the pocket that held a silk handkerchief wrapped about his tobacco, speaking to no-one and finding himself, to his shock, baring his teeth like a dog.

There was movement in the crowd and the resident convicts fell back as officers appeared. One of them, seeing the weaver crouched whimpering by a pilchard-barrel, pushed him with the sole of his boot. Frederick started to move forward but killed the impulse as soon as it was born. It went hard with him to recognize his powerlessness and inwardly he cursed himself for having done so little with his authority whilst he had it. He accepted that Philobeth had been right to urge him to put his position to good use; he hoped that she had been as right to believe that he would flourish in adversity.

The new men were mustered into a dejected group and driven down, with jeers and prods from the cane of a young lieutenant with a look of unwholesome excitement in his eyes, to that section of the ship devoted to stripping the transportees of their last connection with home. As Frederick's head was grasped by the barber, who was to give him the shorn scalp that marked the felon, he glimpsed a merchant ship upon the horizon and, knowing that those vessels were used for carrying prisoners across the seas, his heart lurched within him. They had not been told how long they were to be held in the hulks before their transfer to a ship bound for Australia, and he did not want to draw attention to himself by asking. The thought that he might be locked below decks, sailing southward, before he had discovered a way to escape made him jerk under the barber's hand and be cuffed like a beast for his impatience.

As he ran his fingers over his almost shaven hair, the quartermaster swaggered in, taking the place of the lieutenant, who had watched the first shearings with small squeals of laughter before being summoned above. The quartermaster was solid and square, reminding Frederick of a mastiff he had had shot for meanness, and he fixed his gaze on Frederick as he ordered the convicts to remove their clothes and climb into the tanks of cold water nearby. As the garments were put down, sailors gathered them, holding them up and, with a complacent 'Property of the Queen' from the quartermaster, ran a knife through them and cast them on a pile destined for an old-clothes dealer. When Frederick stood naked except for the bag about his neck, the quartermaster came over to him and, taking his coat from the planks, stroked his thumbs over the material.

'A gentleman's, I think,' he said, looking at Frederick with an eyebrow cocked. 'Were they yours?'

'They were.'

'And what do we have in the bag, gentleman?'

'Necessities for the journey.'

'Would you like to keep them?'

Frederick, his voice carefully not revealing a flicker of hope that corruption was common aboard, said, 'I would.'

'Well, then,' the quartermaster smiled, showing gold teeth, 'I expect you brought a little savings with you. Yes? Then we can come to an arrangement. See those irons waiting there in the corner? Fourteen pounds weight in every one. Fourteen a piece and just waiting for you Johnny Raws, now you've got those gaol-house shackles off. Now you've got to have one, but you don't have to have two. Not if you put a sovereign in my safe keeping.'

'Two guineas,' said Frederick, 'and we all have only one.'

The quartermaster touched Frederick's cheek with the tip of a knife he had been using to rend the clothes. 'Oh, no,' he said. 'Just you. No good turns here. We can't have you getting fond of each other. There's already enough fondness below decks, isn't there, lads?' He turned to the sailors, winking and running the handle of the knife down Frederick's back.

Frederick, conscious of his nakedness and vulnerability, felt a knot of panic tighten his throat, but he spoke calmly. 'Then a sovereign it shall be.' He reached into the bag and passed the coin to the quartermaster, who slid it into his waistcoat pocket. The water in the tanks was slopping from side to side with the rolling of the ship and, in the darkening afternoon, the men's white skin seemed to glimmer in the dusk. Nothing was said, but a subtle change occurred in the atmosphere. The fragile union created by

Frederick's sharing of rum in the coach was broken by the paying of that coin. The men, who had thought vaguely of obtaining some shelter from a gentleman, withdrew their interest and looked away. Frederick sensed a tired hostility born of disappointment, but understood that there was nothing he could do.

'And have we left someone behind us?' the quarter-master asked. 'A doting mother, a bosom friend, a tender-hearted young lady? Someone who can send their lambkin a supply of funds?'

'If they can be sure of achieving their object.'

'A delicate matter, but it can be seen to.' He nodded his head towards the tanks. 'In you get, my gentleman, and tomorrow you and I will have a discussion on your present, pressing financial difficulties.'

As the twilight deepened and the wind rose, pen-etrating the hulk like the intimation of frost, the chain-gangs were rowed back from the dockyards. They descended, sullen and exhausted, to the lower decks where the newcomers were being led to their cells. Frederick and his companions had been assigned to unloading the coal-boats; he watched men black-ened from head to foot, like the Moor in a mummers' play, file into the depths of the ship, too weary to speak or glance at the strangers. He wondered whether his value as one who could summon money would keep him from the degradation of labouring before gloating sightseers, or if pockets would be lined at his expense while officers laughed at his gullibility.

The lower decks stank of mould and stale air. The walls ran with damp that seeped down from the daily sluicing of the upper levels with sea-water as a perfunctory gesture towards cleanliness. Pale, fungoid growths drooped on the wet wood and fingers groping in the darkness sank uneasily into the spongy forms. The cold was growing. The cheap clothes Frederick had been given in exchange for his own – the canvas trousers, the rough shirt and jacket, the loose boots – seemed not to keep out the chill of the dank air, but to wrap it about his shivering limbs. He had never before dressed without a set of undergarments: the discomfort and indignity of the experience acted as a thorn in his troubled flesh.

He was tired. The bleakness of his surroundings depressed his spirits. He had slung his hammock without difficulty, calling on knowledge garnered from happier days when he had sailed in comfort on friends' yachts, but he was reluctant to try to sleep while others were awake. The timbers creaked as the hulk rolled on the deepening swell, the few lanterns that cast a weak light into the obscurity swayed on their hooks, sending shadows reeling into the gloom. It was a place for violence and despair.

Retreating into his cell, he squatted on his haunches for lack of any article on which to sit. His head hung down from his shoulders as loneliness and the problems of his strait filled his thoughts. Through his shirt, he grasped the bag about his neck. His money was gone, as was the handkerchief and tobacco that had been in his coat, but the rest of its contents remained. What was most precious and supporting to him was the bag itself. He had brought no letter from Philobeth nor image of her face, for fear that either would fall into the keeping of a lout, but she had sewn the bag for him and it was strengthening to hold it.

The shadows changed. Three convicts slipped into his cell and stood silently menacing him. He raised himself to his feet. The three were emaciated but he saw the muscles within their leanness. He stood waiting for the one he judged to be the leader to speak.

'We heard there was a gentleman come. Be you that'n?' The convict's accent was a hybrid of West County, London and the genteel.

Even as he prepared to ward off an assault, Frederick was able to guess that here was a quick mind perverted by indignance and depravity. 'I am.'

The convict did not glance at his companions but they both stirred like hounds gaining a scent.

'If you're here for money,' Frederick said, 'you're too late. Apply to the quartermaster.'

'You can get more, can't ee? You'd better. And anything you got now, you give it over.'

Frederick stared at the confidence in the eyes that threatened him. There was no doubt that the man was a villain but, though the felons learnt brutality once in the clutches of the law, the most naturally vicious, the murderers and rapists, did not reach the hulks. It was his class that had saved him from the scaffold; he would use his crime to protect him here.

He lunged forward savagely, gripping the speaker around the throat and pulling him off-balance, bending him backwards so that he must strain not to injure his spine. A hatred and rage, both reckless and calculated, burnt the desolation from his mind. The two henchmen moved restlessly, but dared not risk imminent hurt to their croney.

'What are you here for?' Frederick asked, his voice low and sinister. 'Stealing a sheep? Housebreaking? Theft? I came for murder. I should have hanged.' He pressed his thumbs into the quivering skin. 'I want to hang. I want it. Will you give me my desire?'

*   *   *

At Combehays, there were certain times of day and conditions of light when the autumnal colours of the trees were reflected in the lake in such a way that the water seemed to be a sheet of fire. Carmody, admiring it from an upstairs window, spoke silently to Mahala, as he often did now, telling her of the gold and scarlet that she would have revelled in seeing. His heart was heavy, and yet a painful realization that had first promised to condemn him to continuing sorrow was causing a healing change in his thoughts.

He had not taken well to Philobeth's refusal of his proposal. An uncharacteristic impatience gave him a disapproval of her wayward answer that led him into what he recognized as peevishness. For a fortnight after she had turned him down, he roamed about his mistressless estate finding fault with everything he saw and snapping at the servants, so that they shook their heads and said, with more wit than he, that the master was taking Mrs Carmody's death hard. He had a sense of a contract unfulfilled, a job undone. It was not Philobeth's attractions that consumed his imaginings but Mahala and her yearning to protect her friend. Long, one-sided conversations began to take place in his mind in which he justified himself to his wife, explaining his failure to achieve what she wished and declaring his intention to persevere.

Gradually it began to dawn upon him that, although it would be comforting for him to marry Philobeth, he had mistaken his feelings. He did not love her. She had avoided him since their conversation by the riverbank, but he did not miss her as he missed Mahala. He loved, and his love was for his wife.

The understanding brought him low. It destroyed the happy vision of the future that had upheld him in the last months and delivered him up to the full-blown mourning of the bereaved husband. Regret for the shortness of their time together and the incomplete nature of their marriage tormented him. He castigated himself for not responding to her burgeoning love until, one night, he seemed to hear the laugh she had for life's complications and knew that she had accepted all the strangeness of their situation.

His new awareness gave him a curious freedom. Instead of planning for Philobeth's residence at Combehays, he let himself remember every detail of his connection with Mahala. Memories lapped about him, breathing vitality into a dead house and making him less alone. He talked of his wife to all he met, their reminiscences increasing their intimacy, securing his position as their neighbour. He did not discard the idea of having Philobeth for his wife, but the conviction that his liking and desire were not love meant that his wait for her to need him was not so fraught, and could be endured with the same friend-ship they used to have.

He could not decide whether to tell her. Apart from greeting each other in the road and at court, they had not spoken since he had proposed, except on the occasion when she had tried to persuade him that it had been Miss Farebrother and not Frederick, who had ended Barlow's life. Although he had believed that her story was far-fetched and the consequence of more anxiety heaped upon her grief for Mahala, he had felt that he had let her down. He had wanted to offer her protection and support, but instead he had ignored her whilst brooding on the complexities and vexations of love.

There had been a development that day that made

him eager to talk to her. After giving his own evidence at the trial, he had spent as much time as his duties would allow, listening to the other witnesses. Watching Ellen had made him unsettled and suspicious. Perhaps because she was far across the room and her eyes did not rest on him, he did not succumb to the enchantment that was usual in her presence. The spellbound state that had caused him to grant her request to view the body did not take hold of him in court but, from his vantage point at the back of the onlookers, he saw those closer to her being beguiled as he had been. Her words and manners all seemed false and, though he could not quite bring himself to think that a young woman could kill, the brazen wickedness of standing up in court to tell deliberate lies when a man's neck was at stake struck him to the core with horror.

The verdict had shaken him. He had thought that he had expected and prepared for Frederick to be found guilty, yet when it happened he was outraged. The notion that what was plainly an accidental death could be viewed as murder opened his mind to other possibilities and, almost against his will, his imagination explored Philobeth's proposition regarding Ellen and, despite not finding anything definitive to prove that she was in the lane when Frederick and Barlow had fought, he could see it was feasible that she was.

With an increasing revulsion, he had not welcomed the news earlier that day that the carriage wheels he had heard upon the gravel belonged to Mrs North and had brought Miss Farebrother to speak to him. The episode of a similar arrival that led to her laughing over Barlow's corpse came vividly into his mind as he received her, and the shadow it cast preserved him from being deceived by her attractions. She had come ostensibly to ask him to visit Mrs North the following afternoon, to calm her fears over the potential ills of the coming winter, but it became apparent to him that she was opening a campaign to become mistress of Combehays. He did not flatter himself that she was interested in him – the case was more simple. She had failed to gain Holcombe and was looking about her for another estate. Her intentions were not overt, yet there seemed to be a crudeness in her blandishments that had not been there before. A coarseness showed itself momentarily in her speech without giving her embarrassment. It was as if she had become so confident of her abilities that she felt she did not always have to keep up her guard.

He was troubled. Sitting in the drawing-room, watching Ellen's jewelled hands lifting her cup, he remembered Philobeth's enquiry about the exact nature of the marks on Barlow's face and whether they could have been made by rings. An insistent voice inside his head began to say that, of course, that was how they were made, he had known it at once, and that Frederick did not wear rings. He looked at the figure sitting across the table from him and reflected that, after all, putting a hand across the mouth of an unconscious man did not call for undue strength or daring. He should put aside his prejudice. What could be thought of by one woman could be done by another.

On each occasion that he decided it was possible that Ellen was guilty, his mind drew back, resisting what it contemplated, yet his reluctance to accept it made his sense of failure towards Philobeth more compelling. After staring at the fire upon the lake while he explained the complexities of the affair to Mahala, he collected his hat and set out for Chantry. There was nothing to be gained by continuing the polite estrangement between himself and Philobeth and, whether the reconciliation would lead to the marriage Mahala had desired or not, he wanted Philobeth to feel free to visit Combehays if she chose.

Philobeth was at her desk in the parlour when he was shown in. She had discovered from the Keeper of Dorchester Gaol which hulk Frederick was to board and she was writing to its captain, asking for the date and destination of his new prisoner's journey to Australia. Despite her indignation at the verdict, the fact of Frederick's conviction had calmed her frantic efforts to have his innocence acknowledged; her energies were now concentrated upon her own removal to the southern hemisphere in order to provide him with what comfort she could. The startling revelation, made to her in person by Knowles lest she believe that some malicious trick was being played upon her, that she was the sole possessor of all that Frederick had owned, removed the financial difficulties of emigration and encouraged her to think that enough money paid in the right quarters would secure Frederick a degree of freedom that could eventually lead to them slipping quietly away to a more civilized land.

She had no desire to live out her days on a continent devoted to the punishment of convicts. There were no illusions in her mind about the penal settlements. She expected harshness, cruelty and corruption. Indeed, it could be said that she hoped for the latter. After witnessing the nonsense of the trial, she would not hesitate to enter heartily upon a career of bribery for

Frederick's sake. Nor would she falter in embarking upon the voyage. Her determination to carry out her purpose was absolute and she did not waste time that could be used for preparations in discussion about the wisdom of her actions, nor in pining for what might have been. Even Ellen was set aside in her thoughts, to be dealt with in later years if the opportunity arose. She had written to her father telling him of her decision and had received a bleating reply, warning her of the dangers that beset female travellers, but he had neither tried to dissuade her nor offered to go himself.

His desertion did not worry her. On hearing of her plans, Slater had immediately announced that she would be accompanying her girl, and Philobeth, knowing better than to urge her to stay, did not argue, being glad of her old nurse's loyalty and sure that she would be of far more practical use than Mr Alleyn. It was true that Slater lapsed into scathing remarks upon foreign climates and predictions that they would be eaten by cannibals, but she applied herself to ordering supplies and shutting up the house with a zeal that betrayed a hankering for adventure. This attitude would have been applauded by Mahala, and the conviction that her friend approved of what she was doing braced Philobeth for the myriad difficulties of her expedition, making her feel that Mahala was still close to her.

She was thinking of Combehays when she heard Carmody's voice at the door. Getting up to receive him, she had a moment's misgiving for fear he had come to renew his addresses, but they were bound to meet where they must talk at some point and she reproached herself for wanting to delay the interview. As he entered the room, she was relieved to see that he did not have the aspect of a lover and he, in turn, was struck by the look of resolve about her that had been missing between Mahala's death and the verdict at the trial.

They took chairs on either side of the hearth. It was a cold day with a threat of early frost; a fire was burning brightly, sending out strong licks of flame from the apple wood amongst the coals. The darting light was reflected on the brass fender, the tongs, even Philobeth's swaying earrings as she leant forward to push a log back with the poker. It was a scene that Carmody longed to have enacted in his dark house and, though it did not deceive him into believing he felt more for Philobeth than he did, it made the idea of her in his home more beckoning than it had been since he realized he loved Mahala. He almost seemed to see Mahala as he gazed at Philobeth. The reality of this handsome woman, with her heavy braids coiled about her head and her rich, medieval gown, seemed to bring his wife to him. If he were with Philobeth, it must be that Mahala lay close by; he felt the waft of her fan upon his cheek.

'You were busy when I came in,' he said. 'I mustn't detain you.'

There was a wistfulness in his voice that gave Philobeth a prick of conscience. Since the day of his proposal, when brooding upon his character had led to realizing that it was Ellen who had killed Barlow, she had barely given his side of the question a thought. Seeing him in her parlour, obviously settling himself in for the evening, reminded her that he was a disappointed man. It was tempting to treat him with tenderness for Mahala's sake, but that would not be kind in the long run.

'I did have particular business,' she said, 'but it

245

needn't be done this moment. I was writing to the captain of the *Achilles* to ask him when Frederick is to be moved to a transport ship.'

'I'd heard that his sentence was commuted. There's been a little good sense shown, at least.'

'There was certainly none in evidence at the trial.'

Carmody lowered his eyes. Although he knew that, even if he fully embraced Philobeth's theory about Ellen, he would be no more able to prove it than she, his burgeoning belief made him feel that his part in Frederick's defence had lacked vigour.

Philobeth noticed him flinch. 'I wasn't aiming my remark at you,' she said. 'You were asked for plain details of the body and you gave them. In my opinion, you'd have done well to mention who wears rings and who doesn't, but we'll say no more of that. I've tried to combat the persuasive power of a lovely face and I've failed. I've even been threatened with the law by a J.P. – an old friend of Frederick's, for what friendship's worth – if I open my mouth upon the subject again. And so my mouth will shut.'

'I wouldn't hand you over to the law.'

She looked at him sourly, thinking that his banter was ill-timed, but she saw that he was serious.

'I wouldn't,' he said, 'because I begin to believe you may be right.'

Philobeth laid the poker down in the hearth. A sudden release of tension made her shake and she had to fight against an urge to weep. She had given up all hope of convincing anyone except Slater of Ellen's guilt, and the relief of discovering an ally brought home how solitary she had felt. A catch in her throat prevented her speaking, but Carmody saw that she was affected by his words.

'I wish my conviction could be of service,' he said, surprised to find as he spoke that his doubts were dispelled by the admission of his trust in her judgement, 'but there's no shadow of a fact to prove what happened. Miss Farebrother has already lied in court, knowing what the consequences would be. I can't picture her confessing, even if she were directly accused. She's not a woman to let her conscience trouble her.'

Philobeth straightened in her chair. She had control of herself again and a sensation of light and warmth was cheering her. 'Don't worry about our helplessness,' she said. 'I've accepted that it would be impossible to overthrow the verdict. I look on Miss Farebrother as a form of contagion that arrived from the unknown to destroy our lives. Perhaps she has a soul – I couldn't say. But the harm is done and we must try to repair it by effectual means. I can do nothing for Frederick in England and so I'll cross the seas. I'm now a wealthy woman and in Australia I'll be able to do him good.'

There was no bravado in her manner. Her quiet, firm confidence prevented Carmody exclaiming at her announcement. He understood the change there had been in her demeanour and wondered why he had not anticipated this from the one whom Mahala had chosen as her beloved friend. Admiration for her spirit swept away what lingering thoughts he had on the value of female passivity, and he found a fear of loneliness making him envy a man in chains.

She saw the sadness in his face and regretted having told him so abruptly. To distract him from any intention he might be forming of throwing himself at her feet, she rushed into relating her astonishment at becoming the owner of the North estates. The district being alive with the news, he had already heard much of what she said but he did not interrupt until, suddenly realizing that he might think she felt herself bound to follow Frederick because of her inheritance, she faltered and gave up her tale.

He was touched by her confusion. The awkwardness of their relations could only be smoothed by revealing what sorrow had taught him of his feelings and, though it was hard for him to admit a mistake, it was necessary for her sake that he should put away his pride. 'I'm a practical man, Miss Alleyn,' he said. 'I can tell you something of how a heart beats, but not for whom. You'll think me weak, too weak to know my own mind. Perhaps you'll believe me an adventurer, deliberately deceiving an invalid for my own ends.' He was staring into the fire, unable to watch her as he spoke, too conscious of having failed Mahala to go on.

She leant towards him, her eyes soft and grateful. 'You no longer wish to have me for your wife,' she said gently.

He was glad of her perception, but the baldness of the statement made him feel that he insulted her. 'Forgive me,' he said. 'I mistook what I felt. I loved but I did not know who.'

'It was Mahala.' There was such joy in her voice that he turned his head and both saw that the other looked through tears. Impulsively, she reached out and clasped his hand. 'Forgive you?' she said. 'I thank God that it was not only I who knew her worth. And that my leaving will not hurt you.'

'It will hurt me.' He gripped her fingers and she held his strongly. 'But what would she think of me?' he asked, his voice failing. 'I've broken my promise.'

'What would she think?' Philobeth said. 'She'd think

what many of us are taught. That by giving to someone we love, we are given something more precious in return. That she was, truly, Mahala Carmody.'

The following day, Carmody rode over to Mythe with an unusual variety of medical practice on his mind. Philobeth had described Ellen as a contagion and it seemed to him that she was right. Certainly, Ellen had a way of infecting those around her with the belief that she was as she wished to be. He knew from personal experience how she could induce a state of delusion that was more akin to a form of illness than anything else. The analogy interested him. It called upon his skills as a doctor. He could not bring himself to offer Philobeth the Graham wealth that Mahala had wanted her to have, but perhaps the satisfaction of seeing Ellen turned out of Mythe by his actions would be compensation enough.

He had decided to innoculate Mrs North against Ellen. Just as he might introduce cowpox into a patient's system to protect her from smallpox, so he would drip poison into Mrs North's mind to guard her against the wiles of her guest. It could not be done quickly. Ellen's influence was predominant at Mythe, but he knew the strength of Mrs North's self-love and the steady, implied suggestion that Ellen did not have her benefactress's interests at heart would eventually, he felt sure, lead to expulsion.

It was curious to pull the bell-rope of Mythe's door with his thoughts so dramatically altered since the previous day. He had admitted his longing for his wife, his simple friendship for Philobeth and his belief in Ellen's guilt and the effect was invigorating. Constraints that had hampered his thinking had sloughed away and he told Mahala, as he listened to the footsteps crossing the hall, that life had a purpose again. Not since he had been a student anticipating the outcome of an experiment had he been so intrigued by a possible chain of events.

The maid who took his hat gave him a message from Ellen. Miss Farebrother's compliments and, after the consultation, would he join her in her private parlour to set her anxieties at rest. He smiled a little as he took off his gloves. Tales of her meetings with Frederick in that room had reached him and he thought of her reclining on velvet pillows, with the opulent light of the stained-glass falling on her face, as she waited to beguile him. He had no intention of either entering her lair or letting a refusal bring her to Mrs North, and with a meaningless 'most kind' passed on into the Scarlet Boudoir to see his patient.

The urge to defend herself against any expectation that she play an active part in her grandson's troubles and Ellen's realization that, if the old woman were housebound, she would herself have more freedom, had led to Mrs North becoming prey to fancying a dozen disorders undermining her constitution. Although it was not a cold afternoon, a large fire burnt in the grate and she was wrapped in a woollen rug that did not set off her silks to advantage. Several small bottles cluttered the round table beside her, an apparatus for sending medicinal steam into the air lay in readiness on a cabinet.

Being aware that, beneath her frail appearance, she was as strong as an ox, Carmody was pleased to see these signs of hypochondria. Lifting the tails of his coat, he took the seat placed where he could feel the pulse under the long falls of lace at her wrist and commiserated with her upon her ailments. Talking together in soft tones, they shook their heads over the sad necessity to cosset her health.

'Oh, Doctor,' she said, laying a hand upon her chest, 'such palpitations. If I could say how much I suffer! There are nights when I'm so breathless, I don't think I'll see the dawn. I'm forced to rouse my maid to sit and watch me while I sleep.'

Carmody patted her arm soothingly. 'We must take the very best care of you,' he said. 'You must recruit your strength after such trying times. Have nothing about you that gives the slightest worry.'

'They have been trying.' Mrs North, revelling in the sympathy, put a fine, cambric handkerchief to a tearless eye. 'It has been hard to escape the shame my grandson brought upon him – but he always did take after his mother. There's been a blight on this house, Dr Carmody. Weeks without a suggestion of pleasure. And Miss Farebrother obliged to speak in court! Actually in court with all the world gazing at her. A brave soul.'

'Indeed, yes. She acquitted herself astonishingly. One could almost have thought she had done such a thing before. But, naturally, the strain would be bound to tell upon her nerves. A tonic would settle any little difference there's been in her temperament since the trial.'

Mrs North nodded appreciatively. Much as she relied upon Ellen and enjoyed her flatteries, there had been moments recently when her feelings had been fleetingly jarred by expressions her guest had used. She had not realized it before, but there was a suspicion of over-confidence in Ellen's manner, a usurping of authority that she did not quite like. It was true that

Ellen was taking the household management upon herself only from the best and most generous of motives and yet— Mrs North smoothed the folds of her gown thoughtfully. She wanted to be relieved of troubles, but she did not appreciate being taken for granted. 'Perhaps a tonic would be just the thing,' she said. 'Have one made up, and Miss Farebrother can take her dose when she gives me mine. Then I can see she doesn't forget.'

'Miss Farebrother attends to your medicines?'

There was a trace of apprehension in his voice that puzzled Mrs North. 'Why, yes,' she said. 'Always. Is that wrong?'

'Oh, no. No, no.' Carmody was firm, but a look of misgiving still lingered on his face. 'I wouldn't suppose – of course, one wonders— But we cannot know what experience Miss Farebrother has had. She may be well versed in the administration of drugs. I'm sure there's nothing at all that we need to fear.'

Chapter Seventeen

As autumn deepened, cold settled on the hulks. Frederick, waiting for the boat that would row him to the hospital ship, looked over the side at the heaving slate of the waves and thought that when he was free, he would never again have anything about him that was grey. The lowering sky with its streaks of watery cloud, the sodden timber of the rotting vessel that wallowed on the mounting seas, the shreds of laundry that flapped and cracked in the piercing wind, even his own skin, all were composed of shades of grey.

He walked back and forth along the deck, not so much to keep warm as to counteract the numbing effect of the cold. A clean, bright frost, a shining, brittle freeze would have been easier to bear. The damp that saturated the ship, seeping through the mouldering partitions, dripping from the low ceilings, soaking into clothes and bedding so that the convicts were never dry, had a debilitating quality that sapped the strength of the healthiest men. Decay and despair seemed one in the dank, fetid cells.

His gait was almost normal. The flesh beneath his leg-iron was rubbed raw and would not heal, but he had schooled himself to walk as if the pain did not exist. The weight of the fetter gave a roll to his step that had not been there before, but his impassive face and the lack of hesitation in his stride did not betray his suffering. He practised self-discipline in readiness for escape. There would only be one chance and, to be successful, he must have perfect mastery of body and mind.

He was thinner than he had been and, though he tried to be expressionless, there was an air about him that let him move unmolested through the felons. The violence he had shown on his first evening aboard, his reputation as a murderer who did not care if he were hanged, and his ability to buy the favour of the officers, gave him a safety from assault not enjoyed by other prisoners, but the suppressed aggression in his bearing would have done much to give him the same protection. Anger and determination had so burnt into his heart that had Philobeth seen him standing shorn and gaunt upon the deck, she would have recognized the character she had always believed to be lying dormant.

He had asked her not to visit him. Just as he would not bring a likeness of her to the hulk to be remarked upon by strangers, so he did not want her exposed to the lewd speculations that would follow her appearance. They wrote to each other but, as agreed before he left Dorchester, in the language of brother and sister to shield their love from prying eyes. Their most telling communication, at present, was in the prompt dispatch of money from Philobeth to the ship whenever he required it. His hopes of corruption amongst the crew had been well founded, and the discussion about his financial difficulties that the quartermaster had promised had resulted in an improvement in his conditions directly the first payment had arrived. Convicts could not, officially, possess money but a prisoner able to put gold into an outstretched hand could have his fault winked at and encouraged. His ability to summon bank-notes saved him from the sudden, inexplicable punishments meted out around him, it gave him a full ration of food that would otherwise have dwindled on its journey from steward to cook to convict, it wrapped him in the seaman's jersey he wore beneath his canvas jacket and it rescued him from the degradation of working in the chain-gangs in the docks.

There had been five days of coal-heaving before he was able to pay three sovereigns to be transferred to the hospital ship, and his back still ached from the drudgery it had been. From dawn, when the felons were rowed ashore, to dusk, when they returned to the hulks too weary and starved to rage against their plight, he had carried coal up ladders in holds so thick with dust that he could not see the man next to him, across planks to the wharf with the awkward shuffle of one whose irons would drag him to the bottom if he fell into the harbour, and up into the waiting waggons. The sacks alone weighed twenty pounds, and into each went two hundred weight of coal. He thought the work would kill him. His muscles felt as if they were torn apart and, as he lay in his hammock, his back still seemed crushed forward, driving the breath from his lungs; but worse than the physical agony was the humiliation of finding himself the object of sightseers who thronged the docks, gazing at the convicts as they might gaze at animals in a menagerie.

The ease with which bribes bettered his circum-stances made him wonder whether he could buy his freedom. Could enough money add his name to the list of prisoners who had already sailed? His tentative exploration of the possibility met a blank. It was not in the quartermaster's interest to risk his remunerative position nor for lesser members of the crew to help a convict, who was prominently in their superior's eye. He accepted this with a bragging declaration of what wealth would do for him in Australia and resumed his search for a more independent means of escape.

He believed that he had found it. Its horror was almost unbearable to contemplate but his world was more vile than anything he could have imagined before his arrest, and he would not baulk at the hazards he must face.

The boat he had been waiting for drew alongside and he climbed down to it carefully, remembering that one slip caused by over-confidence would end in drowning. Taking his seat amongst the packages to be hauled aboard the hospital hulk, he nodded to Davies, a clerk with a bronchial cough, whose trembling wife had sold their furniture and allowed a naval arm about her waist to release her husband from dock work. A moment's temptation and an open cash-box had put Davies in irons and, listening to him clear his throat and complain of 'the moist air, sir, a chill', Frederick did not think that he would live to feel the tropical sun.

He went up the ladder onto the hospital ship behind Davies. The clerk was not fit for clambering up slippery rungs and had been known to stand clinging to the ropes, his eyes shut against the terror of the climb above and the water below. With Frederick close by, assuring him that he would not fall, Davies could reach the deck without threats of flogging. Today, a light rain was being blown in icy scurries against their skin as they came aboard and Frederick turned up the collar of his jacket as Davies bent double, propping his arms against his knees to draw hissing breaths through his teeth.

A head appeared from below decks and called to them before disappearing beneath the hatch. The wind prevented them hearing what the order had been but, assuming it was a summons, Frederick and Davies – 'the maids-of-all-work' as Frederick described them – went down the steep stairs into the darkness 'tween-decks. The stench here was different from the ordinary hulks. There was the same gagging presence of mould and night-soil but the tainted sweetness of suppuration and the rank warmth of fever-sweats sullied the already foul air.

It was a place of misery and fear. The transfer Frederick had obtained brought him from the commonplace brutality of the coal-holds to a region where evil lurked in the guise of duty. He had not recognized it at first. It had not been easy to adjust not only to the life of a menial but to the attendance upon patients, whom he could no longer do much to help. His inability to offer the comforts his wealth could have provided was a standing rebuke to him for his idleness in days gone by. He could not look at the pale rows of broken men, consumptive, malnourished, weakened by flux, and think complacently of their punishment. It was not that he sanctioned crime, but he saw few Barlows amongst the sickly wretches, and many who reminded him of Mary.

He had never imagined himself a nurse. The smell of putrefaction, the collecting of pus-soaked dressings flung aside by the surgeons, the swabbing of floors mired with matter he did not care to name revolted him yet, within days, his squeamishness had faded into distaste, and pity triumphed. He had a gentle touch with invalids; he was tender with their alarm and restlessness; he talked hopefully in low tones as he held cups to their lips and wrote their letters home.

In his innocence, he believed that he and the surgeons shared a desire to do good. They showed no friendliness to him or the men they treated but he remembered Carmody's bluntness and gave them the benefit of the doubt. His approval was misplaced. A rough assistance was extended to prisoners likely to get well, but compassion was in short supply. As he watched the casual attention paid to convicts in obvious distress and listened to the callous conversations of doctors, who talked together without troubling themselves that he was there, Frederick was chilled and listened to what he had ignored as rumour with more heedfulness. He still soothed men terrified of being bled, but as deaths occurred – a little unexpectedly in his opinion, a little sooner than they might have done – he found his words ringing hollow in his ears.

He could not say that the men would not have died if that extra pint of blood had not been taken. He could not say for certain. Nor could he say that they had been hurried into their graves – for graves did not greet them. It was the rule that convicts should be buried on Rats' Castle, the cemetery mudbank in the estuary, but the dissectors' agents, who knew the spirit of the docks, would give five pounds for a fresh corpse, and the coffins rowed to their lonely burial held only sand and stones.

This was the final cruelty, an abomination so depraved that he had vomited into the sawdust of the operating-room on learning that it was true. The surgeons, attributing his nausea to the bloody nature of their administrations to a crushed hand and forgetful that they had been discussing the disposal of their patient, laughed and called him 'Kitty', advising him to lose his ladylike ways.

It was not that he believed that men must have remains to rise for the Final Judgement but, that the viewing of a human body as a profitable carcass showed such lack of value for the soul it had housed that he seemed to have fallen into hell. The sights and sounds that met him daily, the desperation, the backs lashed fleshless, the hideous suspicion that the surgeons were, indeed, habitually guilty of the crime for which he had been sentenced might have combined to cast him into a crippling dejection. Instead, it forged a great determination to elude his undeserved punishment and this worst horror was to furnish him with the means of his escape.

Whoever had called to them from the hatchway had not stayed to issue orders but, as Frederick and Davies descended the stairs, Farjeon, a softly-spoken Gloucestershire tailor leant on his mop to tell them that Heyer had died just now and they were to carry him to the mortuary.

A spasm of anticipation gripped Frederick. 'Heyer?' he said. 'He was improving.'

'Ah,' Farjeon looked knowing, 'but 'e were bled yesterday till 'e were as white as a lovesick maid. 'Twas only one outcome then.'

Frederick stared at the wall. His feet were planted far apart to cope with the shift of the ship; there was a defiance in his attitude that made Farjeon nervous.

'Don't you do nothing,' he warned. 'You can't stop un.'

Frederick let out a sigh that was lost in the creak of

the timbers. He beckoned to Davies and the two made their way to where Heyer, his eyes fixed open, lay waiting for them.

Davies hung back. 'I know it's wicked, sir,' he said, his appreciation of Frederick's rank uninjured by their joint situation, 'but this work— If it's a family loss, a normal bereavement, but—' He shook his head.

'We find ourselves in Hades, Mr Davies,' Frederick said, 'and must do what we must.' He watched Davies standing forlornly in the shadows and pitied him. Although he believed his comrade to be doomed, it hurt his conscience to think that his own liberty would deprive Davies of the comfort he drew from their companionship. 'Mr Davies,' he said, 'I hope you'll forgive me and not think it charity, but I know a lady who would be glad to help your wife. Would that be acceptable to you?'

'Oh, sir,' Davies was tremulous, 'if you could understand the relief it would be to me to have my Alice provided for. She's having to find new lodgings, but a letter in the care of the vicar of St Mary's in Yeovil would always reach her. A Mr Standish.'

'Then you may set your mind at rest. Come, take hold of his feet.'

Between them they lifted Heyer onto a stretcher and carried him, wrapped in a blanket, to the mortuary. The cabin was dark, lit only by a lantern suspended from the ceiling, but the shadows falling upon the empty coffin were not as chilling as the realization that the room had been chosen for its mournful purpose because of its proximity to stairs to the upper deck and its separation from the sick by store-rooms, making the removal of the bodies to their market convenient. They placed the young man into the coffin and arranged him decently, despite their awareness that he would not lie there long. Unhappy that no ceremony to mark the passing of a spirit would be performed upon the men they brought here, Frederick and Davies had taken to standing for a moment in prayer when their task was accomplished. This morning Frederick found that the powerful beating of his heart interfered with his meditations. He had resolved to attempt his escape when the next death occurred and he would not go back on his decision, but the dangers that lay ahead and the confusion of feelings caused by benefiting from Heyer dying, agitated him. There was something ghoulish in waiting to take advantage of a death and, though he was sure that Heyer would not have begrudged him his chance, he did not feel at ease with himself.

Throughout the day his thoughts were upon his escape. It was possible that he would die of suffocation, yet the risk was worth taking. Ever since the idea of how he could gain his freedom had occurred to him, he had been conspiring for his presence on the hospital hulk at all hours of the night and his absence from his berth on the *Achilles* to seem normal. He routinely busied himself with extra duties or volunteered to complete paperwork, hated by the officers and needing more education than the other convicts possessed, in order to miss the boat that would have taken him back to his home ship. His scheme had proved successful and it was not a matter of comment to Davies or the crew when he did not muster for the return to the dormitory hulks.

Tonight, when Davies put away his scrubbing brush and emerged into the rain-spattered evening, Frederick was not to be seen so the boat rowed away without him. As he heard the few convicts allocated to night attendance climb down the stairs, Frederick felt a cold sweat break out upon his body. So far, he was doing nothing that could not be given an innocent explanation and he could still discard his plan, but he feared that his intention was written in his eyes and he dreaded being noticed by an officer.

He went down into the depths of the hulk to a little-used cubby-hole where old instruments were packed against the day when someone would clean and sharpen them. Rags, polish and a whetstone that he had secreted days before gave him a reason for being there if discovered, and he did some desultory buffing as the slow time passed. In that isolated hole he had no means of telling what o'clock it was and he had to use his judgement as to when to emerge. The bread he had been given at noon was in his pocket, together with three slices left by patients, and he ate one as the night dragged into the early hours, wondering when he would find food again.

Within the unceasing sounds of a ship at anchor, there was a deep hush when he came out of his hiding place. It was that point of time that seems furthest from the hopefulness of day, and the tension Frederick felt as he walked through the silent men made him clench his fists until his nails bit into his palms.

He reached the mortuary without being observed and, there being no noises from it, forced himself to go straight in. The lantern was still alight and he leant his back against the door for a moment, staring at the flame. He had no excuse for being here, save a wish to pay his last respects, and once he had set about his task, he would be unable to conceal what he was about. His breath juddered in his lungs but he told himself sharply that the scattering of sand beneath the coffin, with its marks of scuffing feet, showed him that the dissectors had possession of a fresh instrument of learning and would not break in upon him. The chaplain would not arrive to be rowed to the cemetery until eight and anyone who died during the night was not usually found until morning. If he were quiet, it was likely that no-one would enter the cabin until the seamen came to carry the corpse to the longboat.

The lid of the coffin had been nailed down but it was in the perfunctory way thought good enough for convicts. He thought he could lever it up without breaking the wood. Going to the cupboard where the tools were kept, he looked for a screwdriver but, finding none, took out a claw-hammer. It disappointed him that there was no implement sufficiently heavy to knock out the rivet in his leg-iron but he could not have attempted to free himself of it on ship and, surely, there would be spades stored at Rats' Castle. He must be patient.

His pulse was beating fast as he inserted the thin edge of the hammer into the crack between lid and coffin, and pressed. He could not risk splintering the boards or causing a sudden rending that might be overheard and he pushed down with a gentle, persistent firmness, his brows dampening, until the half-driven nails slid out of the cheap wood. Inside, four heavy rocks, encrusted with sand and barnacles, were wedged into position with rolled-up sacking. He smiled, drawing in air through his teeth, seeing that he was spared scooping out the mass of small stones he had expected. Where to put the contents of the coffin had been a puzzle. He had thought he would have to chance dropping them over the side, but the cupboard was deep and its lowest shelf was a jumble of forgotten articles that was never disturbed. Carefully lowering the nails back into their holes, he pulled out the ropes, cloths and bags of lint that had accumulated there. If anyone entered now, he could claim to be neatening the stores but the reprieve was short-lived and he removed the lid again, hoisting out the stones and rolling them to the furthest wall of the cupboard. Putting back the debris so that it seemed untouched, he had latched the door and was turning away when he heard steps upon the stairs outside. He stood very still. Two men were coming down towards the mortuary. I'm here for a good reason, he thought, I'm often here at night – but his bowels tightened as the steps came closer. He heard a murmured remark outside the door, a scurrilous laugh in answer and the men went by.

The alarm made him hurry. Lifting the lid from the coffin again, he laid it on the floor and knelt beside it. The two planks that formed its width were held together on the inside by cross-pieces, whose nails protruded through the upper surface of the wood, and he drove a bradle into these, piercing holes into which he threaded loops of twine. He was about to stand up when a horror of asphyxiation came over him with such force that the air in his mouth turned stale and foul. Praying that it would not splinter, he forced a series of tiny punctures into the lid at its head. They were too small to be noticed by anyone not searching for them, but his fear of their being questioned was almost as great as his fear of smothering.

It could not be helped. If he were to be free, he must put aside his qualms. The danger of what he had set himself to do was real and daunting, but if he hesitated he would fail. The chance of liberty was worth the terror.

He rested the lid against the side of the coffin and looked about the room. The hammer and bradle were the only signs that he had been there and he picked them up, placing them in his trouser-pockets. His mind was filled with the sounds of the sea so that his thoughts had to struggle above the waves. Cautiously, he climbed onto the trestles that supported the coffin and then, awkwardly, carefully, into the coffin itself. Dragging the lid from where it was propped, he manoeuvred it until the nails were above their holes and pulled it down. As the light was blanked out, a surge of panic and revulsion almost made him cast the lid to the deck but he mastered himself and lay panting in the darkness until he grew more calm. He could not fit his legs into the lower loops of twine but he pushed his hands through the others and drew on the lid so that it felt firmly in place. He had been afraid that it would seem loose to the seamen, who would be loading the coffin into the boat, but it felt secure and with the twine handles to resist any trying of the nails, he believed he was safe from discovery.

The waiting began. Time had no meaning. He put his lips to a puncture and confirmed the passage of a thread of air yet he had a sense of stifling, and sweat broke out upon his face. He thought that the walls of the coffin were transparent and his concealment would be instantly revealed; he thought he felt earth trickling through the holes he had pierced. Though not subject to supernatural dread, he shuddered at the recent occupation of his refuge by a corpse. His limbs grew numb and his head swam. A giddiness threatened to let his anxiety overwhelm him, but before he lost his self-possession, an effort of will brought him to his senses. To keep his imagination in check, he mentally wrote a letter to Philobeth, describing in minute detail all that had happened to him since he had boarded the *Achilles* and telling her, with the vigour he had denied himself on paper, of his reborn love. He repeated all the poetry – English, Latin and French – that he had ever learnt and when that store was exhausted, he made an inventory of his home, moving from room to room, itemizing the familiar objects. Thirst started to trouble him and he pictured himself as a boy, diving into the cool, green depths of his lake.

He was designing a new flower garden beneath the terrace, when the door to the cabin opened and several seamen came in. The shock he felt made him start and it was all that he could do to suppress a cry. The darkness and isolation of his vigil had brought him to such a state of separation from the world that the intrusion of the men, for whom he had been waiting, caught him unawares. Adrenalin made him alert. He grasped the twine and braced himself to be lifted. The men were talking together in grumbling tones. He could hear them clearly as they roped the coffin. His astonishment that they should be complaining of the previous night's cards when his own concerns were so momentous, made him laugh silently at himself. A plank of wood shielded him from discovery; if he were detected, the flogging he would receive would certainly kill him; if his plan miscarried, he would die, alone and struggling for air. The strangeness of the contrast between his thoughts and those of the sailors amused and revived him as he felt himself raised from the trestles and borne up the stairs.

A sensation of cold relieved the closeness of the coffin as they came on deck. There was a jolt, an upending, an impression of swaying above a great drop and he was lowered into the longboat. He was so near to the men who took the oars that it seemed impossible they could not hear him breathe. It was exhilarating to be moving. With every sweep of the blades he was carried nearer liberation and, for a space, a joy in his enterprise overrode the dangers to come, allowing him a vivid satisfaction in what he had already achieved.

The chaplain, a morose, testy creature, who looked on his duties as an imposition, was on board, huddling into a cloak fit for January, and the oarsmen did not venture to speak in his presence. The steady creak of the rowlocks and the surge of the sea as the boat lifted and fell, surrounded Frederick, an exchange of one limbo for another. A dull, insistent pain from the pressure of the wood throbbed in his back and legs, but he dared not alter his position. The discomfort and fraught seclusion sank his spirits, replacing excitement with sombre anticipation of what was to come. He had taken care to find out how burials were accomplished on the mudbank. As he had suspected, a communal grave was dug and left uncovered until it was full – but what if his was the last coffin to be placed within it? What if the practice had changed? Would he call out as he heard the first shovel of soil fall upon the wood or should he stay mute in the hope that the earth would be shallow enough for him to gain his release? The atmosphere in the box was increasingly sour. Claustrophobia gripped him, making his self-imposed stillness a torment. He raged against the gothic necessity of his incarceration, longing for light.

There was a jarring scrape and the boat was pulled aground. He felt himself lifted again and shouldered across dry land. The wind was louder here, its whining obscuring the words of the priest and broken verses distracted his thoughts.

'"—held my tongue, and spake nothing: I kept silence, yea, even from good words; but it was pain and grief to me.

My heart was hot within me, and—"'

The swaying stopped. His breast tightened.

'"—speak this to your shame. But some man will say, How are the dead raised up? and with what body do they come?"'

He was lowered into the grave.

Chapter Eighteen

At Chantry Philobeth was looking over the laundry lists for Holcombe House. It was not inspiring work but she had set herself to becoming familiar with every aspect of her unexpected acquisition and, having studied her investments with the lawyers, and land management with the bailiff, was now under the housekeeper's tutelage. She did not yet regard herself as a wealthy woman and had no intention of taking up residence at Holcombe. In her eyes, she merely had Frederick's possessions under her protection until she became his wife when, despite the law's vaunting of masculine rights, they would hold their property in common. She did not know what was to be done with the house. As Frederick could never make use of it himself, then, unless he wanted it sold, it should be put up for rent, but she was unsure how attached he was to his family home and did not want to distress him with questions while his life was misery enough.

Her mind was not wholly on her task. She had had no word from Frederick that day and it troubled her. They wrote to each other daily – long, encouraging letters from her; short, exhausted, weekday notes from him, written standing beneath a lantern, staunch, expansive offerings on Sundays – and the disruption of their communication filled her with anxiety. Was he ill? Injured? Was he being punished? Had he been transferred to another hulk? Had he already started for Australia? She scorned herself for the violence of her concern. It was foolish to worry over so short a delay. His letter was probably even now on its way to her door. She tried to push her fears aside, but common-sense told her that there were many dangers awaiting convicts and it would not be realistic to pretend otherwise. The frustration of not being able to contact him made her restless and agitated. She knew she could not endure a long silence. If she did not hear from him for a week, she would go to Portsmouth herself. Grimly, she applied her thoughts to her studies.

Time passed, but whether it was moments or hours, Frederick could not say. Cold had seeped into his bones so that the throbbing of his tortured body had been subdued by a frigid numbness. He began to drift into dreams, pulling himself back into wakefulness, afraid that sleep would slide into death. He needed movement, air and warmth. The safety he would gain by staying concealed until dusk was outweighed by the increasing weakness caused by his confinement. There might be men standing at the graveside as he emerged, willing to drag him back into captivity as their shock faded, but he must take that risk or die of exposure, already entombed.

Tentatively he stretched his stricken limbs, flexing the cramped muscles until he felt the blood flow more freely. Spasms contorted him, twisting his trunk against the coffin's sides, as life returned. When he felt that his body was his own, he placed his hands and knees against the lid and pushed. It did not yield. The drizzling rain that had fallen upon it in the boat had swollen the wood, tightening its grip on the nails: it was not until the fifth attempt, when his heart was beating fiercely, that there was the sound of rending and a rush of dank air.

He cast the lid aside, not caring whether he was heard, and lay gasping, clearing his lungs. It was still dark. A sliver of light showed to his left and he made out the edge of a tarpaulin pegged over the grave. His relief at his deliverance was so great that at first he did not appreciate the foulness of his situation but, as he grew used to wider horizons, he began to taste the rank atmosphere of the covered grave and an urge to be gone completed his revival. Sitting up, he looked about him. His eyes had adjusted to the dim light and he saw a long trench floored with coffins. The effect was melancholy but the glimpse of grass and sky beneath the tarpaulin and the suspicion that his was probably the one body present prevented the eerie imaginings that would have beset him in a vault.

He pulled himself to his feet and stepped out of the box. His legs protested at the unaccustomed motion, threatening to buckle under him, but he steadied himself against the side of the grave until he felt their strength return. To avoid the surgeons guessing how he had made his escape, he put back the coffin lid, scattering it with mud from the trench wall so that it looked undisturbed. The wind was flapping the loose edge of the tarpaulin and he could not hear whether there was anyone in the cemetery, so, walking carefully on the toes of his ungainly boots to avoid leaving footprints, he made his way over the slippery wood of the coffins to where he could see under the canopy.

His view was limited but the desolate nature of the

mudbank and the doleful moaning of the wind had such an air of abandonment that he was encouraged to dig his feet into the wet earth and heave himself out onto the thin grass.

Immediately he felt so exposed that fear of being recaptured made the bile rise to his throat. Even lying, mud-soaked, in a convicts' graveyard, the sweetness of freedom was too great to lose again and he knew that if he saw a pursuer he could not overpower, he would cast himself into the sea to drown rather than be taken to die beneath the lash.

There were no pursuers. The mudbank was empty of all life except the seabirds that hunched beside the sheltering tussocks or stalked the shore, scavenging with angular strides and remorseless eyes. Across the harbour, the hulks rode uneasily beneath the boisterous clouds, as remote a world as the Himalayas. He savoured his success but, remembering that he had a long road to safety, stared around for somewhere to conceal himself until dark. There was a hut a hundred yards away and, though it was too obvious a hiding place to offer security, it might contain tools, stronger than those he carried, that could knock the rivet from his leg-iron.

He could not bring himself to stand up and attract the attention of any telescope trained in his direction. Crawling painfully towards the shed, dragging his fetter behind him, he thought with a wry laugh how unsuited his education had been to fit him for this exercise and how much more alive he felt than he had ever done before.

The hut held only spades and sacking. He had hoped for a pickaxe or mallet, but heavy implements were not needed for grave-digging on the mudbank. His disappointment was acute. The difficulty of walking to Chantry with fourteen pounds of iron around his ankle, even were he able to get to shore, would be minor compared to the risk he would face of being recognized as a felon. Taking the hammer from his pocket, he placed his fettered foot upon a pile of sacks and began striking the rivet as best he could. It was awkward work. The hammer was not heavy enough for the business but, when it skidded off the iron, it dealt a cruel hurt to the raw flesh of his ankle. Just as he had schooled himself to walk as if he were uninjured, he now forced an unflinching endurance as he pounded the rivet with strong, rhythmic blows that drove the metal into his skin. His teeth were bared and all the hatred he had learnt was channelled into the power of his arm.

At last, with a suddenness that made him stagger as he diverted an unneeded stroke into the sacking, the rivet jerked out onto the ground. He stared at it dis-believingly before gingerly unclasping the iron and examining his leg. It was worse than he had thought. The ankle was cut to the bone and blood was trickling into wounds already wet with pus. The lower part of his calf was inflamed and pulpy. He dared not take off his boot, fearing that, once released, his foot would swell too much to be pushed back. He was in no condition for several days' walk, but walk he must and, tearing a strip from a sack, he bound it around his ankle to stop the bleeding. Trying a few paces around the hut, he found that the injured leg, used to being weighted, leapt up of its own volition, and it was with an effort that he was able to control it.

As he walked, it struck him that he did not know how long he had been there – he had forgotten the danger of a second funeral party arriving. Ripping the seam of another sack, he fashioned a rough hood to conceal his convict hair and, picking up the hammer and iron, peered cautiously out of the door. No-one was about and the dismal morning was darkening as the sky became one lowering mass of threatening cloud. It was weather to discourage the chaplain from setting out to the cemetery again, but he did not want to take chances. Tempting as it was to stay within the shelter of the hut, it would not be wise and he left it quickly, upright this time but feeling that eyes were upon him.

He went to the far side of the graveyard to where the yellowing reeds rustled in the wind at the water's edge. It was poor enough cover but it would allow him to slip into the sea if someone approached. He sat down amongst the stalks, disturbing a rat that scuttled into an inlet and swam away with a determination that reminded him of himself. Drinking from a puddle only slightly tainted with salt, he took a piece of bread from his pocket and ate as he watched the feathery heads of the reeds fluttering under the steel-grey sky. He wanted to go on. He thought that, if he could begin his journey, energy would come to him but the prospect of a further wait drained him and made him conscious of the pain of his damaged leg. He lay down, wrapping his arms about his body, and gave himself up to a broken rest that was part look-out and part absorption into memories.

The afternoon passed slowly. A light rain fell in scurries of sharp wind. He was chilled to the bone but it did not concern him. His mind was focussed upon reaching Chantry, and though he registered the dis-comforts of his position, they affected him no more than they would have a jockey poised for the race. He wanted freedom and Philobeth, and his spirit offered up a reserve of strength and resolution never previously tapped. He felt himself to be shedding a skin to emerge as another, better man.

When night had fallen and the half moon had risen above the lights along the coast, he prepared himself. Eating the last of his bread, he threw the hammer and leg-iron into the sea and stood with the waves lapping at his feet, considering the distance he must swim. He judged that the tide and wind were in his favour but still the water stretched, black and treacherous, before him, promising exhaustion and the slow filling of his lungs. It was necessary to risk taking off his boots and he hung them around his neck by the laces. Darkening his face with mud, he dragged a stout piece of driftwood from its lodging and, propelling it before him, waded out into the sea.

The cold was intense. He had not thought he had any heat to lose but he had been wrong. A deadness gripped him as the waves rushed against his chest, biting into his limbs as if it had drawn off his blood, and he plunged forward before it numbed his reason, automatically thrashing his legs as the shore fell away. The motion revived him but, as he swam, he shuddered with the bitter shock of the water and his hands, locked on jagged branches of his buoy, lost all sensation so that only sight told him that he held on.

The waves were high and turbulent, casting him this way and that, swamping his mouth as his sodden boots dragged his neck downwards. He could not guide the driftwood. All his exertion was needed to keep afloat. Confusion clouded his thoughts. He could not understand why there was water above and below, and only by wrenching his wits from an enveloping faintness, could he recognize that the rain had grown heavy.

Chance brought him aground at a stretch of mud in the shelter of a ramp to a badly kept boat-house. He was too weak to move at once but, as he lay shivering on the strand, amongst a litter of rope-ends and discarded tackle, he gave thanks for being delivered into a ramshackle district where no nightwatchmen would challenge his right to be there.

Painfully he got to his feet and took his bearings. In the shade of the ramp he made himself as like a respectable labourer as possible, but there was little he could do to avoid being taken for a vagrant. The rain washed off much of the mud and excused the wetness of his clothes. Once away from the area, he would be dismissed as a man on the tramp but in Portsmouth the danger of being known for a convict was strong and encouraged him to leave.

He began to walk. This part of the town was unknown to him and the stars were too obscured to give him his direction but it was more important to reach the country than to head west and, keeping to the shadows of the buildings, he chose roads that seemed to lead away from the docks. He passed through streets of run-down warehouses and workshops, where pigs and hens were kept in the gardens of cottages that had once stood alone. An increasingly rural aspect began to colour his surroundings but, as dawn streaked the sky and he was no longer solitary, he dared not feel secure. Apprentices were opening shops; workmen, their hats pulled down against the lessening rain, were trudging stoically through the rivulets; seamstresses, with skirts hitched above their ankles, were hurrying towards backrooms at expensive dressmakers; none had eyes for Frederick, yet at every turn he expected to be challenged. Only one, a butcher overseeing the loading of his van, looked at him speculatively. Seeing the suspicion, Frederick, falling into the Irish accent he had mastered when staying with a squireen of his schooldays, touched his brow and asked the way to the workhouse. Receiving the curt reply that a man of his age should be seeking employ not charity, he slipped down a passage as the butcher was diverted by the dropping of a side of beef and was questioned no more.

He walked steadily all day, his heart lightening as he found himself amongst fields. Avoiding the road that had brought him to Portsmouth, where guards escorting convicts might recognize he was a felon, he kept to lanes that added to his route but decreased his danger. His pulse quickened at every sight of a traveller but the poor merely gave him a greeting and gentry ignored him. A thin clergyman in a high hat reined in his cob as Frederick passed and, pointing his whip, enjoined him to be off and not try to be a charge on the parish. Frederick, suddenly Irish again, claimed softly to have work at Duntish and his persecutor rode on, grunting. His injured leg grieved him but his habit of scorning its pain stood him in good stead and he did not let up his pace. He ate well from the hedgerows, filling his mouth and pockets with blackberries, sloes and hazelnuts.

On the second day he could not help but limp. He had walked until he could barely stand and then slept for a few exhausted, restless hours behind a fallen tree on a verge, disturbed by dreams of capture. It was tempting to find a barn to protect him from the wind or snatch a turnip from the edge of a field but he was haunted by the fear of being taken up for some crime of vagrancy before he reached Chantry and preferred to endure any deprivation rather than jeopardize his escape.

That night he slept within a double hedge and awoke feverish and stiff. Weakness and despondency kept him on his back, gazing listlessly at the black twigs above him until amusement at lying pining for kippers broke his lethargy and set him on his way. At noon, a woman, feeding her fowls and seeing his eyes upon her pail, gave him a handful of corn meal and, eating it with gratitude and relish, he realized that here, thirty miles from Holcombe, she might have been someone who would have recognized him.

He could no longer travel by day. Sheltering until nightfall in a bramble thicket, he went on through the darkness, keeping to the roads for fear of being suspected of poaching if he met keepers on the paths. By dawn, when the east wind could not cool the heat that racked him, he was a dozen miles from home. To be so near to Philobeth and yet divided from her by a hundred people who would know his face, was a torment more agonizing than the wound on his leg. He yearned to go on but it was not wise. Climbing into a spinney, he sat down to wait.

'Shall I light the lamp?'

'No, the fire is enough.'

Slater went out, leaving Philobeth sitting alone in the parlour. The room was warm, scented with fircones and coffee and flushed with the red glow of the coals, but its comforts did not soothe its mistress. She had not heard from Frederick for five days. That afternoon she had gone to Holcombe and given instructions that the carriage should be made ready to take her to Portsmouth the following day. She could not wait a full week without word from him. Something was wrong and she would discover what it was.

She sat on, watching the flames and listening to the wind rattling branches of jasmine against the windowpanes. Her life stood still. She must live in hope of letters, in expectation of Australia but, now that her preparations to cross the world were made, she could only curb her active spirit and strive to be patient. A vigorous scraping told her that Slater was riddling the kitchen grate. When that had died, the quietness in the parlour seemed more intense. The coals rustled as they slid into ash, the clock ticked, the wind was intrusive but the sounds only emphasized the solitude in the room. She longed for the presence of the lost and the dead. An hour passed. The wind rose higher. There was a tapping at the window that was not made by jasmine. It forced itself into her notice. Rising, she went behind the curtains and looked out.

There was nothing to be seen, then, suddenly, a face that had drawn back into the shadows was before her beyond the glass. A gaunt, bearded face that stared at her with pained and hungry eyes. Her heart moved. She lifted the catch and pushed the window wide against the wind. Cold air rushed into the room as she reached to grasp Frederick by the arms and pull him over the low sill. She lowered him into her chair and ran to close the window and curtains to screen him from view. There was no doubt in her mind that he had escaped and before they had spoken, she was devising means to keep him safe.

She went back to the chair where he lay against the

279

wing, panting and watching her as though she were water in a drought. She was horrified by what she saw. The marks of suffering upon his face were nothing to the blood that soaked one leg and glistened on his boot. She knelt beside him and eased the canvas and sacking from his ankle. He stiffened as she touched him, one hand gripping the chair, the other laid lightly on her shoulder. A stench of suppuration came from the wound and Philobeth, seeing the pus-filled gash, the discoloured swollen calf, the fever on his brow, wanted to cry out but, instead, laid her cheek upon his hand.

'You have come back,' she said, 'and I will make you free.'

Chapter Nineteen

July 1848. Dalarna, Sweden.

Philobeth put down her palette and walked a few
paces to the lakeside, considering the view. It was late
afternoon but the sun that would extend day into night
was still high and glittered so brightly on the water that
her eyes were dazzled and the fir trees on the far bank
seemed one dark, serrated mass.

She moved into the shade of a rowan and, sitting on
the folding stool placed there, untied her wide straw
hat. Her loose, white clothes took on the pattern of the
leaves and she raised one hand, holding the shadow of
young berries on her palm. To her left, a silver birch
had succumbed to last winter's storms and subsided
into the lake, where small fish were darting between
the trailing twigs. The water's edge intrigued her. It
was as perfect as a Giotto landscape and yet came of
nature more severe than any that flourished on Dorset
hills. The long grass, with its flowers both foreign and
familiar, ended in a border of smooth stones, shining
where the ripples lapped them, and the sinuous curve
of exposed roots. Beyond the shore, the yellow cups
of lilies raised their gleaming heads amongst their
spreading pads.

She had crossed this same lake by sledge in January,
travelling, wrapped in wolf-skin, to her new home,

when sky and land were white and the forest was radiant with ice. Today she could not imagine frost but the exhilaration of light had not left her, and the paintings she created were bold and luminous with the impression of her world.

Turning her head, she smiled. A voice carried down from the verandah where Slater, unhampered by the difference in language, was instructing the maids how a kitchen should be run. Philobeth looked across the plumes of meadowsweet to the stretch of mown lawn that lay below the house. She was glad they had come here. When she had opened the window at Chantry to find Frederick, wounded and pursued, it had been the inspiration of the moment to hide him in the wide, Northern woods she had travelled in the past. Who would look for them there? The ports for France and America might be watched but a couple touring quietly to Norway with their servant would greet no suspicion. Had his health been strong, she would have taken him away with no-one the wiser but she dared not risk treating his infected leg herself. She had grown to trust Carmody and he did not fail them.

For three anxious days, whilst bills offering a reward for the capture of the escaped convict were posted all about and a constable came to warn Philobeth that the fugitive might make for Holcombe, Frederick lay hidden in the cellar. His determination to be gone was checked only by Carmody's insistence that if they left rashly and were caught Philobeth would be charged with aiding a felon, and Slater's tart inquiry whether it was his intention to make her girl a widow before she was a wife. Their greatest problem had been in leaving the valley without Frederick being seen. He believed that he could trust the discretion of his coachman but Philobeth had been uneasy. It was Carmody, telling his household that he had to collect scientific equipment, too delicate to entrust to any driving but his own, who drove the Chantry party to the railway platform at Bristol. In the guise of a respectable and staid family group, they had made an uneventful journey by train to Newcastle and taken passage for Oslo.

They had married on board ship. There had been no priest nor legal binding. The respect they had once had for the rules of society had died a bitter death and they were not prepared to hazard their financial security for the sake of outward form. They pledged themselves, each to the other, with mind and heart and soul – and Philobeth remained mistress of their wealth. Both felt that Mahala would have approved.

Philobeth lifted her face to the scatter of sunlight that fell through the leaves. She had had no moment of regret. The man she had thought Frederick could be had been roused by vicissitude. The prevarication and indolence that had left her dissatisfied had been replaced by vigour. She was expecting him now. In her position as owner, and with his agreement, she had sold Holcombe to a cloth-merchant who wished to be a gentleman, and together she and Frederick had bought this estate. There was timber to be managed and flax to be farmed, but these did not take up all his energies. It was the mine, whose rich veins of iron-ore had cost them dear, that was his interest and absorbed his days. His increasing mastery of the industry and dialect pleased her with its activity and enthusiasm. She did not know if this would be their final home but, for this time, she was content.

There was only one matter on which they differed. A

conviction that Ellen had been guilty of Barlow's death had grown upon Frederick as he encountered the inhumanities of the hulk, yet he did not share Philobeth's desire for revenge. He wanted to separate himself from the misery that had brought them to the forests: brooding over wickedness that could neither be proved nor punished seemed a fruitless endeavour. Philobeth would not agree. She could not lay aside a hatred of the evil that had harmed her lover, knowing that its perpetrator lived without blame or conscience. In her heart, she acknowledged that Frederick's course was wise and yet she continued to await the effect of Carmody's slow dripping of poison into Mrs North's ear.

It had met with greater success than either of them had expected. She reached into the folds of her skirt and drew out a letter from Carmody. The news it contained had caused her such satisfaction that she suspected her own character could not stand up to scrutiny. Surprise had given it added delight for she had thought that her hopes of seeing Ellen brought low had been achieved as far as would ever be possible. The escalation of Ellen's autocratic ways at Mythe, and Carmody's fuelling of Mrs North's resentment and misgivings over her guest's probity, had reached the happy conclusion of Ellen being told to leave the house she had intended to inherit and not return.

So much Philobeth had learnt from Carmody's previous letter, but the one she held in her hand, tilting it to allow the leaf shadows to bring out the words, had carried intelligence of a wholly startling and gratifying nature.

'My dear Philobeth and Frederick,' it read, 'you will

think, from the time it has taken me to reply to your last, that a plague of infirmities has stricken the county and I have not had leisure to write. It was not so and it is not so and God forbid it should be so, as Mr Fox says in the tale. The delay has been occasioned by the workings of the law; workings that have taken more of my attention than is proper for one who should be about his business but, alas, I am a sad fellow and, far from regretting my idleness, I cannot congratulate myself enough for the turn our affairs have taken.

'Can you recall that Miss Farebrother was to be expelled from Mythe, bag and baggage with, no doubt, the fire-irons flung after her? I think it may have lodged in your memories. I claim all the credit, but could not have imagined the extraordinary outcome. Madam went as desired, but in the company of Mrs North's set of garnets and the emerald necklace that should rightly be yours, being, I believe, a family heirloom. How could she show such folly? Mrs North is not one to relinquish her jewels. A hue and cry was raised and Miss Farebrother apprehended with the ornaments in the lining of her trunk.

'Newspapers embraced the event. A gentlewoman – a distressed heiress of an unusually lovely countenance – turning thief does not happen every day. The likeness you drew of her, Philobeth, was copied by printers and a Mr Deverill of Virginia, travelling in Europe for lack of anything else to occupy him, was outraged to recognize one Margaret Miller, a servant, who left his employ somewhat abruptly with, as you may guess, his wife's trinkets in her pocket. Inquiries were made. It would seem that Miller, then known as Marsh, had set sail for England as the maid of the genuine Ellen Farebrother and assumed her name when the unfortunate lady drowned in the storm. The judge took a poor view of such social-climbing and Miller is to board ship again – this time for Australia and for life.'

A flock of soft-brown ducks with material designs upon Philobeth were floating expectantly on the gently rocking water close by, but finding that bread was not forthcoming they drifted away amongst the lily-pads. She did not see them. Her thoughts were of a woman cast up upon the shore and, for a moment, she did not know what she read.

'—and by-the-bye,' the letter went on, 'it had been my assumption that Mahala's disposition was formed from a pattern on her father's side but I happened to be called to the home of her mother's cousins this day week – as much to look at me, I think, as to use my skills – and sat a while drinking unwanted tea as one does. A daughter of the house came in, a girl not yet eighteen. Selena. She is fair and there was nothing of Mahala in her appearance until she heard my name. Then a certain expression came into her eyes. "Ah," says she, all cool and dry, "you are the doctor that snatched bride and property from beneath the Grahams' hands." This did not suit Mamma and Miss was sent upon an errand, but she came back directly and drank her cup. I believe I shall call on them again.'

She heard cheerful voices and, turning, saw that Frederick was calling out to Slater as he passed the verandah. His wet hair glinted in the sun and he was fastening the cuffs of a white linen shirt as he walked. He came down across the lawn and through the long grass, untroubled by the limp he would always have. Despite the hours he spent beneath the earth, his face was brown and had the aspect of a man at peace with himself. He stopped to examine her canvas and came to her, raising her face to his before sitting on the ground beside her, an arm about her waist. Love and trust enfolded them.

'Each one is better than the last,' he said. 'When will you leave me for your Exhibition?'

'I will exhibit,' she said, 'but I will never leave you.'

She leant her head to his and, together, they looked forward to where the light shone brightly on the water.

THE END

A SELECTED LIST OF FINE WRITING
AVAILABLE FROM BLACK SWAN

THE PRICES SHOWN BELOW WERE CORRECT AT THE TIME OF GOING TO PRESS. HOWEVER TRANSWORLD PUBLISHERS RESERVE THE RIGHT TO SHOW NEW RETAIL PRICES ON COVERS WHICH MAY DIFFER FROM THOSE PREVIOUSLY ADVERTISED IN THE TEXT OR ELSEWHERE.